WELCOME TO MURDER WEEK

ALSO BY KAREN DUKESS

The Last Book Party

WELCOME TO
MURDER WEEK

A Novel

KAREN DUKESS

SCOUT PRESS

New York   Amsterdam/Antwerp   London
Toronto   Sydney/Melbourne   New Delhi

Scout Press
An Imprint of Simon & Schuster, LLC
1230 Avenue of the Americas
New York, NY 10020

For Linda and Laura

What is it about the English countryside—why is the beauty so much more than visual? Why does it touch one so?

—Dodie Smith, *I Capture the Castle*

PART I

The Booking

CHAPTER ONE

FEBRUARY

The long-stemmed roses on the counter are technically beautiful, even I can see that. But they're also ridiculous, and not only because they're too elegant for my kitchen with its warped linoleum floors and ancient, putty-colored refrigerator. I lean against the sink and stare them down, trying to make the whole arrangement spontaneously combust. A gust of wind blows snow off the garage. The birds in the dryer vent rustle.

I put down my coffee mug and pick up the glass vase. Still in my pajamas and fuzzy slippers, I carry it along the snow-crusted path from my house to the cottage out back. It's only eight fifteen, but Mr. Groberg opens the door fully dressed, his shirt buttoned smoothly beneath his cardigan.

I hold out the flowers.

"For you."

"These are from the handsome fellow with the pickup truck and the dog?"

"That's the one."

I follow him into the kitchen. He sets the vase on the counter beside the chocolate babka his daughter sends from Brooklyn.

"What happened?" he asks.

"He got starry-eyed." There's nothing like romance to kill a perfectly good casual relationship.

Mr. Groberg gives me a familiar look of kind exasperation. He picks up a serrated knife and holds it above the babka.

"So, he likes you, he's got good taste; is it a crime that he wants to take things up a notch?" He slices a piece, puts it on a napkin, and pushes it toward me. "You know, Cath, one of these days, you've got to—"

I put up a hand to stop him, to remind him of our unspoken deal. I don't raise his rent, and I make him a hearty soup every week. He pays on time and doesn't meddle in my personal life.

I don't think of myself as an orphan—it sounds so nineteenth century, and also, at thirty-four, I'm not a child—but Mr. Groberg is as close as I've got to a relative. The business that he started in 1972, Robert L. Groberg Opticians, where I began working after school and on weekends when I was sixteen, is now mine. He didn't pass it down to me but let me work off a zero-interest loan with my salary. Three years ago, after my grandmother died, leaving me alone in the old Victorian where she'd raised me, Mr. Groberg, by then retired, decided his house on the east side of Buffalo was too much for him. The day he moved into my cottage, I felt like I'd won the lottery, and not because of the monthly rent.

I pull off a warm, gooey piece of babka, put it in my mouth, and pretend to swoon.

"If you talk to your daughter soon, thank her for me," I say, as if I don't know that his adoring daughters call every evening.

"Tell me you're doing something extraordinary today," Mr. Groberg says. "By which I mean, literally out of your ordinary."

I wipe some chocolate off my lip.

"Can't. It's Saturday. I've got a list."

Buy rock salt, change the batteries in the smoke alarm, match odd socks, make soup. I also should toss the shriveled plant in the front hall that I forgot to water.

"On a glorious morning like this, you should take a walk," Mr. Groberg says.

Through the window, the sky is the bottomless blue of a cold winter day. It's profoundly reassuring when the seasons clock in and out as they should, a crisp golden fall giving way to piles of snow. I don't like warm days in winter the same way I don't like unexpected visitors appearing on my front porch. Change is fine, as long as it's predictable.

"I'm doing the boxes today."

"I see." Mr. Groberg is too kind to state the obvious, which is that I vowed to tackle the boxes last week and also the week before. "It will take less time than you think, and you'll be unburdened when it's done."

How could three cardboard boxes be so daunting? They've been sitting in my back hall, unopened, since they arrived from Gainesville more than two months ago, a few weeks after I flew to Florida for the "celebration" of my mother's life, a nonsensical ceremony of songs, bad poems, and chants under an ancient oak tree dripping with fuzzy strands of Spanish moss. I wore mascara that day, which dismayed my mother's friends, few of whom I knew. They tut-tutted my "rookie mistake" and handed me tissues just in case. I didn't need them.

"Here," Mr. Groberg says, wrapping another piece of babka in a napkin. "Fortification."

Walking back to my house, the babka cupped in my hand, I notice fat icicles hanging from the eaves. I should have been more diligent about cleaning the gutters. I remind myself that the contents of the boxes will be mundane, with few surprises. No cause for hope, no fear of disappointment.

One day when I was ten, my mother showed up unexpectedly at my grandmother's house with a present for me. Young enough to be excited by the substantial size of the box, I giggled as I ripped off the wrapping paper and cut the packaging tape, reveling in the way my mother watched me from the couch, leaning forward and smiling. Inside the box was a badminton set—a net, four rackets, and birdies. I wanted to put it up immediately so my mother and I could play, but the yard was flooded from days of rain.

"Tomorrow," my mother promised.

The next morning, I ran downstairs in my nightgown, swinging a racket hard enough to make a satisfying swoosh against the air. My grandmother was drinking milky coffee at the kitchen table.

"Where's Mom?" I asked, already sensing the silence of her absence.

"Gone."

"On an errand?"

She sighed. "She left."

I waited for her to say more, my stomach tightening from the truth. "She went to meet a new boyfriend at the racetrack in Saratoga Springs."

It was a pattern I would come to know well.

I dodge the icy patch at the end of the path and open my back door. Inside, I stand above the boxes, kick one lightly with my foot. Whatever's in here is not even for me; it's what remained after my mother's friends sorted and gave away her clothes and furniture and books. But Mr. Groberg is right, getting this done will be a relief. Maybe it will put behind me this strange state of not being able to celebrate my mother's life or mourn her death. I put down the babka to save for later and drag the first box into the kitchen to begin.

CHAPTER TWO

The clanging of the kitchen radiator keeps me moving. I'm on the second box, making quick decisions on what to keep and what to throw away. There are unpaid bills, unopened bank statements, and overdue notices from the library. There are stacks of catalogs with dog-eared pages marking luxuries my mother had dreamed of buying but could not afford. A tufted leather ottoman. A seafoam-green cashmere wrap. An Instant Pot. There is a fat folder of letters from old boyfriends, some handwritten and many more printed out from emails. There are even copies of love letters my mother had sent. As I leaf through them, phrases jump out from her looping cursive: "your manly, musky scent," "my soulmate, my bodymate." The recycle pile grows.

This is the opposite of nostalgia; there's nothing here to make me slow down and indulge in memories. Instead, I glance and toss, glance and toss. A photograph of my mother and the man who lured her to Gainesville, who'd always say "Hey, little lady," when she'd make him get on the phone to talk to me. A newspaper clipping from a Napa Valley newspaper about the opening of her tea shop, which she closed in less than a year when she decided she'd be happier in New Mexico. A list called "Romantic Things" that includes mostly clichés (sunsets, wine-red roses, silk lingerie) along with a few wacko entries (marshmallows, hailstorms, spider plants).

There's a blue file folder that's so thin I assume it is empty. It looks new, so I fling it to the keep pile. But a paper floats out, its heading in bold: "Your Unique English Village Holiday!"

Another of my mother's pipe dreams. When I was little and ready for bed, I'd lie on my stomach and she'd tickle my back and talk about the trips we'd take: to Manhattan to eat frozen hot chocolate at a place she'd seen in a movie or to Arizona to ride mules to the bottom of the Grand Canyon. Even after she left me, she'd call to share her ideas about where we should go and what we should do. *Do you want to see the wild horses of Chincoteague?* Of course I did, but mostly I wanted her to keep talking, to not hang up the phone, to come home.

As I lean over the box to grab more papers, I notice the phrase "paid in full" on the errant paper. I pick it up and scan the words, getting more confused as I read. How could my mother have paid for a weeklong holiday for two in a cottage in the English countryside? She was always tight on money and never good at keeping a job. For the past few years, she'd claimed she was too broke to come up north. How could she have afforded a trip to England? It makes no sense, but it's here in black-and-white: Skye Sanders Little booked a two-bedroom cottage in a village called Willowthrop, on the edge of someplace called the Peak District.

I google Peak District, only to learn that it's "an upland area in central-northern England, at the southern end of the Pennines," about 150 miles north of London. The Pennines, I read, are a mountain range but not in the American sense. On average, the tallest "peaks" are only half as high as the Adirondacks or the Catskills. The first of the national parks of England and Wales, "the Peak" as it's known, includes the mostly uninhabited moorlands and gritstone plateaus of the absurdly ominous sounding "Dark Peak" and the steep limestone valleys, gorges, and rolling hills of the "White Peak." According to Google, visitors are drawn there to hike the beautiful countryside, go rock climbing, and visit the area's quaint, historic villages.

What I read next is even more surprising. In addition to renting the cottage, my mother paid $1,600 for two participants to solve a "genuine fake English-village murder mystery." Incredulous, I read on. The mystery will be plotted by "one of England's noted mystery writers" and enacted with the participation of actors and local villagers who will play the roles of "victim, red herrings, innocent bystanders, and culprit." The event will include an opening-night dinner at a local restaurant (choice of steak and kidney pie, fish and chips, or chicken tikka masala), the examination of "an actual, simulated crime scene," and the questioning of suspects. At the end of the week, the winner (or organizers, if there is no victor) will reveal all in an Agatha Christie–style wrap-up—fancy dress encouraged— which will be capped off with sticky toffee pudding, "inclusive of your choice of custard or vanilla ice cream." The award for solving the case is the opportunity to be the "understudy for an already deceased on-camera victim" in a future television murder-mystery show. I assume this means that you get to step in, or, more likely, lie down, if the card-carrying actor playing the dead body takes ill or needs an extended bathroom break. It's unclear whether travel expenses will be paid for that return trip.

I am so confused. My mother wanted to go to England to play a game? I read further. Participants in this unique event will be helping the tiny village of Willowthrop, as all proceeds will go toward restoring the much-loved but dilapidated community pool. And then at the bottom of the paper, a notation, initialed by my mother, that the cost of the "murder week" is nonrefundable under any circumstances.

Nothing about this makes sense. For the first time since my

mother died, I am overwhelmed with missing her—not to have more time together but to grab her by the shoulders and ask what she'd been smoking when she booked the trip. Instead, I call my mother's best friend and astrologer.

"Such a shame!" Aurora says. "Skye was so excited. She even found a pair of rubber rain boots at the thrift shop. She called them wellies."

"Had she recently gotten into murder mysteries?"

"Not really."

"How could she be so irresponsible?" I eye the unpaid bills that are now my problem.

"On the contrary, she had me check the planetary alignment to make sure the timing would be auspicious."

"Which obviously it wasn't." I don't have to say "sudden stroke" to make my point.

"I'm an astrologer, Cath, not a clairvoyant."

"My mother was in debt."

Aurora sighs. "Money is such a millstone."

"Who was she going to travel with?" I ask Aurora. "Had she met an Englishman? Fallen for an Anglophile?"

I long ago stopped trying to keep up with my mother's love affairs. I was only two when my father was killed by a drunk driver, after which we moved in with my dad's mother. I assume my mother went through a period of mourning and celibacy, but I can't remember a time when she didn't confide in me about her romances, sparing few details. Only during college did I begin to understand how deeply weird it was to know how your mother best achieved orgasm and with whom. It was a big day for me when I suggested that she treat her relationships like a new pregnancy and keep them secret until she'd passed the twelve-week mark, a milestone she rarely reached. Thankfully, she never filled the new void in our conversations by asking about my romantic life, which was fine with me, as there's not been much to tell. I've had a handful of relationships, mostly with guys who wanted to keep things as casual as I did. In between, I've been fine on my own. I'd rather stay single than chase love like my mother did.

I have to ask Aurora to repeat herself.

"I said, she was going to take you," she says.

"That's impossible."

The last time my mother and I traveled together was on a fall weekend when I was nine and we drove from Buffalo to Vermont. We held hands as we hiked along a gorge, visited a toy museum, and stayed in an old hotel where we slept together in a canopy bed. The next day, we moved into an ashram. My mother gave me an old book about girls in boarding school, which I read while she did hot yoga. At the end of the long weekend, we drove to Rochester, where my mother put me on a bus back to Buffalo, my grandmother's address and phone number scrawled on an index card she'd zipped into my jacket pocket. For weeks, she said she'd be home soon, but by Christmas, she'd moved in with a massage therapist she'd met in a silent meditation. From then on, she never returned to Buffalo for more than a few days at a time.

"What made her think that I'd agree to go?" I ask Aurora.

"Again, astrologer, not mind reader."

"But why me? Why on earth would my mother book this ludicrous trip to England with me?

"I haven't the foggiest," Aurora says. "I suppose that's another mystery for you to solve."

CHAPTER THREE

Dear Miss Little:

I am so sorry about your mother. I had the fortune of corresponding with her at length and am deeply sorry that her untimely death has prevented her from indulging in what she said would be the fulfilment of a dream: to visit England with her only child.

In answer to your inquiry, no, we are not monsters. As such, we will graciously refund half of your mother's payment. The other half, which she was chuffed to bits to allocate for you, is unfortunately not refundable, as you are not presently deceased.

However, you can recover a portion of the payment made by transferring from the two-bedroom cottage your mother selected to one of our shared accommodation offerings, Wisteria Cottage, along with two other participants, each traveling solo. The three of you can work as a team. See details in the attached reimbursement notice.

I trust this will suit you and we look forward to seeing you on the 27th of May, when the festivities begin!

Yours most sincerely,

Mrs. Germaine Postlethwaite
Owner, The Book and Hook
Willowthrop Village
Derbyshire, England

———

It is 9:50 a.m., ten minutes until the shop opens, and I read the email again. Who is this Germaine with the unpronounceable last name? And why does she assume I want to fly to England to solve a fake murder? I have nothing against English-village mysteries; I've spent hours watching them on television with Mr. Groberg. We watch only at night or on rainy days, always with tea and gingersnaps, though I never drink the tea. Mr. Groberg usually identifies the culprit well before I have the slightest idea of whodunit. My mother used to make fun of me for watching "dowdy people solve crimes in bad weather with no sex." It didn't occur to her that what I loved was not so much the shows themselves as the time with Mr. Groberg. Had she thought I'd be into this trip?

I rest my head on my desk, not looking up when the antique sleigh bells on the door jingle and a blast of cold air rushes in. I know by the scent of patchouli that it's Kim. The tinny sound of electronic dance music escapes from her earbuds.

"Everything okay?" Kim shouts.

I lift my head and nod toward my computer screen. "I got a response."

Kim takes out her earbuds and pulls off her wool beanie, a mess of long blond ringlets tumbling down her back. Unraveling her scarf, she reads the email over my shoulder.

"Wisteria Cottage sounds lovely," she says.

"Wisteria is an invasive species."

I walk to the door, pull up the blinds, and flip the sign to "We're Open." Outside, it's still snowing, thick flakes making slow-motion cartwheels to the ground. The plow has been through once already, but the street is white again. Across the road, the shops look warm and inviting. These are my favorite days, cold and muffled and clean, in the city where I've lived my whole life, the place my mother fled without looking back.

"How can you *still* live there?" she'd said the last time we spoke, about a month before the stroke that killed her at fifty-five.

She had never intended to settle in Buffalo. She was twenty when she left home in Indiana to seek adventure in a big city. Buffalo was supposed to be a pit stop, an overnight visit with a friend at the state university. But down the hall in her friend's dormitory was Ben Little, the bearded, soft-spoken resident adviser. He was a senior, an English major who wrote poetry without punctuation and played Spanish guitar in the stairwell, where the acoustics were good. Within a few days, my mother was ensconced in Ben's single room. When he graduated a month later, they moved into a garage apartment near Anchor Bar. My mother took a job at a coffee shop while he prepared to start teaching high school English. Within a year, she was pregnant with me.

Buffalo may have been an accident for my mother, but for me it has been the source of everything good. Here was love and consistency. Here was my beloved paternal grandmother Raya, who stepped up when my mother left. Who took me to the public library every week, attended my parent-teacher conferences, combed the knots out of my thick hair, suffered my brief stint playing the oboe, and indulged my love of Polly Pockets. Who taught me how to bake challah, make a sundial, hang wallpaper, and catch and cook a brown trout. Who told me stories about my father, who used to read to me every morning and every night from the same books she'd read to him when he was a child.

"A week away from home could be what you need," Kim says when I'm back at my desk.

I know exactly what she means. I've been a cranky mess since getting back from Florida. Last week, a customer came in with an adorable little schnoodle, one of those hypoallergenic breeds, and I snapped "no dogs" and made them leave, even though I love dogs and keep a box of Milk-Bones in my desk drawer. Yesterday, I talked a perfectly nice woman into choosing a pair of frames that made her eyes look beady and her nose gargantuan. Luckily, I came to my senses before the order was final and suggested a more flattering pair.

Kim thinks I'm in some sort of "grief purgatory" because my mother's so-called funeral didn't give me proper closure. She doesn't understand that I don't need to mourn. I was already used to my mother leaving me.

"You haven't had a vacation in years," Kim says. "A long weekend cat-sitting at Lake George does not count. And this one is paid for."

The bells jingle and a customer walks in, thankfully stopping our conversation. But all day, fitting glasses, adjusting frames, and cutting lenses, I can't stop thinking about my mother's payment to Germaine What's-her-name. Not getting what you paid for is like throwing money away, which makes my skin crawl. But the English countryside? It hasn't exactly been on my bucket list. I went to Greece after college with a girlfriend, and everything about it was luscious—the weather, the turquoise sea, the olives and feta cheese, a vacationing med student named Gregori. An English village seems like the opposite. If Greece is a sarong tied around your waist in a sexy knot, England is a pair of galoshes. There's nothing enticing about sitting in front of a fire with a bunch of old biddies doing needlepoint and debating whether it was the colonel with the cricket bat behind the field house or the vicar in the parsonage with the candlestick.

After work, I bring Mr. Groberg a Tupperware container of chickpea soup and tell him about the email and the partial refund. He's so enchanted by the whole trip that I suggest he go as my proxy.

"When you crack the case, we can share the glory," I say.

"Is there a prize?" he asks.

I tell him about getting to be the backup victim in a murder mystery and he says, "What's second prize? You get to understudy two dead bodies?"

He pours some soup into a bowl and puts it in the microwave. While it's heating up, he tells me his travel days are over. And then he shakes his head and says, "For all her faults, that mother of yours had a real joie de vivre."

The comment stings. The first time my mother met Mr. Groberg, she waltzed into the store unexpectedly while I was working. I hadn't even known she was coming to town. I was embarrassed by the way she hugged me for too long, and I apologized to Mr. Groberg for the intrusion. Before he could say anything, she'd said, "Nonsense! I'm your mother, and I couldn't wait to see you." But then she spent nearly an hour talking to Mr. Groberg, asking him all sorts of questions about his life, his business, even his childhood. I'd worked for him for nearly a year by then, but until that day I had no idea that he'd had polio as a child and had once dreamed of being a famous ventriloquist. The longer they talked the angrier I got, though I'm still not sure if I was jealous of Mr. Groberg for getting all my mother's attention or if I was envious of how easily she got him to open up. What bothered me even more, though, was that my mother never again mentioned Mr. Groberg other than to ask when I was going to get a more exciting job.

Mr. Groberg takes the bowl of soup from the microwave and dips in a spoon for a taste.

"I have two things to say," he tells me. "One, nice touch of cumin. Two, you should go to England." He sits down at the table, tucks a napkin over his shirt. "Travel is never a mistake. Even if the trip is not fabulous, it will give you a new perspective. You know that moment when you fit a customer with new glasses? And everything they've gotten used to seeing as blurry or distant suddenly pops into focus? You've made everything old new for them. Going away from home for a little while can do the same thing."

That night, I have trouble sleeping again. I think about what Mr. Groberg said about bringing things into focus. Maybe travel offers that, but do I need to see my life more clearly? Do I want to? There's nothing wrong with my routine. It's reliable and familiar, even if I can't pretend that lately it hasn't felt off-kilter. Since returning from Florida, I haven't slept straight through a single night. Maybe Kim is right that I need closure. Could this trip provide it, a way to say goodbye to my mother for good?

I roll over onto my stomach and punch the pillow. The light of the clock is a penetrating blue. It's 4:00 a.m. There's no way I'm going to be in a better mood tomorrow. I flip onto my back and tuck the quilt around my legs. I think about crossing the ocean. Landing at Heathrow, taking a train north to the distinctly low "uplands." Maybe I should call Aurora, pretend I believe in astrology, and ask what the stars say. Should I do this for my mother? For myself? It's 4:15. An eon later, it's 4:25. By 4:45, I'm bargaining with the gods of slumber. If I take this cockamamie trip to England, can I sleep through the night?

At work that morning, Kim reminds me that I use a credit card for the shop's expenses and that I've probably accrued a lot of points. "I bet you could fly business class," she says.

"Very funny," I say.

We both know it would physically pain me to spend more to sit in the front of an airplane that's going to get me to my destination at the exact same time as the people in the back. But flying on miles sounds good, like traveling for free.

"What about the shop?" I can't remember the last time I've been away from work for an entire week. "Spring is busy."

"I can handle things here," Kim says. "And what would you miss anyway, the chance to watch another woman try thirty different frames, ask your opinion on each, and choose the first pair you suggested?"

She's right. It's a routine business. She can manage it easily.

"I'll even house-sit," Kim says. "I can water your plants."

"I don't have plants."

"I'll bring mine."

I open my desk calendar and flip to May 27.

"We're getting the new display cases that week."

"And I know exactly where they're supposed to go," Kim says.

"What about Mr. Groberg? He relies on my hearty soups."

Kim folds her arms and nods. "His favorite is lentil. I know."

"But no onions. They give him gas."

"Noted."

"And you'll remind him to feed his fish? Sometimes he forgets."

"The fish will be fed." Kim is smiling now, rubbing her palms together. "Bravo. I knew you'd go!"

PART II

Murder Week

CHAPTER FOUR

THREE MONTHS LATER—END OF MAY
SATURDAY

I can't sleep on the plane, or the train from London, but by the time I'm in the taxi that promises my first view of "the Peak," I can't help nodding off. When the cabdriver says, "Here we are, love," I'm groggy and disoriented. I've seen nothing of the countryside or the village that will be home for the next week. We are on a steep, cobblestone street, parked in front of a wrought-iron gate that opens not to the freestanding, thatched-roof cottage I'd imagined, but to a row of two-story attached stone houses, each with a small garden in front. A sign by the first door says Wisteria Cottage, but I see none of the vine I'd assumed would cloak the cottage in bushy, lavender blossoms. A few rows of purple iris line the stone walkway to the door. I pay the fare and step out of the car.

As I'm unlatching the gate, hoping I'm the first to arrive, a voice from above says, "Good morrow, fair maiden!"

A man is leaning out the casement window and tipping an imaginary hat. The Shakespearean act is weird, but the accent is even more worrisome; I thought my cottage mates were supposed to be

American. Please let him not be part of the ruse, in character already. At least not until I've had a cup of coffee and a shower. My mind, which is still somewhere over the Atlantic second-guessing this entire venture, needs to catch up with my body here on the other side of the looking glass.

"Alas, I am mistaken," the man says, a finger out as if to test the wind. "Morning has given way to the noonday sun, and we know who that's fit for. Mad dogs and Englishmen!"

I ask if the door is unlocked, though I'm reluctant to go in.

"Hold on, I'll be right down." He now sounds 100 percent American, which is a relief.

My suitcase wheels bump over the path. The man from the window opens the door. He is extraordinarily tall and gangly, with boyishly bright red hair. His cheeks are sprinkled with freckles. He looks like he's in his early forties.

"I'm Wyatt Green." He shakes my hand and then hoists my suitcase over the threshold, all the while looking beyond me furtively, like he's checking the perimeter for threats. "Come on in, but watch your back," he whispers. "There's a murderer among us."

"Doesn't that start tomorrow?"

Wyatt shrugs. "Beats me." He rubs his eyes. "I'm sorry. I'm jet-lagged and I get loopy when I'm tired. I adore my husband, but this was the most bizarre gift. I can't believe I'm really here."

"That makes two of us." I introduce myself and step into the living room to put a little distance between myself and this marionette of a man. At five foot ten, I don't often look up to people.

Wyatt says he'll show me around.

The main room is sparse, free of the doilies or needlepoint wall hangings I'd feared. There are leather couches and a plush armchair positioned around a woodburning stove. The living area opens into a bright kitchen with lemon-yellow cabinets and a few open shelves for dishes. A vase of sunflowers as big as pancakes is on the windowsill above the sink. Wyatt opens the cabinets, which are surprisingly well stocked. There's a French press and what looks like good coffee, a box of tea, some cookies, a jar of olive oil, and a bottle of champagne.

"And this," Wyatt says, opening a closet, "is a combo washing machine–dryer contraption, big enough for a full load of Barbie clothes."

"Small country, small appliances?"

"I guess so. At least the bathtub is American-size. Come, I'll show you."

He grabs my suitcase and carries it up, taking the stairs two at a time. On the second floor, I poke my head into the bathroom, which looks freshly renovated, all clean white tiles and sparkling fixtures. The tub is extra-long and deep. I hope there's enough hot water to fill it. Each of the three bedrooms has a queen-size bed, although they probably don't call them that here. Wyatt has taken the smallest room, which faces the back. It's a generous gesture, considering that he arrived first. I choose one of the front rooms and ask Wyatt to put my suitcase there. The room is pretty but simple, with a fat white comforter and four fluffy pillows on the bed and a small dresser with an attached mirror. The mullioned windows open outward with levers and overlook the village, from this high vantage point all slate rooftops and narrow lanes. There is a church spire, lilac ballooning over stone walls, and, in the distance, velvety green hills dotted with what I assume are sheep. It's a charming view, soothing and quiet, the placid mood interrupted only by what sounds like the clip-clop of horses. And there they are, two women, perhaps a mother and daughter, riding up the lane on shiny brown horses with swishing tails. They pass right in front of the cottage, backs straight and elbows tucked, chatting as they go as if it's the most ordinary thing in the world.

Leaning against the door, Wyatt says he's glad he's not the only singleton who signed up. "I mean, not that I'm single. Or not that there's anything wrong with being single. I'm just here solo. Like I said, this trip was my husband's big idea."

"Because you love murder mysteries so much?"

"Maybe. I mean, I do love mysteries. I've watched them *obsessively* for the past year, but that's because I couldn't help myself. It's a long story. Bernard, that's my husband, owns a birding shop, New Jersey's best, Hi, Hi Birdie!—I know, it's not funny even in an ironic way—but that's Bernard. I work with him at the shop, where I'm mostly just comic relief, which means I can binge-watch mysteries on my phone. Anyway, Bernard said he thought I'd love this, and I'm not saying I won't—I'm hoping the whole thing is campy, you know? But it also wouldn't have been disappointing if he'd bought us a trip to Aruba."

Wyatt looks a little self-conscious, folding and unfolding his long arms. But his nervous babbling puts me at ease. Maybe sharing the cottage with him will be all right. He nods toward the light on the bedside table. The lampshade is brown plaid flannel, with a few pleats and a russet-colored feather poking out at an angle. "Do you think you're supposed to turn on the hat or wear the lamp?" he says, and I laugh, relieved that he is not at all the kind of housemate I expected.

CHAPTER FIVE

"Helloooo? Anyone home?"

In the garden below is a petite woman in a belted trench coat standing beside a large aluminum suitcase on wheels.

"Oh, look," says Wyatt, now standing beside me. "A lady detective." He leans out the window in the same way he greeted me, but this time he says, "Tally ho, petal!" And then to me: "Shall we go welcome our housemate?"

In the front hall, the new arrival introduces herself as Amity Clark from Northern California. She has a soft, pretty face and, up close, looks younger than she had from above. She's maybe in her early fifties, about my mother's age, but with an entirely different vibe; I'm pretty sure she doesn't have a tattoo of a baby armadillo above her clavicle. She reminds me of some of my wealthy customers back home, with the same understated, forgiving, but obviously expensive clothes. Her silvery shoulder-length hair is thick and well cut.

Amity doesn't wait for a tour to walk through the cottage.

"An umbrella stand! Delightful. A woodburning stove! Hopefully we'll have some chilly nights." She touches the blankets in a basket. "Cashmere. Nice." She runs a finger along the books in the built-in shelves and pulls one out. "Hello, my pretty." She opens the book, brings it up to her face, and inhales its pages. "Did you know that Mr. Darcy lived in Derbyshire?" She looks at me with a playful smile. "You're young and lovely. Are you married?"

"No," I say. She'd better not be the matchmaker type. "And I'm fine with that."

She squints at me.

"So, you're not looking for a single man in possession of a fortune stepping out of a pond in a wet shirt?"

"Blimey," Wyatt says.

Amity giggles. "Forgive me, occupational hazard. I'm a romance writer."

She moves into the kitchen, where she opens the refrigerator, peers into the cabinets. She takes out a package of Hobnobs. "Biscuits!" She touches jars of jam. "Do you think they have Marmite? I'm dying to try some." She looks around, hands on hips. "This is all just what I'd hoped. So cozy and pretty. So English." She picks up the kettle. "Fancy a cuppa?"

Wyatt says sure, and I decline. I don't like tea. I tell them I'll make coffee and ask Amity to put some extra water in the kettle for me.

Amity opens a bright red tin. "Oh dear, tea bags. That's disappointing. We'll do a pot anyway." She takes a ceramic teapot from the shelf, lifts off the top, and drops in two tea bags.

Wyatt sits at the kitchen table, his long legs stretched out toward the middle of the room. Amity is smiling at each of us in turn, apparently as delighted with her cottage mates as she is with the cottage itself.

"How extraordinary that we each came alone! And I thought I might be the only person traveling solo. It's new to me, you know. I'm a recent *divorcée*. That's an elegant word for it, don't you think? Much prettier than 'jilted wife.'"

She doesn't seem too crushed about it.

The water boils, and Amity fills the teapot. I take the kettle and pour some water into the French press. Wyatt and Amity are both so talkative; I hope they don't expect the same from me. How can I explain why I'm here when I'm still not sure myself?

"Are you working on a romance while you're in Willowthrop?" Wyatt asks Amity.

"Me? Fall in love this week?" Amity winks at me, a hint that she's deliberately misunderstanding Wyatt. "As my sons' Magic 8 Ball would say, 'Outlook not so good.'"

She takes the teapot and two mugs to the table.

"You have little kids?" I ask.

"Ha! You're adorable," Amity says. "No, my boys are 'grown and flown,' as they say. They're twenty-three and twenty-five. They haven't lived at home for a while now, but I'm sentimental about their things. The Magic 8 Ball is just one of their old toys I couldn't bring myself to give away. Will I ever play Apples to Apples again? I will not, but should you need it, my basement playroom's the place." She fills Wyatt's mug and then her own.

"I meant, are you here to research a new novel?" Wyatt says.

I push down the plunger, pour myself a coffee, and join them at the table.

"Oh, no, this is pure pleasure," Amity says. "I've always wanted to travel to the English countryside, and murder mysteries are so much fun. Now that I'm solo, here I am. It's a much-needed break from my routine. For the first time ever, I've been experiencing writer's block."

Amity tells us she's had four books published, all of which found enough of an audience that her editor wanted more. But for the past year, she's been struggling. "I'm still good at the meet-cute, the falling in love, even the steamy sex, and at creating an obstacle to pull my lovers apart. But I can't seem to find plausible ways to bring them back together. I keep writing stories that end in misery."

This is unexpected. Nothing about Amity suggests a dark nature.

"My latest is about an oyster farmer and a mezzo-soprano who meet at a benefit on Cape Cod. He's shucking oysters while she's performing *Carmen*'s 'Habanera' and the noise of the shells hitting the pail throws off her cadence."

"Nice setup," Wyatt says, putting one and then another heaping teaspoon of sugar into his tea.

"Then what happens?" I ask.

"They fall in love," Amity says, "but when everything is going swimmingly, she's asked to fill in for an opera star whose appendix burst at the start of a lengthy tour through Eastern Europe. She's reluctant to leave her new love but it's an offer she can't refuse, so she ends things with the oysterman and goes off to Riga, where she discovers what had been missing from her singing to take it from good to great."

Wyatt leans forward. "What was missing?"

"Heartbreak," Amity says. "She gets standing ovations at every performance. She's stuck with a choice—stay for fame and misery or go home for true love and mediocrity. And I'm stuck with a story going nowhere."

"It's a good ending," I say. "That's life. I like it."

"So does my writing group," Amity says. "But that's not the kind of story I want to write. Despite everything, by which I mean the predictable saga of how Douglas—that's my husband, oops *ex*-husband—dealt with turning fifty, I believe in romance. I can't help it. I like making readers feel so tingly they want to go back to page one and bathe in the whole experience again. I want only enough tension to make it absolutely delectable to arrive at bliss."

Amity takes a sip of tea. On the back of her hand are a few sunspots. My mother always chased a happy ending too. But somehow, Amity's searching doesn't seem frantic. The visions dancing in her head seem harmless, even pleasant, not dangerous at all.

"What about you?" Amity asks. "How'd you end up here solo?"

"That's the million-dollar question," Wyatt says. "It was ostensibly a gift from my husband."

"Why ostensibly?" Amity tops off Wyatt's tea.

"I'm not sure who the real beneficiary is." This time, Wyatt puts three teaspoons of sugar into his tea. "I think Bernard wanted a break from me."

"And shipped you all the way across the ocean?" Amity says. "That can't be right."

I'm afraid Wyatt might get offended, but he just laughs and says, "Let's hope not," though he doesn't seem too convinced of it.

"I can't compete with Bernard's passion for birds," he says.

"Is he an ornithologist?" Amity asks.

Wyatt shakes his head. "Technically, an ornithophile."

"A bird lover?" I say.

"Through and through."

"My neighbor has a bird feeder," I say. "He calls it a squirrel jungle gym."

"Tell him to get a squirrel baffle for the pole," Wyatt says with absolutely zero enthusiasm. "Nineteen-inch width. $23.99 plus tax."

"I've never really understood bird-watching." Amity takes a sip of tea. "My husband and I went on a safari in Kenya for our honeymoon, and one day we were joined by an English couple on a birding trip. We'd be looking at a lion tearing into a gazelle or a baby giraffe wobbling on its long legs and the woman would be completely uninterested. She'd have her binoculars up to the sky saying, "Oh, look, Nigel, I do believe that's a cinnamon-breasted bunting."

"Pair of twitchers there. That's what they call birders in England," Wyatt says, and takes a big gulp of tea. His Adam's apple bobs up and down his long neck. "I adore Bernard, but sometimes I wish he'd put down the binoculars and watch me instead. That's weird, right?"

"Not in the slightest." Amity reaches across the table and pats Wyatt's hand.

After a few moments of silence, I have the sinking suspicion that it's my turn.

Sure enough, Amity says, "What brought you here?"

I try to figure out the best way to put it, to not elicit more sympathy than I want or deserve, yet also not sound callous. In the end, I blurt out, "My mother bought this trip for the two of us but didn't tell me, and then she died, and here I am."

I can tell from their expressions that this information didn't land the way I'd hoped.

"You poor dear," Amity says. "You're much too young to lose a mother."

She has no idea.

"So sorry," Wyatt says. "That must have been tough."

"It's okay," I say. "We weren't close."

"Is that so?" Amity says. "I always thought having a daughter would be like having a best friend."

That's so far from my experience that I share the truth.

"She left me when I was nine," I say. "My grandmother raised me."

Now it's my turn for a tender hand pat from Amity.

"Oh my." She takes a sip of tea. "But your mother must have cared about you to plan a surprise like this. It's a lovely gesture."

It figures that Amity likes surprises. Optimists generally do.

I don't feel like saying more, so I push back my chair and, trying to sound casual, say, "Well, I guess I'll unpack and take a shower before I'm totally crushed by jet lag."

"You mean you've just flown in?" Amity says. "You didn't visit London first?"

30

Coming early never occurred to me. Signing on for the full week was almost more than I could handle.

Wyatt looks at his watch. "How about you two unpack and shower and then we'll go check out the village before death comes a-knocking? I'll wait down here; I've already had a kip and a scrub."

"Have you now?" says Amity, looking delighted.

"A what and a what?" I ask.

"British English, pet. A nap and a shower," Wyatt says. "Sorry, I always fall into foreign accents. I've been doing it since I was a kid and discovered Monty Python. Imagine ten-year-old me on the playground: "'Your mother was a hamster and your father smelt of elderberries!'"

"I think it's good fun," Amity says. "You feel a Britishism coming on, accurate or not, let it rip. You do you."

"Hear, hear," I say.

"By golly, you two are enchanting," Wyatt says. "We're going to have a cracking good time solving this murder."

Amity claps her hands and says, "Indeed we are."

I've never been much of a joiner, but Mr. Groberg made me promise to throw myself wholeheartedly into the game, to get into the spirit and all that. There's no way I'm going to match the enthusiasm of these two, but I figure I'd better at least try. In my best British accent, which is admittedly pretty pathetic, I say, "By Jove, we're going to be bloody brilliant."

CHAPTER SIX

When my mother told me to pack for our trip to Vermont, I had trouble filling my overnight bag. Two changes of clothes and underwear, my pajamas, scrunchies for my hair, a hairbrush and toothbrush, and I was done. But my mother filled a large suitcase, the same vinyl one she'd brought from Indiana years before. She packed sweaters, skirts, jeans, yoga clothes, pajamas, and slippers. She also took the mohair throw she liked to wrap around her legs when she watched television on the couch, a framed photograph of herself as a bride, her *Espresso Yourself* coffee mug, and an inlaid wooden box filled with beaded necklaces and earrings. We both had to sit on her suitcase to zip it closed. After I was back home in Buffalo for a month and my mother still hadn't returned, I thought about that overstuffed suitcase and decided that staying away without me must have been her plan all along. And maybe it had been. But in time, I saw that she always overpacked, filling that old suitcase even for a mere weekend in Buffalo. Traveling light, she once told me, is overrated.

I would have packed more for this trip, but I'd been warned against checking a bag. I shake out my rain jacket and hang it in the closet, along with my two dresses and two blouses. I toss my sandals and boots in the closet and put the rest of my clothing in the dresser. I tuck my nightgown under a pillow, plug in my phone charger by the night table, and set my toiletries case on the dresser, which seems like a more considerate place to keep it than in the shared bathroom. I close my empty suitcase and stash it in a corner.

It's strange to have so few possessions. Usually, I'm surrounded by so much *stuff*. My own things, my grandmother's things, things that belonged to my grandfather, who I barely remember, and my father, who I don't remember at all. My grandmother's house—and I still think of it as hers even though it's been mine for three years—is brimming with paintings and books and tchotchkes of all kinds. There are baskets of yarn left over from the blankets my grandmother crocheted, old copies of *Field & Stream* and *The New Yorker*, fly rods and fishing reels. There are everyday dishes, my grandmother's wedding china, and pantry shelves filled with candlesticks, tablecloths, and old Haggadahs. The linen cabinet in the upstairs hallway holds not only the sheets I got on sale at Target last month but also my father's baby blanket, pale green with a white ribbon running through it, and the old cotton sleeping bags my grandmother would unzip and use for picnics. The house is toasty with history and personality, and I love it.

But standing in this spare room, knowing how little the drawers and closet hold, I feel buoyant. Like I've Marie Kondo'd my life, but instead of bringing only items that spark joy, I packed things that have not had a prior life, that have never belonged to anybody but me. I have the basics that I will need to dress, and bathe, and sleep, and nothing more. I've never felt burdened by my home, but being in a place that holds so little of my past makes me feel like anything is possible.

CHAPTER SEVEN

I t's a short walk to the village center, down the hill and then four blocks along a two-lane road with a sidewalk so narrow that we have to go single file. Wyatt takes the lead. Amity, who is reading as she walks, lags behind.

"According to this itinerary, we have two hours and fifteen minutes before we have to be at the parish hall for the opening assembly," she says. "More than enough time. It says here that Willowthrop, population 1,853, is one of the smaller villages in Derbyshire."

Wyatt stops by a red cylindrical pillar, which turns out to be a Royal Mail postbox. He rests an elbow on it and takes a selfie. His jaunty pose reminds me of Dick Van Dyke in *Mary Poppins*, a film I watched a zillion times on VHS as a child and that my mother loved to ridicule.

"Chim Chim Cher-ee?" she used to sneer. "God help us."

"How many villagers are part of Murder Week?" Wyatt asks.

Amity flips through her pamphlet. "Here we go: 'The mystery has a cast of twenty-five characters, some of whom will be playing characters while others may seem to be characters but will be playing themselves, albeit with adjustments to their words and actions to adhere to the storyline of their given characters.' Goodness, I hope the quality of the mystery exceeds the quality of the writing."

She continues.

"'As you perambulate through Willowthrop investigating the crime, you may question anyone you meet, but only Murder Week players will reveal significant clues.'"

"Hopefully they'll all be lousy actors and it will be easy to tell who's bona fide and who's bogus," Wyatt says.

"Lucky for us this isn't Stratford-upon-Avon," Amity says.

We come to the village green, an inviting expanse of lush emerald grass with neat beds of red and yellow tulips. The streets are lined with shops, each with a colorful painted sign and some flying the Union Jack. Over the narrow lanes leading away from the center are strings of bunting, red and blue triangles flapping in the breeze. And there are flowers everywhere, climbing walls and trellises, spilling from window boxes and planters, and overflowing baskets hanging from lamp posts and wrought-iron hooks attached to the old stone buildings.

"Quaint-orama," Wyatt says, taking pictures.

Hands on hips, Amity surveys the scene. "'Think of the deeds of hellish cruelty, the hidden wickedness which may go on, year in, year out, in such places.'"

Wyatt and I wait for her to say more.

"It's Sherlock Holmes, in *The Adventure of the Copper Beeches*. Isn't that what we're here for? A pretty village and a sordid crime?"

"Also shopping," Wyatt says, stretching out an arm to display the stores within sight.

He suggests we start at the Willowthrop Cheese Emporium. We follow him inside, where the air is musty with milkiness. Chunks of veiny Stiltons and rounds of cheddars fill the display cases. The shelves are stacked with fruit chutneys, jams, and crackers. Wyatt buys a jar of Old Hag Real Ale Pickle for his husband, who he says will appreciate the gift and the joke. The cheesemonger, a slight man with pink cheeks, is pleasant but not particularly interested in us. As we leave, we agree he's not playing a part of any kind.

Next door, at the Willowthrop Sweet Shoppe, we look at the glass jars of candies, pointing out the ones we've never heard of, like aniseed balls and honeycomb cinder toffee. The woman behind the counter seems to be listening to us and then, without any greeting, starts talking to us like we're already in the middle of a conversation.

"As I said, he's got to stop making trouble. She didn't want to be married to him anymore, and that's that. Enough with the threats and carrying on. Does he think he's the first husband to be given the boot?"

The three of us look at each other, wide-eyed. I mouth: "*Bogus.*"

"Already?" Wyatt whispers. "No one's been murdered."

"But it might be a clue," I say.

Amity steps toward the shopkeeper.

"Exactly who are we talking about?" she asks sweetly.

"Oy, did I speak out of turn?" the woman says. "Don't mind me. I do prattle on. What can I get for you? Some strawberry bonbons? Jelly babies?"

I buy a bag of rhubarb and custard sweets in hopes of getting her talking again, but a group of Dutch backpackers comes in asking for salty licorice and the shopkeeper turns her attention to them.

We spend the next hour or so checking out more shops. Amity buys a Peak District National Park dish towel, and I get a tin of tea and a package of stem ginger biscuits for Mr. Groberg. Outside a beauty salon, a young woman with spiky red hair vapes and looks us up and down with enough disdain to suggest she'd rather die than play-act murder. We're less sure about the man sweeping the sidewalk and whistling an Adele song in front of the haberdashery. When he winks at us like he's in on a secret, we decide he's definitely, possibly bogus.

We come to a pet shop advertising "all things for birders," which Wyatt starts to pass by but then says, "Oh, why not, let's just have a quick sticky beak."

The store smells like sunflower seeds and wood chips.

"Look at this!" Wyatt says, touching a bright red feeder in the shape of a classic British phone box. "And oh my god, this!" He points at a birdhouse that looks like a pub and is customizable with the name of your choice.

"Bernard would adore these."

We follow Wyatt around the store.

"I used to have such fun working with him. We met a few weeks before the pandemic, and during that first year, it was just the two of us at the shop, filling orders for people to pick up outside, giving advice—well, Bernard gave advice, I stood by and admired my smart, sexy beau. I loved being with Bernard all the time. It didn't matter what we were doing, I liked doing it with him. But once the shop opened again, things gradually changed. Not for Bernard, who could talk about birds all day, but for me. I learned enough to help customers with the basics—bird feeders and birdbaths and birdhouses—and I amused myself by trying to stump the regular customers with weird bird trivia."

"Such as?" I ask.

"Did you know that hummingbirds are the only birds that can fly backward? That the flamingo can eat only with its head upside down? I could go on, but I'll spare you. In fact, I'll spare you all of this. We can go now." He leads us outside.

I don't realize how hungry I am until we're standing in front of a gourmet store displaying a wide variety of small pies. Inside, we're greeted by a young woman with skin so dewy and glowing it doesn't seem real.

Amity whispers, "English rose."

I'm too famished to care if the woman is an actor or not. The array of savory pies is mind-boggling: short ribs and Roquefort; steak, bacon, and ale; beef and potato; Gruyère, butternut squash, and pork sausage; and something called "four-and-twenty chicken-and-ham pie," which turns out to be layers of nuts, fruit, chicken, and "gammon," which Amity thinks is a kind of ham.

We agree on the four-and-twenty chicken-and-ham pie for the name, and also choose the one with bacon, and the beef and potato pie because it sounds reliably simple. We eat them cold on a bench outside the shop.

"My sons wouldn't like a lunch like this, a few little pies on a bench," Amity says.

"They're picky eaters?" Wyatt says.

"Not in the slightest, but they'd need scads more food," Amity says. "When they were teenagers, there was no better value than taking them to an all-you-can-eat buffet. It's a wonder they didn't put some of those restaurants out of business."

"My mother attributes most of her wrinkles to raising boys," Wyatt says.

"We loved having boys," Amity says, looking wistful. "They could be feral, of course, but also so sweet. Whenever there was a thunderstorm, one of them would yell, 'Front porch!' and the four of us would pile onto the wicker couch to watch the rain and count the seconds between the lightning and the thunder. The boys would be all squirmy and excited, but then they'd settle down and cuddle with us."

"You must miss those years," I say, remembering how I used to ride out thunderstorms in my grandmother's bed.

"I do, though not as much as I thought I would," Amity says. "When my boys were little, I used to feel sorry for people with older kids, who just didn't seem cute. But then I discovered that the older my boys got, the more interesting they became. I knew I'd always love them, but I didn't know how much I'd genuinely like them."

"They didn't want to join you here?" I ask.

"On a mystery week?" Amity laughs. "I didn't even suggest it."

"They're not BritBox watchers?" Wyatt says.

"Goodness, no. But they adore making fun of my shows. *Stay tuned for scenes from next week, when Lady Esmerelda drops a teacup and Lord Croptopton scandalizes the county by burping!*"

"In these parts, I believe it's known as belching," Wyatt says.

The pies are not bad but vaguely disappointing, less like something intentional than like leftovers eaten straight from the fridge the morning after a holiday dinner. Maybe they'd be better warm.

Wyatt goes off to find a cold drink, and Amity and I decide to stay put. The scene is so calm and orderly that I imagine all the activities are on a loop. That, eventually, I'll see it all repeat just as before. First a pack of children, running with that school's-out burst of energy, and behind them the harried-looking woman in a skirt and sensible shoes telling them to slow down. Then the double-decker bus, the jolly driver waving at the postman before pulling over just past the King George Inn, a stone's throw from where the lady walking the terrier takes five steps, stops, and turns away as the dog crouches to relieve itself.

Now entering stage left is a woman, maybe in her late sixties, in a misbuttoned flowery blouse, jodhpurs, and boots. She's wearing leather gloves and holding a long pair of hedge clippers.

"Incoming bogus," I say to Amity, who is sitting beside me with an actual paper map spread out on her lap.

"Have you seen the hunt?" the woman says, not really looking

39

at us. "I had to prune the roses, so many roses, the floribunda was in a shambles, and now I've lost them."

She's doing a bang-up job at acting distressed.

Amity puts down her map and stands up.

"How absolutely dreadful," she says to the woman in the kind of posh English accent you might hear at Buffalo's best dinner theater. "The hunt is long gone. It was quite the spectacle. A veritable whirlwind of hounds and trumpets."

Amity winks at me and takes a pen and notebook from her purse. She asks the woman her name.

"My name?" The woman puts a hand to her chest. She looks terrified. "You don't know me?" She looks over her shoulder. "I think I'm being followed. I fear I'm. . . ."

"About to be murdered?" I say, surprisingly excited.

The woman gasps. "Am I in danger?"

As she steps back, a startlingly handsome younger man rushes up and puts an arm around her.

"Okay, everything's fine now, come with me," he says. He's got thick dark hair nearly to his shoulders and warm-brown skin. He's got to be an actor; he's way too gorgeous for this town. Giving us barely a glance, he starts to usher the woman away.

"Wait," I say. "Can we please ask a few more questions?"

He stops and turns back. Even scowling, he makes me catch my breath. He's several inches taller than I am, with dark eyes, a long, straight nose, and a beautiful neck.

"Whatever for?" he says. Tied around his waist is the white apron of a chef or a waiter.

Amity waves her notebook. "Clues? We're on the case."

"You're on the—" He runs a hand through his hair, pushing it back off his forehead.

I feel a little lightheaded, like I should have eaten more of those pies.

"Oh, that." He sounds annoyed. "It's not what you think."

"Come now," I say, trying to be playful, like we're all in on the joke. "Riding gloves? A brooch of the Union Jack on her blouse? Seriously?"

He steps forward, putting himself between us and the woman.

"She's got dementia," he whispers. He looks genuinely concerned; the man is not only hot, but he can act.

"Oh, does she?" How gullible do these villagers think we are? "And you happened to swoop in before she could say more?" I feel Amity's hand on my arm, but I shake it off.

"I happened to have 'swooped in,' as you say, because she's my *mother*," the man says. The woman gazes up at him with watery blue eyes.

I turn my attention back to the man, who I realize resembles the woman though she is white and he is not.

"Not used to mixed-race families in Arkansas?" His face is hard to read; I'm not sure if his smile has a tinge of a smirk or vice versa.

As he turns away, I find myself quietly uttering "I'm from Buffalo," as I realize that nothing about what just occurred was bogus and that I've been a bona fide ass.

CHAPTER EIGHT

The parish hall is only a few blocks from the village green. When we arrive, Wyatt and I talk Amity out of taking seats in the first row and settle in the third. Two women in front of us twist around and introduce themselves as sisters from Pittsburgh, retirees who love traveling together.

"We've been cramming for months, watching reruns of *Grantchester* and *Father Brown* and deconstructing the cozy mysteries of M. C. Beaton," one of them says. "We love Agatha Raisin. Wasn't *The Quiche of Death* delicious?"

I have no idea what she's talking about.

"A delightful book!" Amity says.

"I don't do quiche," Wyatt says with a wave of his hand. "Lactose intolerant."

The people gathered look middle-aged and older. I count about thirty participants, most of whom are seated in pairs or small groups, which makes me glad I'm also part of a team.

On the stage, a woman wearing a corsage taps on the microphone. Her blouse is untucked and hangs over a denim skirt that nearly reaches her bright green Crocs. The ensemble strikes me as more hippie school principal than English countrywoman, but the parish hall is not particularly quaint either. With rows of folding chairs and the small stage edged by a faded maroon curtain, it's the kind of place you'd expect to watch a spelling bee.

"Maybe we have it all wrong," I whisper to Wyatt. "Maybe what looks bogus is bona fide and vice versa."

I'm still confused by my encounter this afternoon with the mother-son duo and hoping that it will become clearer who's part of the mystery and who's not.

The microphone squeaks. The schoolmarm leans in.

"Welcome to Willowthrop's first ever Murder Week! We are delighted to have you here in our humble village. We trust that you all are well and truly afflicted with what the great nineteenth-century novelist Wilkie Collins called 'detective fever.' You see, our local constable is a lovely chap but unfortunately is a few egg whites short of a soufflé, if you catch my meaning. So, in the case of a murder in our midst, we will rely on you."

Ripples of applause. The speaker introduces herself, and I'm disoriented all over again. *This* is Germaine Postlethwaite? Of the imperious email and the extensive correspondence with my mother? I'm not sure what I expected—more tweed, less shlumpiness? At the least, more intimidating. I should have pushed harder on the refund.

"Before we begin," Germaine continues, "I'd like to state, at the request of the head of the parish council, that Willowthrop is utterly and completely safe. There has not been a suspicious death here since 2012, when the village orthodontist unexpectedly expired."

"That explains the teeth," Wyatt whispers.

Amity shushes him.

"There was an inquest—" Germaine continues.

"Ooh, an inquest! Like in *Rebecca*," says one of the Pittsburgh sisters, eliciting a wink from Germaine.

"—and it was determined that the orthodontist had died of natural causes. An undetected heart condition. Not murder."

Murmurs of disappointment throughout the hall.

Germaine goes over the ground rules.

"You are to gather at the village green tomorrow morning at nine, at which time you will be informed that a murder has occurred. You will be briefed on the case and then taken, by groups, to the scene of the crime."

Excited chatter. Germaine raises a hand and waits with the practiced patience of a kindergarten teacher. The room falls silent.

"Each team will have an opportunity to examine the crime scene and interview witnesses and suspects, some of whom may be in character and some playing themselves, but with minor adjustments to adhere to the storyline. In other words, it is up to you to decide who is real and who is not and which information is relevant to solving the crime. If you identify a suspect whom you would like to interview and their location is not easily discernible, you may ask us how to locate them. If they are not part of the game, that information will not be forthcoming. We want you to be challenged, but we have no desire to send you on a wild-goose chase.

"You will have five days to investigate the crime. Your written solution must be turned in by seven o'clock on Thursday evening. You must provide not only the *whodunit* but also the *howdunit* and the *whydunit*. Obviously, your conclusion will contain some theories that can't be proven. Fingerprinting and DNA testing have no role in this challenge. You may not use the internet, which would be of no use anyway, as all background facts pertinent to the crime are fictional. The team that comes closest to the truth will have the honor of presenting the details at our evening finale. If you believe you have figured out the crime before then, please keep it to yourself so that we may all enjoy the denouement together."

Germaine glances to the wings of the stage.

"I'd now like to introduce our special guest, who has been quite instrumental in the development of our mystery." She clears her throat, looking like she's tasting something unsavory. "Ladies and gentlemen, please welcome Willowthrop's very own Mr. Roland Wingford, author of *Murder Afoot*, the first in his series of eleven murder mysteries featuring Cuddy Claptrop, the crime-solving farrier."

Silence but for the sound of Germaine's clapping.

"A furrier? How fabulous," Wyatt whispers.

"*Farrier*," Amity says. "Who shoes horses. A blacksmith."

"So much for Anthony Horowitz," grumbles the man sitting behind me. "Hey, Siri, tell me something about Roland Wingford."

From the man's phone, a robotic voice: "Winsford Devine was a Trinidad and Tobago songwriter who composed over five hundred calypsos."

"I said," the man repeats, sounding irritated, "who is Roland Wingford?"

Siri doesn't answer.

"You have to say, 'Hey, Siri,' again," whispers the woman next to him. "But quietly."

"Hey, Siri," the man rasps, "tell me who is Roland Wingford."

"Sorry, I didn't quite get that."

"No phones," someone hisses.

A white-haired man dressed all in tweed—jacket, vest, and slacks— has joined Germaine at the microphone.

"Good evening." Roland Wingford is barely audible. He leans a bit closer to the microphone, which squeaks, catapulting the author a step back as if he's been bitten. He tries again. "Uh, good evening."

Germaine, standing beside him, says, "Go on, then."

"I am Roland Wingford." He waits, presumably for applause; none comes. He clears his throat. "I am a most devoted acolyte of the works of the golden age of detective fiction, classic murder mysteries written between the wars. I am, I believe, soon to be selected for membership in England's famed Detection Club."

The Detection Club sounds like a spin-off of the Baby-Sitters Club, but Roland Wingford says that it's a prestigious "secret" society established in 1930 by a group of legendary British crime writers (no thriller writers, only "detective novelists") that included Agatha Christie, Dorothy L. Sayers, and G. K. Chesterton.

"Membership in the Detection Club, which exists to this day, is by invitation only," Roland says. "Initiation involves a candlelit procession in the dark. New members place a hand upon a skull, known as Eric the Skull, whose eye sockets are illuminated from within by red light bulbs."

"How can that be real?" I whisper to Amity.

"Oh, no, I've read about it. Though apparently a doctor's analysis strongly suggested that Eric the Skull is female."

"*Sacre coeur!*" whispers Wyatt.

Amity giggles.

As Roland Wingford speaks, Germaine appears to be scanning the audience in search of someone or something, until her lips twitch and her gaze stops on me. Or at least I think it does. I look over my shoulder. Perhaps she's looking at someone else, maybe the guy behind me who was talking to Siri and has offended her by having his phone out again. When I turn back, she's still focused on me. Am I supposed to wave? I shift in my seat so I'm no longer in her line of sight.

"Here we are," the man behind me says to his companion. "According to this article, Roland Wingford published his first book in 1995 . . . it was reviewed by the *Times* of London, well, that's something. Oh. They called the book 'not unaccomplished.' The other ten books were self-published."

"Upon induction into the Detection Club," Roland continues, "members take an oath, which I abide by myself, promising that their detectives shall detect the crimes presented without reliance on nor making use of divine revelation, feminine intuition, jiggery-pokery, coincidence, or act of God."

I peek out at Germaine, who is looking at her watch.

"What's wrong with feminine intuition?" Amity whispers. "And how will they know if we use it?"

"Thank you, Roland," Germaine says, moving to take over the microphone. "That was quite elucidating."

Roland doesn't budge. He is now close enough to the microphone to kiss it. "To solve the crime I have devised, you must use ingenuity and employ the arts of observation and deduction. In accordance with the rules of detective fiction set out by the American crime writer S. S. Van Dine in 1928, I have not employed any of the clichés of the amateurs. To wit, the perpetrator will not be identified by comparing the butt of a cigarette left at the scene of the crime with the brand smoked by a suspect. The culprit will not be the newly discovered identical twin of a suspect. Servants, such as butlers, footmen, valets, gamekeepers, cooks, and the like, will not be chosen as the culprit. And a dog that does not bark will not be your indication that an intruder was familiar. In addition, the motive for the crime will be personal, not political. A golden age detective story, or an English-village murder mystery, for that matter, must be kept gemütlich."

Germaine frowns.

"Which, of course, is the German word for 'pleasant and cheerful.'" Roland steps back.

"A cheerful murder is really the best kind," says one of the Pittsburgh sisters.

"Well, that clarifies things," Wyatt says. "We're going to solve a gemütlich crime that doesn't involve cigarettes, a twin, a servant, or a dog."

"Easy peasy," I say, though I'm pretty sure it's going to be nothing of the kind.

Germaine asks if there are any questions. One of the Pittsburgh sisters raises her hand.

"I have a dodgy hip. Will all suspects be located in the village center, or will we have to walk far?"

"Walking is encouraged but not required. Most of the action occurs in the village, with a few suspects farther afield and reachable by foot, bus, or taxi," Germaine says.

"What happens if more than one group solves the crime?" asks the man who'd been conversing with Siri.

"Such confidence," Amity whispers to me.

"There are many details to the crime scenario," Germaine says. "The team that identifies the most details will be the winner. If all details are identified exactly the same way, we will have to investigate the crime of cheating."

Roland Wingford leans in.

"All participants are requested to adhere to the motto of the Detection Club, which is 'Play Fair.'"

Germaine invites us to proceed to dinner, which is not, as I'd thought, at the swanky King George Inn but at another establishment, The Lonely Spider, down the block. As we rise from our seats, Germaine catches my eye again. Her interest makes me nervous, like I might need to pay more money or something, so instead of walking toward her, I beckon Wyatt and Amity and suggest we hightail it to The Lonely Spider so we can be first in line at the bar.

CHAPTER NINE

We are assigned to the same table as the Pittsburgh sisters, Naomi and Deborah. Both have ruddy cheeks, brown eyes, and curly gray hair, but Naomi, the older sister, is plump and Deborah, only a year younger, is thin, which makes them look like a before and after of the same person in a weight-loss ad.

They barrage us with questions, eager to know how each of us came to sign up for this adventure alone. They're delighted that Amity also was drawn to England by Austen, the Brontës, and *Midsomer Murders*. They seem genuinely disappointed that Wyatt's husband didn't come too, because they are avid bird-watchers. And when they hear about my mother, they shower me with affection, which makes me feel a little guilty for not being as broken up as they assume I must be, but is surprisingly comforting. Naomi rubs my shoulder, and Deborah pats my back. Being touched by strangers usually makes me cringe, but I have a strong desire for these sisters to wrap me in their arms and hug me tight. They remind me of my grandmother.

"We know loss," says Naomi, as we take our seats. Four years ago, she says, her wife died of pancreatic cancer, and a year after that, Deborah's husband dropped dead from a heart attack. They've lived together ever since.

"Had you and your mother spent a lot of time planning this trip?" Naomi asks.

She looks shocked when I tell her that my mother booked it as a surprise and that I have no idea why.

"She hadn't expressed interest in traveling to the English countryside?" she asks.

"Never. She'd never gone abroad and didn't seem to care."

"But she read a lot of detective stories?" Deborah says. "Fancied herself an amateur sleuth?"

"Not in the least. She loved romance novels and Jane Austen."

"She was an Anglophile? Of the Masterpiece Theatre variety?" Amity says.

"Not really. But she liked *The Great British Baking Show*. She liked trying the recipes, usually ones with funny names, like jam roly-poly and spotted dick."

"Oh my," Wyatt says.

"She was very impulsive," I tell them. She called it spontaneity, but I always had the feeling she was running away.

"There's got to be a reason she wanted to come here," Amity says.

"I agree," Wyatt says. "And we should get to the bottom of it."

I'm tempted too, but I tell them not to bother.

"My mother was eccentric and unpredictable, all impulse and no reason. Following her trail will lead to a disappointing dead end. Trust me, I know."

"If you say so," Amity says, but not without a quick glance at Wyatt, who winks at her and then looks down at the table. I have a hunch they're not going to let this go. They're like cops in a television drama who've been officially taken off a case but are damned well going to continue to investigate.

"It's an enticing puzzle," Naomi says.

"Did someone say puzzle?" It's the man who'd been talking to

Siri behind me in the parish hall. "Bix Granby, venture capitalist. My wife, Selina." Bix and Selina, with nearly identical pageboy haircuts, are both in tight sleeveless tops. Their upper arms look professionally toned. Pulling out a chair for Selina, Bix says, "We're puzzle people. We do them all."

"Not jigsaw puzzles, of course," says Selina, unfolding her napkin. "We prefer puzzles that require mental gymnastics, a vast vocabulary, and considerable knowledge about, well, everything." She bites her lip as if she feels bad for being so smart.

"I love the Sunday crossword. I do it every week," says Amity.

"What's your best time?" Bix says.

"I don't know, usually in the late afternoon? Before dinner?"

"We usually finish a Sunday in under eighteen minutes," Selina says.

"Impressive," Naomi says, narrowing her eyes. "Will you be solving the murder in record time too?"

Her sister reaches out and puts a hand on her arm, as if to warn her against saying more.

"I can't imagine it will be too challenging," Selina says, as the waiters start asking who has the fish and who the chicken.

No one has ordered the steak-and-kidney pie. Bix and Selina have arranged for plates of roasted vegetables.

"In any case, this is a warm-up for us," Selina continues. "An amuse-bouche. We're going cycling in the Tyrolean Alps next week. Do you know Backroads?"

There's an empty chair at the table, and the waiter asks if we're expecting another diner. Did someone forget that my mother wasn't coming, that I was traveling alone? The waiter picks up the extra place setting and takes it away, but the chair remains, like the specter of Skye Little. I wonder what she'd make of this crowd. She'd probably complain about how old everyone is, not realizing that the only people not in the average age group are Wyatt and me. But then she'd charm them all anyway, ask question after question, her intense interest getting them to spill their secrets and their dreams. I used to hate the way she grilled everyone. I never understood why people rarely seemed bothered by it.

"You're nosy," I told her once.

"I'm curious," she answered. But all I could see was that she was collecting more people to leave behind.

"We're doing a particularly challenging bike trip," Bix says. "We're hoping to do the steepest climbs faster than we did last time."

"Well," Wyatt says, with a sultry gaze at Bix. "I hope you don't do *everything* quickly."

Bix looks embarrassed and fiddles with his silverware. Wyatt winks at me. I give silent thanks that I've landed with Amity and Wyatt. For no apparent reason, we seem to have clicked. People often think they're going to like each other because they have a lot in common, but it doesn't always work that way. This is why even if I were looking for love, which I'm not, I wouldn't use one of those dating apps that sends you to dinner with someone because you both like film noir, hate the beach, and never eat the ginger slices that come with your sushi.

Amity tastes her fish and chips and, as I've already come to expect, is ecstatic.

"Scrumptious," she says. She lifts up a little metal cup as if it's a golden chalice. "Mushy peas!"

I think Amity's enthusiasm is rubbing off on me and that my chicken tikka masala tastes better because of it. Selina is smiling as she picks at her vegetables, but I'm pretty sure she's side-eyeing my naan as I tear off a piece and take a bite.

CHAPTER TEN

The dinner conversation, about mystery books and television shows, is a blur of names, only some of which I know. There's DCS Foyle, a favorite of Mr. Groberg's, and two women, Annika and Vera, who apparently don't need last names. There's someone called Josephine Tey, who was both an acclaimed mystery writer and a detective in a series of books, I'm not sure how, and Flavia de Luce, which sounds like an aperitif but turns out to be a fictional eleven-year-old aspiring chemist who solves crimes in her English village.

Amity asks the table what kind of person we think "our culprit" will be, and, before anyone offers up ideas, Deborah tells us about an essay that George Orwell wrote in 1946 in which he suggests that the British public's most satisfying kind of killer, in the true crime cases that drew widespread attention, was middle class, a dentist or solicitor, and here she does air quotes, "a quiet and respectable little man" who commits murder, often via poison, out of passion and in fear of public scandal.

"What about greed?" asks Bix. "I've seen some money lust that's downright murderous. My ex-wife—" He jumps like he's been kicked under the table.

"Bix, please," Selina whispers.

"In Nancy Drew, the culprits were usually seedy guys from the wrong side of the tracks," Amity says.

"Seedy guys?" Deborah says. "And what do you think that's code for? Nancy Drew books morphed over the years, but the earliest editions were classist, racist, and anti-Semitic. Quite a trifecta, no? The 'criminals' were always poor and uneducated and often described as being dark-skinned or having stereotypical Jewish features."

Murmurs of surprise. I finally see an entry in this conversation that's been swirling around me.

"I read an old Nancy Drew that I found at my grandmother's house. It was definitely dated, I remember Nancy drove a 'blue roadster,' but I'm sorry to admit I liked it. My favorite was Nancy's friend George, probably because she was tall, like me, and not afraid of anything."

"Oh, don't apologize, I loved them too." Naomi puts a hand to her heart. "George Fayne was my first lesbian."

Selina freezes, fork in midair. "There weren't any homosexuals in Nancy Drew."

"Eye of the beholder, honey," Naomi says, touching Selina's hand, which Selina snatches back.

After a lull, Amity turns to Selina and asks if she's always been an avid mystery reader.

"I've long been a voracious reader," Selina says. "I read everything—mystery, literary fiction, poetry, nonfiction, even thrillers. Every category you can think of—except romance, of course."

"Why is that?" Amity says, sitting up a little straighter.

"They're so predictable," Selina says.

"Lots of people think romance is silly," Amity says. "And to that I say, you find love superficial? Well, then, I'm sorry for you." She tosses back the rest of her wine. "What's more important than the pursuit of love? Of cherishing someone and being desired in return? If

WELCOME TO MURDER WEEK

a romance is written well, it's a story of being fully human—of firing on all cylinders, sexually, emotionally, and intellectually. There's nothing more exciting."

"That settles it," Wyatt says. "I'm downloading one of your books tonight."

Selina's cheeks go red. "You're a romance writer? I didn't mean—"

Amity waves a hand. "Not to worry, I've heard it all before."

"Where should I start?" Wyatt says.

Amity looks at Wyatt like she's sizing him up.

"I think you'll enjoy *Comely Comeuppance.*"

"Scrummy," Wyatt says.

"Sounds adorable," Selina says, picking at her zucchini.

An awkward silence follows.

"Time for another beer," I say, standing up. "Anyone up for a second round?"

"I'll take a glass of white wine," Amity says. "And make sure it's a big pour."

CHAPTER ELEVEN

The restaurant is closed for our event, and there doesn't seem to be a bartender on duty. I wait a few minutes, hoping one of the waiters who served our drinks will appear. No luck. There are wineglasses and a few open bottles of white on the counter. After waiting some more, I go ahead and pour a glass of wine for Amity. The beer poses a trickier problem. I can't exactly serve myself, which would require walking around the bar. Just as an experiment, I stretch out my hand to see if I can reach the beer tap. As my fingers touch it, I hear a man say, "Try that in a real pub and you'd get kicked out."

It's the guy from the village, the handsome one with the mother I thought was an actor. He's not scowling, which is a relief. He picks up a glass. "May I?"

"Sure, I'll have the lager." I want to apologize for my mistake this afternoon, but I don't know how. As he hands me the beer, I say, "You're a good son."

He considers me for a moment, and his face softens. "She's a good mum."

It seems so uncomplicated the way he says it, like it's possible to have that kind of relationship with your mother. Like she raised him well, with love and constancy and patience, and he's returning the favor.

He picks up a cloth and wipes down the bar and then tucks it into the waist of his pants.

"I'm sorry about yours," he says.

"Pardon?"

"You're Catherine, right?"

"Cath." No one has called me Catherine, or even Cathy, since I read *Wuthering Heights* in high school and forsook my namesake. Catherine Earnshaw might have been beautiful, but she was a petulant brat enmeshed in the world's most dysfunctional, obsessive romance. I still don't understand how my mother could have named me for her.

"Sorry. Cath. I heard about your circumstances." His eyes are dark and serious, but he exudes warmth.

"I wasn't aware that my circumstances were common knowledge in Willowthrop."

"Germaine's an old family friend."

"And also the village gossip?"

He smiles a little and shakes his head. "I don't think she spread it around. I was helping her with some logistics, and it came up. She means well."

"So you *are* part of the week's activities."

"Can't say."

"Can't, as in you're not allowed to say because you're playing a part? Or can't because you don't want to?"

He looks serious now. "I can tell you one thing: that was my mother this afternoon. And she wasn't acting."

"I am so sorry about that."

"It's okay. I didn't mean to react so harshly. It's just that I get a bit of a stick in these parts."

"Meaning?"

"You know, people asking where I'm from and being shocked when I say London. The follow-up question is always 'But where are you *really* from?' As if a bloke who isn't white can't have a mum from Willowthrop."

"I was sure you were part of the game."

"Did I say I'm not?" He looks confused for a moment and then laughs. "Nah, I'm just taking the piss. I'm helping out tonight, making and serving drinks. I've got my own bar in town, and I've started a little distillery. Artisanal gin."

"That's a thing?" I honestly don't know whether to believe him, but his banter is very attractive.

His face lights up. "Absolutely. Small batch, made with different aromatics."

"I thought gin was made from juniper." I'm impressed with myself for knowing that much.

"Juniper is the basic ingredient. But then there are other botanicals— verbena, cardamom, lemon, bay leaves. I try to source local when I can. I've got a batch flavored with rhubarb from my garden." His speech has changed. He's talking faster and with an unabashed eagerness to share.

"Isn't gin one of England's biggest exports?" I ask.

"Yes, it's popular."

"So there must be hundreds of distilleries."

He smiles and says, "My gin is *really* good."

He's brimming with something, maybe optimism or excitement, neither of which I've felt in a long time. It's alluring; not only is there no trace of that scowl, but his dark eyes shine and his lips curl into a sweet smile. He seems to have forgiven me for my earlier offense, which is more of a relief than it should be considering I barely know the guy.

He takes out a cocktail napkin and scribbles an address on it. "That's my bar. Pop in one night and say hi."

"It's really your bar, not a stage set?"

"Come see for yourself."

"That's not an answer," I say.

"Isn't it?" He holds out the napkin. "I'm Dev, by the way. Dev Sharma."

"Real name?"

"Does it sound fake?"

"Another deflection."

"Excellent observation," he says. "But of course, you're a detective, so . . . "

He's enjoying this, and so am I. Until I remember that even if he's telling the truth about his mother, his flirtation may be scripted. And I'm not going to be the gullible American who falls for his lines.

"Thanks," I say, taking the napkin. "I'll try."

Without looking at what he's written, I shove the napkin in my pocket, crumpling it in the process. I pick up the drinks and walk away.

CHAPTER TWELVE

SUNDAY

"What a misty, murderous morning!" Wyatt throws his head back and breathes in the damp air.

We're standing on the village green with the other contestants, waiting to hear who's been bumped off during the night. The grass is shimmering under swaths of fog. It's barely raining, more like moist air, but we Americans are dressed for a deluge, in slickers and ponchos and rubber rain boots, some of us under black umbrellas. It's like we're gathered for a funeral, though we don't yet know who has died.

A man in a police uniform steps up to a podium, his big belly pressing against his jacket, the buttons of which are mismatched. He introduces himself as Constable Bucket. I wonder if he's just playing the part of a constable or if he's the real constable playing the part of a fictional one. Flanking him are Germaine Postlethwaite and a young woman in a tightly belted black trench coat holding a clipboard.

"Good morning, ladies and gents," the constable says. The paper in his hand is shaking. He might have a bit of stage fright, although he could be worried about impersonating a constable, which might be a crime even if you are one. "I regret to inform you that at eight thirty this morning, the body of Mrs. Tracy Penny was discovered, dead, at Hairs Looking at You salon." He gestures to the block behind him, where blue-and-white police tape is strung across the front of a three-story building. "Mrs. Penny, forty, was the owner of the salon. Upon arriving at work as usual, the salon assistant, Dinda Roost, found Mrs. Penny on the floor, with apparent trauma to the head. The coroner estimates the time of death to be last night between eight o'clock and ten o'clock. The precise cause of death will be ascertained by an autopsy, the results of which will be distributed to you in due time. Mrs. Penny and the entire crime scene will be available for viewing and photographing throughout the morning. Each group will have fifteen minutes to examine the scene. In addition, you will have the opportunity during the week to visit the residence of Mrs. Penny, which is located above the salon, to search for clues."

The constable takes out a cloth handkerchief and mops his brow. He announces the order in which each group will examine the crime scene. Selina and Bix are first. They high-five and speed-walk toward the salon. Next are the five members of a mystery book club from Tampa, Florida, who jump up and hug one another. Amity, Wyatt, and I are third. We settle on a bench on the edge of the green to wait our turn.

"A hairstylist was not what I expected," I say.

"I wanted to murder my stylist once," Amity says.

"Do you think Mrs. Penny was a churchgoer?" Wyatt says. "I'd love to interview the vicar."

"Is there a vicar here?" I ask.

"There's always a vicar," Wyatt says.

"I hear their vicar is a looker," Amity says.

"A dishy vicar?" Wyatt says. "Yes, please."

I take my notebook out of my bag and write VICAR on the first page. I have a rush of being eleven again and pretending I'm a spy. I used to roam our neighborhood, recording the movements of the residents. I never saw anything criminal, and never found any mysteries to solve, but I witnessed some moments meant to be private, like when Sissy Lampkin, the prim president of the Junior League, stood at her kitchen sink picking her nose. My grandmother hooted when she heard about this, though it hadn't surprised me. By then I already knew that people weren't always what they seemed. My grandmother said I was cynical beyond my years, which I always took as a compliment even though she never sounded pleased about it.

I'm starting to settle into the fact that, as strange as it is, I'm here in England to solve a fake crime and that I might even enjoy it.

Selina and Bix, after their allotted fifteen minutes, come out of the salon looking miffed at each other. Another fifteen minutes pass and the Tampa book club ladies exit laughing. I guess the crime scene is suitably gemütlich.

CHAPTER THIRTEEN

We enter the salon and practically trip over Tracy Penny, who lies face down on the floor, wearing a silky bathrobe printed with green vines and bright red poppies. She has long, wavy dark hair, luxurious for a woman of forty, but not totally surprising, as stylists always seem to have fabulous hair the way dermatologists have skin as unblemished as a baby's bottom.

As we circle Tracy, I try to ignore the gentle rise and fall of her torso. I take several pictures with my phone, not only of Tracy's body but of the crimson liquid on the floor. Maybe that's a clue? At least it was in one of the old shows I watched with Mr. Groberg. *If you look carefully, you'll see that the blood splattered forty-five degrees due northwest, which means the culprit could only be left-handed. Constable, arrest Lord Dastardly immediately!*

I'm finding it hard not to laugh, but Wyatt is all seriousness, opening and closing the front door. "No sign of forced entry."

The constable informs us that the front door was closed but unlocked when the assistant arrived to open up.

"Did Tracy usually lock the door at night?" Wyatt asks.

The constable turns to Germaine, who's watching from the side of the salon. She gives a quick, approving nod.

"Mrs. Penny's habit was to lock the door," the constable says.

"So, then, the murderer was known to Mrs. Penny?" Amity says.

"Or had a key," Wyatt says. He pulls a notebook from his pocket and scribbles in it.

"And left in a hurry, not bothering to lock the door," Amity says.

The salon is sunny and clean. Three seats, one of which has a robe draped over the back, face a wall of mirrors. A shelf runs the length of the mirror. On it are two glass jars of blue disinfectant filled with combs and scissors and a chrome shaving set with a wood-handled blade and a shaving brush in a small bowl. There is also a damp towel.

I pick up the shaving brush, which is sticky, and am about to ask Wyatt if it's real animal hair when the constable barks, "No touching!" and I drop it. In the back of the salon are two sinks for washing hair and a small washing machine and dryer. I walk over to the washing machine and ask the constable if I can open it. He nods. But inside is nothing but a single black nylon robe. The dryer is empty. The back door opens to a vestibule where there is a staircase leading to the apartments on the second and third floors and another door, bolted from the inside, which opens onto the parking lot.

"You said Tracy lived upstairs," I say to the constable. "Did she live alone?"

"She used to live there with her husband, Gordon Penny, but he moved out six months ago," he says, and hands me a business card for an establishment called Gordon's Cha Cha.

"Is that a strip club?" I ask.

"In Willowthrop?" The constable looks as shocked as a Downton Abbey butler asked to serve dinner with only one footman.

"This is a *cozy* mystery," Germaine says. "Gordon's Cha Cha is a dance studio."

I pocket the card and turn my attention to the framed photographs on the walls. They're all of Tracy Penny, captured in excellent light in a variety of hairstyles. Here she is in hiking clothes on the shores of an emerald-green mountain lake (hair in braids). Here she is on a sun-drenched terrace (hair in a sleek short bob) hoisting a margarita glass as big as her head. Here she is in her wedding portrait (hair in a glamorous updo and her head bent into a bouquet of white calla lilies). There's also a framed magazine article about a stable, featuring a full-page photograph of Tracy, now with a perm, standing in the middle of a corral, holding the reins of a speckled pony on which sits a little girl with unruly red hair. The caption says, "Staff member Tracy helps little Ambrosia get comfortable in the saddle." I take photos of all the pictures on the walls and move on to examine a shelf of hair products with labels that look homemade. When the constable turns his back, I open one and take a sniff.

"If it smells like almonds, it could be cyanide," Amity says.

"More like Froot Loops."

"It's one hundred percent organic, love," comes a whisper from the floor. Tracy is peering up at me. "If you want to buy some, stop in at the end of the week after I've been resurrected."

From the side of the room, Germaine tsks and rolls her eyes.

A toilet flushes, and a young woman in a white smock appears. She is holding a washcloth to her face, dabbing her eyes, which look red from crying. The constable introduces Dinda Roost, the salon assistant. Wyatt asks Dinda if there was anything unusual about her arrival at the salon this morning.

"Other than my boss on the floor dead as a doornail?"

"Answer the question, please," Germaine says.

"Well, the door was unlocked, which was unusual. I'm always the one who opens up at eight thirty. Tracy usually comes down at eight forty-five."

"Was Tracy seeing anyone?" I ask.

"Like a boyfriend? She wouldn't tell me if she did. We weren't exactly besties." Dinda looks at her fingernails.

"Can you think of anyone who might have a grudge against Tracy?" Wyatt asks.

Dinda purses her lips. She shrugs.

"How long have you worked here?" I ask.

"Going on a year now." She sounds proud, like this is an enormous accomplishment.

"Was she a good boss?" Amity says.

"I don't like to speak ill of the dead."

Wyatt is behind the reception desk, looking through the appointment calendar.

"Who's this L. M. Blanders who came in for the last appointment of the day yesterday, a blow-dry at four o'clock?" he says.

"That's Lady Magnolia Blanders," Dinda says.

"A lady?" Amity's voice rises with excitement. "Was she a regular here?"

Dinda laughs. "Lady Blanders a regular? Don't be daft. Toffs like that don't come here unless they have to. Tracy acted like she was annoyed by the booking, like she'd be damned if she'd have to treat Lady Blanders like the Queen or something. But I could tell she wanted to make a good impression. She was probably hoping she'd get more business out of it. She even made me google Lady Blanders to find out what kind of tea she drinks and what she likes to gossip about. Rather full of herself, if you ask me. I found an article about how she's getting some kind of award from a children's charity, something about being a model wife and mother."

"I'm sure she does her best," Amity says.

"Don't count on it," Dinda continues. "Lord Blanders is even worse. Total snob. In that same article, he said he married Lady Magnolia because she was 'a fine specimen,' who would ensure that their children would be a credit to the Blanders line. Can you imagine? He called their boys 'perfectly bred' in every way—well-mannered and handsome, accomplished athletes, scholars, and gentlemen. And they're only seven and eight years old!"

"And how was Lady Blanders in person?" Wyatt asks. "As horrid as you expected?"

"I wouldn't know. Tracy made me leave early. She even did the hair wash herself. Probably didn't occur to her that I could use the tip."

I'm standing by the sinks and notice in one of them a plastic face shield, the kind people used to wear during the pandemic.

"Did Tracy always wear a face shield?" I ask.

"Are you kidding?" Dinda says. "She wouldn't even wear a mask during Covid."

"So Lady Blanders made her wear it?" Wyatt asks, looking up from his notebook.

"Like I said, I wasn't here," Dinda says.

The constable clears his throat and says, "As far as we know, Lady Blanders is the last known person to see Tracy Penny alive. Which makes her a prime suspect." He hands us a paper with the address for Hadley Hall, the home of Lady Blanders, a schedule of interviews (ours is tomorrow at eleven thirty in the morning), and directions for getting to the house by foot, bus, or car.

I take photographs of other pages of the calendar—last month's and the coming months. The salon was busy; Tuesdays through Saturdays have back-to-back appointments for cuts and color, and, on the Friday following, a notation about a court date. Mondays are blank except for a standing appointment for someone's blow-dry on Mondays at three. I ask who that would be.

Dinda peers over my shoulder at the calendar. "Dunno. We're closed on Mondays."

The constable looks at his watch.

A sneeze. Again from the direction of the floor.

"Gesundheit," Amity says.

"Could you hand us a tissue, love?" Tracy whispers.

Amity takes a tissue from her purse. "May I?" she asks Germaine.

Germaine sighs and nods. Tracy reaches up to take the tissue and winks.

The door opens, and Naomi, the older and plumper of the Pittsburgh sisters, pokes her head into the salon. "I believe it's our turn."

Behind her, Deborah calls out, "Is it gruesome? I hate the sight of blood."

CHAPTER FOURTEEN

Outside, Wyatt turns to the left and leads us along a narrow alley to the back of the building and a well-tended parking area. There are five spaces marked for cars and, hidden behind a white fence covered with golden honeysuckle, blue recycling bins and black garbage bins. On either side of a narrow dirt path leading away from the parking lot are rosebushes, about to bloom, that look like the ones my grandmother tried to cultivate. The path dead-ends at a slightly wider trail, where a sign on a wooden post reads PUBLIC FOOTPATH. It has two arrows, one marked for the direction of the King George Inn and one pointing the other way, to the "fairgrounds." Beyond the path are more bushes and pastures that blend into gently rolling hills.

When we're back in front of the salon, Wyatt suggests we discuss the crime scene while it's still fresh in our minds.

"It's sad, isn't it?" Amity says. "Tracy Penny had a full life. All those photographs. A vibrant woman."

"There, there, Amity." Wyatt pats her arm. "I think she's going to pull through in the end."

"I haven't forgotten that it's pretend," Amity says. "I'm just trying to imagine how this would feel if it were real. Understanding who the victim was as a person and being angry at the murderer for cutting her life short might help us crack the case. We must think like psychologists."

"Not like detectives?" I say.

"Both," Amity says. "Do you think it's coincidental that Sigmund Freud loved detective stories? They're not only about evidence, they're also about the workings of the human mind. Tracy Penny may be fictional, but we've got to analyze her like she's real. And to that end, I'd say she was vain."

"Why do you say that?" Wyatt asks.

"Because all the photographs in the salon are of Tracy Penny. Did you see that large portrait of herself as a bride? There's only one reason a woman displays her wedding portrait after her marriage ends. Because she knows she looks gorgeous. That's the memory she's conjuring, not the wedding itself."

I get her point, but I still don't understand why anyone would want to display evidence of their own naive hopefulness.

The sun is coming through the clouds, and the air is warming. I take off my rain jacket and fold it over my arm. We review the crime scene and agree that it was strangely tidy. No sign of a struggle, no messy fingerprints or bloody tracks on the floor. It was as if someone entered the salon—either with a key or after Tracy let them in—waited for Tracy to turn her back, thwacked her on the head a few times, and departed, closing but not locking the door.

"It was not a crime of passion," Amity says.

"Not sudden anyway." Wyatt unzips his jacket.

"A premeditated murder," I say slowly.

The way Amity and Wyatt look at me, it occurs to me that if anyone is going to be playing the Watson role in this investigative trio, it's me.

Wyatt asks if we noticed the nylon robe left on the back of the chair. It was an ordinary black robe, the kind that snaps around the neck and that you put on when you get your hair cut or colored.

"It was an extra-large," he says. "And the shaving brush on the shelf opposite that chair was still out—not in its holder—and was dirty. As was the towel beside it."

"In an otherwise clean salon," Amity says.

"Tracy insisted that Dinda leave early," I say. "I guess she didn't have time to tidy up?"

"But if, as Dinda suggested, Tracy wanted to impress Lady Blanders, wouldn't she have cleaned the place before her arrival?" Wyatt says. "Perhaps the mess suggests that Lady Blanders was *not* the last person to see Tracy Penny alive. Someone else was there after her appointment."

"And that someone was a man!" I say.

"Or someone wants us to *think* that a man was there," Wyatt says.

"Ooh, you're good," I say.

"A real sleuthhound," Amity says.

"Never heard that one," Wyatt says, though he stands a little straighter.

"It's in A. A. Milne's *The Red House Mystery*," Amity says.

"Next to *The House at Pooh Corner*?" Wyatt says.

"Entirely different. Milne wrote eclectically, you know. First, he was a humorist at *Punch*, and when he told his agent and publisher he was going to write a detective novel, they told him that what the country wants from a humorist is more humor. Then, after the success of *The Red House Mystery*, when he said he wanted to write nursery rhymes, they insisted that his public wanted a new detective story. But Milne was adamant that the only reason to write something is that you want to write it. He said he'd be as proud to write a telephone directory 'con amore' as he would be ashamed to create a blank verse tragedy because someone else wanted him to."

"Sound advice," says Wyatt.

Amity looks up at him, like she's giving it serious thought.

"I suppose it is."

CHAPTER FIFTEEN

Amity takes out her map and says, "Next stop Gordon's Cha Cha," which still sounds slightly obscene.

Wyatt looks at his phone. "We have to walk three blocks to the river, over a bridge, and across a big parking lot."

Before we head toward Gordon's, Germaine approaches and asks to have a word.

"With me?" I ask.

Germaine is exactly my height but makes me feel small.

"We haven't formally met," she says, "but you know who I am and vice versa. All is well? Wisteria Cottage suits you?"

"It's lovely."

"Roommates amicable enough?"

My roommates are standing there with me.

"They're great."

I introduce Wyatt and Amity. Germaine greets them warmly but seems only interested in me. I smooth down my hair, which I sense has wigged out from the humidity.

"I wanted to say something about your mother," she says.

"Oh, no worries. It's been months now. I'm fine."

"Not condolences, my dear. I believe I already expressed them in my email. I hope it's not too strange to be here without her."

How do I explain to Germaine how much stranger it would be to be here *with* my mother? If we were in England together, would she still find a way to cut out early?

"It's unusual to be here, period," I say.

"I'm sure," Germaine says. "But what I'm eager to know is, are you going to continue her quest?"

"What quest?"

"To find whomever she was searching for, of course."

This is apparently of great interest to Wyatt and Amity, both of whom take a step closer. I tell Germaine I have no idea what she's talking about.

"No? How peculiar. Your mother, whose many emails were delightful, led me to believe she had a very particular reason to be here, maybe even to find someone. She was coy about it, but in a delightful manner, like she was anticipating something wonderful. I'm so sorry she died. I feel we would have been good friends."

Another person charmed by Skye Little.

I fold my arms. I know I look defensive, but I don't care.

"My mother often got carried away. It's totally possible she convinced herself that she had ancestors in England and that with a little digging, she'd trace her lineage back to some landed gentry. Or that like Sara Crewe in *A Little Princess* she'd discover some wealthy relative who'd been trying for years to find her to make good on a promise to bestow an inheritance."

My mother had given me *A Little Princess* when I was a girl. I'd loved the book as she had, but even then, unlike my mother, I knew that miracles like the ones in books don't happen in real life.

Germaine looks skeptical.

"It seemed more grounded than that," she says.

Behind us, the salon door opens. The constable leans out, again wiping his brow with a handkerchief, and tells Germaine that she's needed urgently inside. Maybe the "corpse" is getting chatty again.

"Let's continue this conversation later," Germaine says. "I'll share what I know, and you'll do the same. Stop by my shop this afternoon. *The Book and Hook*. On Crane Street. Impossible to miss. Any time after two o'clock."

"You see?" Amity says, once Germaine is gone. "There's something there. I knew it."

"You'll go talk to her, won't you?" Wyatt says.

I want to say I won't, that I know better, but there it is again: that tiny spark of hope that never fails to emerge no matter how badly my mother has let me down. Even the finality of her death can't extinguish it.

"What's the harm?" Amity speaks gently, as if she knows how loaded this is for me. "I mean, you're here, you might never be back. Maybe you're right and it's nothing, but what if there's something you'd like to know?"

"Is it totally out of the question that it's something good?" Wyatt says.

"You too?" I ask.

He shrugs. "Would I be here if I could resist a good mystery?"

Amity and Wyatt look at me expectantly. I may not be here with my mother, but nor am I alone. Maybe digging a little with Amity and Wyatt will be more of a lark than a threat. If we come up with nothing at all, I'll have confirmed that I know my mother as well as I thought I did. If we find something ridiculous, we can have a laugh at my mother's eccentricity, toast her fanciful approach to life, and put it to bed. And if my mother's quest was for something worth finding? I don't allow myself to consider it.

CHAPTER SIXTEEN

Before we set out for Gordon Penny's dance studio, Wyatt holds up a hand.

"Wait," he says. "Check out that window."

It's an ordinary first-floor window in a narrow stone building. Lace curtains inside, a window box with bright red flowers outside.

"What are we looking at?" I ask.

"Give it a minute."

The curtain lifts, and a woman's face appears. It's hard to make out her features, but then she seems to press her entire face against the glass, so much so that her nose and lips are smushed by the pressure until she looks like a melting clown. I don't understand what I'm seeing until Wyatt says, "That, I believe, is the nosy neighbor."

"Oh, yes," Amity says. "There's always a nosy neighbor."

Mr. Groberg says we're all nosy neighbors, unable to resist the allure of what goes on beyond closed doors, to expose what others are hiding. I think he's right. Why else would Germaine, Wyatt, and Amity be so interested in my mother's alleged quest? Why else would all these Americans have paid good money to pretend snoop in a village planted with fake secrets?

We cross the street, and Wyatt rings the bell. The door opens to reveal a plump, gray-haired woman with reading glasses hanging around her neck on a metal chain.

"Finally! I've been lifting and dropping that curtain all morning. I thought I'd never be noticed. Too subtle, that's what I told Germaine, too subtle. But she insisted, promising me that this was a good and vital role."

She introduces herself as Edwina Flasher and ushers us into her sitting room, which is decorated in early Jane Marple. Shag carpet, couch and easy chair upholstered in beige corduroy, and lace doilies on dark wood furniture. A black rotary phone that looks like a prop sits on a small round table. I'm tempted to pick up the receiver to see if there's a dial tone. Edwina shakes Wyatt's and Amity's hands with brisk efficiency but stops when she turns to me.

"Nice to meet you," I say. "I'm Cath."

"You're American?"

"We all are."

"Yes, of course." She still looks befuddled. "Forgive me. I'm an old woman, and I tend to get things mixed up. Please, have a seat."

Amity, Wyatt, and I squeeze onto the couch. Edwina perches herself on the edge of her recliner. She takes a pair of opera glasses from the side table and holds them up. "If you hadn't noticed my curtain routine, I was going to resort to plan B, which was standing outside on the pavement with these. Plan C was to set up a telescope. Thank you for sparing me that indignity."

Edwina smooths her skirt, thrusts out her ample bosom, sits up taller.

"You said you wanted to question me about a crime?"

We'd said no such thing, but as she seems to be in character now, I decide to go full method too.

"As you no doubt are aware," I say in my most officious voice, "Tracy Penny was murdered last night in the hair salon across the street. We thought perhaps you saw something suspicious. Particularly between eight o'clock and ten o'clock?"

"Bravo," Amity whispers to me.

"Let's see." Edwina Flasher furrows her brow and puts a finger to her pursed lips like an amateur actor demonstrating deep thought. "I went to bed as usual at nine o'clock, but I couldn't sleep, so I got up to make myself a glass of warm milk."

"What time was that?"

"I don't know. I couldn't see the clock clearly. I left my glasses upstairs. But I know I took my milk and sat right there"—she points to a chair under the window, her lookout, presumably—"and tried to think dull, sleepy thoughts—about crochet patterns and cream of mushroom soup—when I saw the lights go on at the salon."

"You hadn't seen anyone enter?" Amity asks.

"I'm afraid not."

"Could you see anything through the salon window?" I say.

"The blinds were drawn, but I could see two people moving about. And then only one person, until the light switched off; the front door opened, and I saw an umbrella."

"How's that?" Amity asks.

"Whoever was there opened a large black umbrella before stepping out. The umbrella completely shielded his face. He was tall and he walked that way, to his left, and out of my view entirely."

"If you couldn't see his face, how did you know it was a man?" Wyatt asks.

Edwina looks confused. "I don't know. I suppose it was his height? I can't say exactly why, but I'm sure it was a man."

"Any idea who?" Amity says.

Edwina shakes her head. "But, you know, it wasn't unusual for Tracy Penny to have a late-night visitor, if you understand my meaning. Since the separation, that is. Sometimes I worried that poor

Gordon, that's Tracy's ex, was going to encounter her paramour one day when he came for his allowance."

"His allowance?" I ask.

"Her paramour?" Amity says.

"Affirmative and affirmative." Edwina looks pleased with herself, as she should be. Her line delivery is excellent. "Gordon came by weekly, always looking rather dejected on the way in and the way out. Must have been terribly humiliating for him. Fortunately, he rarely came on Mondays, when the salon was closed. That's when Tracy dolled herself up to go out. She'd sit there in one of the big chairs and do her own hair and makeup. Then she'd leave, and when she returned, her hair was disheveled." She presses her lips together like she's said something untoward. "Sometimes she received a guest after hours. He was tall and broad-shouldered. Marvelous head of dark hair, which I suppose was important to her, being a hairdresser and all."

"Did they go upstairs to her apartment?" Wyatt asks.

"Sometimes they did, and sometimes they did *not*."

There's the slightest bit of titillation in her tone, a little Peeping Tom to round out the Nosy Neighbor.

"Anything else unusual? Any thoughts on why someone might want Tracy Penny dead?" I say.

Edwina leans forward.

"She wasn't well-liked. Poor Dinda Roost, I believe, was beginning to learn why. She'd been so happy to get hired at the salon as assistant. And good thing too; it had been her last resort. She'd worked everywhere else in town—as a house cleaner for the King George and some others, at two of the local pubs, at the bakery, and at a tearoom. She didn't think she'd like the hair salon, but it turned out that coiffeurs were her calling. Shortly after she started, she told my friend Velma—Dinda still cleans for her once a week—that she loved her job. But I don't think that lasted. Yesterday, I was taking my morning constitutional and passed in front of the salon. It was a lovely day, and the front door was propped open. I couldn't help but hear Tracy and Dinda arguing. A snippet of it anyway."

"Which was?" I ask.

"Dinda said she wanted to be paid fair and square. And Tracy, whose voice was at quite an angry pitch, said, 'And what makes you think I don't?' And then Dinda told Tracy she was cruel and selfish and that she'd suffer for this. And Tracy called Dinda an utterly irresponsible parent. That's all I heard anyway. I didn't want to pry. And it's so strange because Velma never mentioned to me that Dinda had any children at all."

Edwina jumps up and goes back to her window, where she pulls back the curtains, peers outside, and then drops them again. She counts to five under her breath and does the curtain routine again. Across the street, the Pittsburgh sisters are looking at their notes, oblivious to Edwina Flasher's smoke signals.

Wyatt asks where Dinda lives so that we can interview her again later. Edwina tells us that poor Dinda has been quite pressed for money and has been living in an apartment above a garage on the end of town.

"Beware her dog," she warns us. "Her name's Petunia, but don't be fooled. She's a holy terror."

CHAPTER SEVENTEEN

Sticking to our plan to question Gordon next, we follow a cobblestone lane down to the river. It's a bucolic scene, with tall weeping willows on the far bank draping their strands in the water. The side closer to us is walled and edged by a wide walkway for strolling. Young couples push baby carriages, and some schoolboys are skipping stones. The river looks calm, but the ducks paddling upstream and then being pushed back down hint at a deceptively strong current.

As we cross a low bridge over the river, Amity stops to take pictures of two swans gliding beneath us. "Aren't they regal?" she says.

"They're literally regal," I say. "Owned by the British royal family."

"Those two particular swans?" Wyatt looks doubtful.

"All the swans in England. Queen Elizabeth the First wanted to corral some swans and was told their owners might resist giving them up. So she took the issue to court, which ruled that she had a right to any swan on open waters."

"She nationalized the swans?" Wyatt says.

"How ever do you know that?" Amity says.

"I'm not sure. I might have heard it from my mother. She used to concoct stories for me all the time. It's probably not even true."

Amity scrolls through her phone. "She didn't make it up. It was in the 1500s, and since then the royal family holds a ceremony on the Thames every summer where a census is taken of the local swans, weighing them and inspecting them for injuries. Pity, it's in late July. I would have liked to have seen that. A swan inventory, imagine that."

The other side of the river is not as densely built as the village center. We pass a few buildings, still old but not particularly charming, and find Gordon's studio next door to the community pool, which has a sign on the front that reads, CLOSED. SORRY FOR THE INCONVENIENCE. In the studio, four elderly women are paired up, dancing the rumba. A man in the obligatory dance instructor outfit—black V-neck top, stretchy black pants, and soft black shoes—none of which flatter his slightly paunchy physique, swirls around them chanting, "And back, side, together. And forward, side together." When he spots us, he glides our way, calling over his shoulder, "Hips! Activate your hips, ladies!" He stops in front of us, his feet turned out in a ballet dancer's first position.

"Looking for lessons?" he asks.

Wyatt flips open the top of his notebook with Sam Spade panache. "Are you Gordon Penny, husband of Tracy Penny?"

The flash of disappointment on Gordon's face suggests that he'd forgotten about the murder mystery. He rubs a hand over his head as if he's pushing hair back, but it must be an old habit, because other than a few lonely strands crossing his scalp, he's bald.

Gordon sighs. "The one and only," he says.

"If you don't mind, we have a few questions," Wyatt says.

"Give me a moment." Gordon turns back to his students and

claps his hands. "Okay, ladies, brilliant work today. I'm afraid we've got to wrap up early."

Gordon switches off the music. There are some oohs and aahs as the women seem to recall what's going on in their village this week. A plump woman with purple-tinged hair swats Gordon on the hip. "I hope you didn't kill anyone, you cheeky fellow!"

"Do you need an alibi?" another woman asks. "I'll tell them you were with me *all night* and that I know it for sure because we didn't sleep a wink!" More laughter.

The women pick up their things and head out of the studio. Gordon leads us to folding chairs lined up on the wall. He pulls out a chair and sits down opposite us.

"Our deepest condolences," Amity says, patting Gordon on the knee. "Such a shock to lose a dear one in so brutal a manner."

I love how sincere she seems. It's interesting how taking all of this so seriously, acting like we really are detectives investigating a crime, makes it more fun. My drama teacher in high school used to say the first rule of improv was to agree with whatever scenario anyone else created, but I was too self-conscious to listen.

"Yeah, yeah," Gordon says. "Cry me a river."

"Were you married for long?" Amity asks.

Gordon gives us the rundown. Tracy and he were married for fifteen years. Seven years ago, they moved down from Sheffield with plans to run the dance studio together. "I thought she'd finally found her thing after changing her mind all the time. First it was scuba diving and all 'Let's move to the Bahamas and run a dive shop.' And then it was horses—she said she'd never been as happy as doing horse therapy over in Whitby."

"Helping anxious horses?" Wyatt asks.

"Nah, helping kids with horses. You know, troubled kids. With various issues, brain damage, born with differences, that kind of thing. They live in a special school over there, next to the stables, which they visit once a week. Tracy still volunteers there."

"You must mean equine therapy," Amity says. "I've heard of that. Working with horses, communicating with them, can be very calming and help with impulse control."

"If you say so," Gordon says. "Anyway, Trace settled on the dance studio, until she didn't. Then it was hairstyling and certification lessons and, voilà, she opened the salon. And made a solid business of it. Good for her, but I'm left with this place on my own. As if that was *my* big dream."

It's hard to imagine it was. The dance studio is dreary. The chairs are old with ripped vinyl seating. The music comes not from the upright piano in the corner but from a dated-looking boom box. Gordon seems genuine, and I'm guessing Roland Wingford kept his storyline close to the truth to make it easier for him. Maybe Gordon and Tracy are actually husband and wife and he was dragged into this role once she agreed to be murdered.

"Tracy didn't have any enemies?" I ask.

"Like unhappy clients? Not that I know of. The landlord was a bit of a thorn in her side, complaining she was negligent about the salon. She thought he wanted her out. I guess the problem's solved now though."

I write down LANDLORD and ask where we can find him. Gordon tells us his name is Bert Lott and he runs the stationer's shop in the village.

"And where were you last night?" Wyatt asks.

"I was here, working until about five, then down to the local for a pint. Then back here to watch telly. Been sleeping here. Just temporarily you know. There's a room in the back."

"What did you watch?" Wyatt asks.

"The horse races. I'd put a few bets on earlier and wanted to see how I did."

His tone is casual, but something in it makes me think he's trying to justify his gambling or make light of it, like it's not something he takes seriously or does too often. One of my mother's old boyfriends used to sound that way when he talked about betting, like it was just a silly diversion and not something he cared about or put too much time and money into, despite the fact that he spent weeks at Saratoga every summer and had an OTB account. Nevertheless, his gambling was a deal-breaker for my mother, who broke up with him because of it. And he was a good guy, as I recall, even-keeled and funny in a kind way. That's how much she despised gambling.

Wyatt is still talking about the races with Gordon.

"And how'd you make out?" Wyatt asks.

"In the first race, I put a fiver on Hopeless Romantic to win. I lost."

Amity laughs. Gordon glares. He's taking his role awfully seriously.

"And after that?" Wyatt says.

"In the second, I had Cloudy Day to show, and he didn't even place. Had a tricast on the third, no good there either. Then I had an exacta in the last, betting on Raisin Spring and Mud Flat to win and place. Finished with thirty pounds in my account. I came up all right in the end."

"Raisin Spring, you say?" Wyatt asks.

Gordon nods, and Wyatt writes it down with great care, like he's going to look up in a moment and say, *But you can't have won on Raisin Spring, old chap. Raisin Spring was pulled from the race just before entering the gate. Constable, arrest this man immediately!*

Gordon starts fidgeting.

"Is that it?" He stands up, starts ushering us out. "I have a private lesson coming in."

We're about to leave when Wyatt asks if Gordon still has a key to Tracy's salon and apartment.

"Sure, what of it?" Gordon says. "You think I killed Tracy? And why would I do that? She'd already dumped me. Killing her wouldn't bring her back now, would it?"

CHAPTER EIGHTEEN

We go directly from Gordon's Cha Cha to the nearest pub, where we sit outside at a table under a red umbrella and have a lunch in which the only vegetables are the red onion on my hamburger and the crushed garden peas that come with Amity's cottage pie and Wyatt's steak sandwich.

I ask Amity if she ever writes about married people, and she says never, that she only writes about what she calls "the three p's—prelude, plummet, and perfection," otherwise known as flirting, falling in love, and living happily ever after.

"No one wants to read about how people gain weight once they marry, or spend evenings doing crosswords separately, each on their own phone, or how divine it is when your husband goes away on a business trip and you can eat scrambled eggs for dinner and wake up in the morning with the sheets barely rumpled. Just flip back one corner, and the bed is made. It's practically orgasmic."

"Sounds . . . exciting?" Wyatt says.

Amity laughs.

"It's not, but that's okay. Married love ebbs and flows. Soon enough, your husband makes you snort with laughter, or says something so perceptive you're blown away by how well he knows you, or you're watching a *Seinfeld* rerun together and find yourself holding hands. If you didn't drift apart now and then, you wouldn't get to rediscover each other." She pokes at her cottage pie with her fork. "That's how I saw it anyway." Amity pushes back her plate. "But we didn't come here to talk about my marriage. What's next?"

I'm weighted by jet lag and a food hangover, and I need a nap. Wyatt feels jet-lagged too, and says he'll walk back to the cottage with me so he can change and go for a run, which he thinks will revive him. Amity, despite being the oldest of our trio, says she's filled with energy and is going to take a bus to visit a nearby village called Bakewell where Jane Austen is said to have stayed.

As Wyatt and I cross the village green, I'm thinking about our conversation at lunch. I ask Wyatt what he thought of Amity's "three *p*'s."

"She writes fiction, enough said."

We cross the street. Edwina stands at attention at her window, lifting and dropping her lace curtain. I wave, and Wyatt gives her a little salute.

"I don't really buy that 'plummet' thing either," I say.

"Speak for yourself, pumpkin. I plummeted hard."

"Seriously? How'd you guys get together?"

"It was at an Audubon Society fundraiser. I'd recently quit law school, an absurd idea from the get-go to everyone but my lawyer parents, and I was working for my sister. She was catering the gala. Bernard and I chatted during the cocktail hour. He liked my barbecued pulled pork on wonton crisps with jicama slaw and I liked his jawline."

"Excellent prelude."

"When Bernard told me he owned a birding store, it made me laugh. It was so tweedy and grown up, yet weirdly sexy. He was older than me, by a decade. I mean, he knew things—about wingspan and migration patterns and our fine feathered friends. What did I know about anything? Bernard was so earnest, and it didn't hurt that he seemed to be hiding the body of a triathlete beneath his blazer and corduroys. It was so unexpected, you know? Bernard asked for my number and called the next day. By which I mean, he didn't text. He made a phone call."

"How sweet."

"Bernard took me to an early dinner at a tavern a few towns over. He said he wanted to show me 'the swallows' before dark, which I figured was some exclusive gay bar. But after dinner, he drove us to the river and led me to the water's edge. We just stood there. I had no idea why. I mean it was pretty, but nothing dramatic. He said to wait. We waited. I fidgeted. And then I saw them, tiny dots in the distance. A blur at first, and then more dots, until there was a swarm of vibrating black spots filling the sky."

"What was it?"

"Swallows. Hundreds of them, swooping and turning like they'd been choreographed. They twisted up in the air like smoke signals or ribbon dances or, I don't know, waterspouts. Dissolving into shapes and new shapes like images on an Etch A Sketch. Bernard called it a 'murmuration.' I didn't even know that was a word. It's how swallows protect themselves. Strength in numbers. Anyway, it was beautiful. Like something I hadn't known I was looking for, delivered to me in a magnificent swoop. I watched the birds spin themselves into a tornado, which narrowed at the bottom like the birds were being funneled into the ground. And then the sky was clear. Bernard said, 'That's where the birds will settle for the night. Shall we settle in too?'" Wyatt smiles, like he's savoring the moment all over again. "Within a month, I'd moved in with Bernard and was working at Hi, Hi Birdie."

I stop him, my hand on his arm.

"You just jumped into his life, leaving everything behind? That's very impulsive." What had Wyatt been thinking? No wonder he's having troubles now; he rushed in *way* too fast.

"I was all in," Wyatt says. "It was thrilling. He's still everything to me, but he seems frustrated by having me around. He keeps suggesting I find more fulfilling work, as if he could imagine anything more fulfilling than birds."

We pass the cheese shop and the stationer's shop, and we hear music. It's jazz piano, and it's coming from the place on the corner, a narrow space with rustic wooden floors, a few tables with mismatched antique chairs. Inside, a man is sweeping. Just as I realize that it's Dev, he steps close to the door and pushes a pile of dust outside. Wyatt and I both cough.

"Terribly sorry. I didn't see— Oh, Cath, hello." Dev has his sleeves rolled up. His brow glistens with sweat.

"No worries," I say. I introduce Wyatt.

The two men shake hands.

The sign above the bar reads simply, MOSS.

"Interesting name," Wyatt says. "Is it after a person? Moss Hart?"

"Who?" Dev says. He looks a little embarrassed. "It's just for, you know, moss. The green stuff? I've loved it since I was a kid. I used to lie down on it. It feels amazing." He laughs, looks at his feet.

"That's a sweet image." And then my mind travels from sweet to something entirely unexpected. While I'm standing there like nothing odd is happening, I'm imagining being stretched out beside Dev on a velvety bed of moss, his fingers between mine, his gaze intensely loving. I don't even know if he's for real, but Dev's presence is stirring something inside of me, like he's giving off some kind of force field that I can't resist. But that's ridiculous. Maybe one of Amity's heroines would think she'd found her soulmate, but that's not me. I don't "plummet."

Wyatt peers inside the bar. "Looks like a cozy spot."

"It's a start." Dev rocks the broom handle back and forth in a way that makes me think he's about to waltz with it. He says, "We open at eight in case you want to come by."

Is he looking only at me?

"Good to know," I say.

When we resume walking, Wyatt asks if there's anything I want to share.

"No." The tips of my fingers are tingling. I'm probably dehydrated.

"Do we add the handsome barkeep to our list of suspects?" Wyatt says.

"I think he's only helping out." And then I realize that I don't know for sure, that I never got a read on when he was kidding and when he was not. Maybe that's why he's having such a strong effect on me; it's not attraction, it's confusion.

Back at the cottage, jet lag finally catches up to me. I crawl under the comforter and fall into a deep sleep. When I wake up, I'm surprised to see I've been out for nearly three hours. I fill the tub and take a long, hot bubble bath. The citrus scent tickles my nose and is at once relaxing and invigorating. I sink down into the water, let my hair swirl around me. I stretch my legs, wiggle my toes. I am on vacation, free of responsibilities. I imagine myself on a map, across the ocean, up from London, in the heart of the Peak District, in a village, in a cottage, in the bath. I stretch out and give silent thanks for this extra-long tub.

By the time I get dressed, I'm famished. Wyatt's back, and I ask if he wants to join me to get something to eat.

"You're not going straight to cocktails? At a nice little place that opens at eight?"

I can't pretend I haven't thought about it. But what would be the point?

"Food first," I say.

Wyatt declines my offer. I walk back down to the village center and buy some sausage rolls, which I've heard are popular in England. With the first bite, I have to laugh. Of course they're popular. They're pigs in a blanket. Why in God's name have we not made them into fast food too? They're delicious, greasy, and salty, and they leave me with an undeniable thirst. I come upon a pub and look through the window. Inside, there are two tables filled with people I recognize from the parish hall. Naomi and Deborah and some other wannabe detectives. I'm not in the mood for more mystery talk. I walk slowly to the place on the corner, which is still playing jazz. There aren't many people inside. Maybe I'll have one drink.

CHAPTER NINETEEN

"You came."

Dev plants his palms flat on the bar in front of me. He looks happier than last night, which probably has to do less with being in my presence than in being at his own bar instead of helping out at a dinner for tourists.

"I figured I should try artisanal gin," I say.

"Which is, indeed, a thing."

I think he's making fun of me, but he's smiling, so I don't mind.

Dev gestures to the bottles behind him and says, "What's your fancy?"

"Gin and tonic?"

"Not on my watch."

He hands me a small menu in the shape of a bottle. I scan the cocktails. I point to something called a Bramble and say, "This sounds good, but I have no idea what crème de mûre is."

"It's a French liqueur, from blackberries."

"My favorite berry." I remember getting stains on my fingers from picking the wild berries that used to grow behind my grandmother's house. I should have taken better care of the bushes.

"One Bramble, coming up."

Dev fills a cocktail shaker with ice. He runs his fingers over a row of fat little bottles with blue labels—his gins, I suppose—and pulls one out. With the excited focus of an artist starting a new canvas, he pours in gin, and simple syrup, and squeezes in some lemon juice. He flicks the shaker back and forth, watching me watching him, and then strains it into a tumbler of crushed ice. He picks up a bottle with a long, thin neck and displays it for me the way a sommelier would present a fine wine.

"Voilà, le crème de Mûre."

I lean in and say, "I concur."

He has a warm laugh. I want to believe what he told me yesterday, which is that he was not playing a role in the fake murder. Until I remember that even if he was telling the truth about his mother, his flirtation could be scripted. I'm going to have to observe him carefully. Slowly, he pours the liqueur into the drink, which turns a purplish pink, and tops it with a lemon wheel and two blackberries. He places it on a cocktail napkin in front of me. Eyes on him, I take a sip. It's a perfect blend of sweet and tart.

"Not bad."

There are three women at the other end of the bar now, members of the mystery book group from Tampa. They glance my way but show no signs of recognition, maybe because I'm not with Wyatt and Amity. Dev walks over and says something that makes them all laugh. One of the women tucks a loose tendril behind her ear. Another whoop of laughter. I remember that bartenders are professionally social and that it's their job to make customers, especially women, feel comfortable and even desirable.

My drink goes down easy, like lemonade. Dev is busy now, making drinks for the Tampa women, who are getting louder, leaning in toward him. When he looks my way, I hold up my glass and mouth, "Another?" He nods, keeps moving, pouring and shaking, delicately placing herb sprigs and citrus slices. When he brings my second drink, he says, "Cheers," and turns to wipe down the bar where he'd been working. A few more customers come in. By the time Dev comes back my way, I'm buzzed.

"You're sure you're not an actor? Never been on the stage?" I ask.

"If you must know"—he looks around, like he's checking to see if anyone's listening—"at school, I was in *You're a Good Man, Charlie Brown.*"

"Which role?"

"Linus."

"With an American accent?"

"God, no. But the critics said I sucked my thumb with great panache."

I peer at him, too dramatically, but I can't help myself. "Why do you live here, really? Are you trying to single-handedly bring down the village's average age?"

He laughs.

"After my parents got divorced, my mum moved back here and my dad moved to Delhi to find his roots. I left London two years ago, when mum took a turn for the worse."

"You live with your mother?"

If he says yes, he's definitely not acting; even Roland Wingford wouldn't script that detail into a character meant to be the local heartthrob.

"I live in a cottage on her property. Alone."

"Oh." I give myself a moment. "I live alone too." I pick up the cocktail menu and look like I'm studying it, but I don't register the words. Should I not have said that? But when I look up, he's leaning in close, dark hair flopping onto his forehead, and pointing to the menu. He recommends the Hanky Panky, and I have to make an extra effort to swallow.

"It's gin, sweet vermouth, and Fernet-Branca," he says.

I have no idea what that means.

"It's an Italian brand of fernet, a kind of bitters," he adds, turning and taking a bottle off the shelf.

I ask what's in it.

"The recipe has been a secret since it was formulated in 1845, but if I had to guess," he says, opening a bottle and taking a sniff, "I'd say it has gentian, probably chamomile, maybe Chinese rhubarb, definitely peppermint and saffron, and myrrh."

"Get out. Like frankincense and myrrh? From the Bible? They're real?"

He gets that excited look on his face again. "They're resin extracted from trees. They're brilliant, really. Chemists in Italy discovered a molecule in myrrh that affects the brain's opioid receptors and acts like an analgesic."

"Well, then, make mine a double."

He looks amused. He mixes the ingredients, strains the blend into a glass with ice, garnishes it with an orange twist. The drink is a luscious red.

"It's good."

"And good for you," he says. "Bitters have cancer-fighting properties."

"You sound like a scientist."

"That was the plan. But chemistry led me to distilling, which is a lot more fun." He folds his arms, leans onto the bar. "So, what do you do when not solving pretend murders?"

It's hard to think with him so close to me.

"I help people see," I say.

"You're a fortune teller?"

I shake my head.

"A psychotherapist?"

I laugh. "That'd be a joke. I tried therapy once in college, and it was kind of a bust." The only secret I revealed is that I don't like talking about myself.

"You're an art history professor?"

"I don't even like museums," I whisper.

He's scrutinizing me like my face will reveal what I am. I'm not a fan of being interrogated, but I want him to keep guessing wrong so he'll have to keep looking at me. He shrugs and says he's stumped. I'm reluctant to tell him. I've never felt ashamed of my job, but any pride I take from it has been more about keeping a local business afloat than loving my work. It's what I do: I live in the same house where I grew up and have worked in the same establishment since high school.

"I'm an optician."

"Ah, I see."

"Then you don't need my services?" For a second, I regret how flirty that sounds, but Dev says, "On the contrary. It's been ages since I've had my eyes checked."

I lean closer. "Your eyes look *very* good to me. And that's a professional opinion."

"What do I owe you for the diagnosis?"

"No charge." I explain that I don't do eye exams, just fit people with glasses. I imagine him in dark frames that would complement his thick brows, warm eyes, beautifully curved lips. "You'd look sexy in geeky glasses," I say.

"Or geeky in sexy glasses."

I'm not exactly spinning, but I'm feeling the effects of the Hanky Panky. My hands are on the bar, tantalizingly close to Dev's forearms. Arms that have been deep in the dirt of his garden, making things grow. Rhubarb. What a funny word. I whisper it. *Rhubarb.*

Dev asks if I'm okay. I squeeze my eyes shut and open them again.

"Please tell me you're not drinking on an empty stomach," he says. The familiarity of the remark reads more like genuine concern than bossiness.

"Does a sausage roll count?"

Dev goes to the end of the bar and comes back with a packet of cashews and a bright yellow bag of something called Scampi Fries.

"These seem like a weird match for fancy cocktails," I say.

I push the bag away and tell him the nuts will do fine. He shakes his head and walks off to take someone's order. I nibble cashews, watching him. The nuts awaken my appetite. I reconsider the Scampi Fries, which according to the bright yellow packet are "a cereal snack with a delicious scampi and lemon taste." I open the bag and take some out. How about that, they look like Cinnamon Toast Crunch. Worth a try. Bursts of buttery, lemony, bacony, fishy heaven. A few more. Why don't we have these at home? I polish off the rest of them, tip my head back, and shake the bag to pour the crumbs into my mouth. When I right myself, I'm face-to-face with Dev. He looks at me like I've done something hilarious. I hiccup and put my hand to my mouth. Smiling, Dev turns away to get drinks for a couple who's just settled at the bar. I figure I'd better leave before I get sloppy, but as I push off my stool, Dev is back. He takes the towel from his waistband, and for a second I think he's going to undress. Clearly, it's time for me to call it a night. He asks if he can walk me back to my cottage. I tell him that would be nice. He folds the towel and places it on the bar. He calls to a waiter and says he'll be back in ten.

Outside, the air is cool and damp. The village is eerily quiet. The whiz of a car passing by. Footsteps in the distance. It reminds me of a stage set for a murder mystery, which I suppose it is. The stone houses are close to the street. Through lace curtains, I see the flickering glow of a television. A woman reaching for a light switch.

The sidewalk is too narrow for both of us, so Dev walks beside me in the street. Without looking, I can sense him glancing at me.

"Do you often walk inebriated customers home?" I ask.

"No, I wouldn't say that," Dev says. "This is a first." A few more paces. "Do you often get too sloshed to manage on your own?"

"No, I wouldn't say that." I'd like to be able to say this is a first, but the year after my grandmother died was rough.

We turn off the main road and up the lane. Dev stops at the gate in front of Wisteria Cottage. I'm surprised that he knows where I'm staying, but then I remember he's pals with Germaine. Dev opens the gate and waits for me to cross into the garden.

"I should get back," he says.

"Right." I turn around.

"Good night," he says.

We don't move. We each reach for the gate, and our hands touch. Does he think I did that on purpose? I grasp his hand and give it a firm, businesslike handshake.

"Thank you for the safe delivery," I say.

He looks amused.

"Thank you for being a valued client," he says.

He's still holding my hand.

"Good night," I say.

"Good night, Cath."

The way he whispers my name is as intimate as a kiss.

CHAPTER TWENTY

Inside, I lean my head back against the door with my eyes closed like a young woman in an old movie after a dreamy date.

"Interesting evening?" Wyatt says.

Wyatt and Amity are on opposite couches, Amity in a floral nightgown and matching robe and Wyatt in flannel pajamas. They're each cradling a wineglass, and there's a nearly empty bottle of red on the coffee table. Something about Amity seems off.

"Is everything okay?" I ask.

"Amity's feeling bamboozled," Wyatt says.

I ask them to give me a minute and I go upstairs to the bathroom, where I pee and splash cold water on my face. I take two Tylenol and go back downstairs. When I'm settled in the armchair, Amity tells me about her day. That afternoon, she went to Bakewell as planned to visit the Rutland Arms Hotel, where, according to several guidebooks and websites, Jane Austen had stayed while writing *Pride and Prejudice*. Amity's tea was delightful—crustless sandwiches with watercress and scones with clotted cream. Before leaving, she bought a history of the hotel, which she read that evening, upon which she made the unpleasant discovery that it was all a myth, cooked up as a marketing ploy more than a hundred years ago and embellished in a 1936 guidebook by the Bakewell town clerk, apparently in cahoots with the proprietor of the Rutland Arms. In truth, Jane Austen had never visited Bakewell or anywhere in Derbyshire.

"I was hoodwinked!" Amity says. "I so wanted to walk in Austen's footsteps. Isn't it rotten when the facts ruin a good story?" She pours herself more wine and gives me a good long stare. "Enough about me, tell us why you look so *glowy*."

Wyatt swivels around and up onto his knees. "You were with the beautiful bartender! Is he for real?"

I sink into the upholstered chair.

"Maybe?"

"Does it matter?" Amity says. "Role-play can be extremely sexy. In my last novel, the main characters met in an improv class."

"Proximity to danger is also a turn-on," Wyatt says.

"So true," Amity says. "Douglas and I used to make love on the trampoline in our backyard. Hidden by tall hedges, but transgressive enough to be very exciting."

"And Cath might be sleeping with a murderer!" Wyatt says.

"I'm not sleeping with anyone," I say, my stomach taking a little tumble at the thought.

But they're not wrong. The element of mystery is probably why flirting with Dev is so irresistible. And if something happens, and I'm still not sure either of us wants it to, it will be temporary by default. It will have the same predetermined expiration date that gives summer romances their freedom and ease. You can be all in because when time's up it's an easy-peasy *Cheerio, old chap, it's been grand.*

"Whatever you do, don't get so blinded by lust that you miss important clues," Wyatt says. "At this point, our culprit could be anyone. Your bartender, Germaine, even Constable Bucket."

"Would they do that, make the people running the show part of the crime?" I ask. "Wouldn't that go against the Detection Club's motto to play fair?"

Amity waves a hand dismissively. "Agatha Christie broke the rules all the time. In one of her best-known mysteries, *The Murder of Roger Ackroyd*, the man recounting the story of the murder turns out to be the one who did it."

"He manages to describe the crime without incriminating himself?" I say.

"Absolutely. Christie almost got kicked out of the Detection Club for making the narrator the culprit, but in the end, Dorothy Sayers voted to keep her in."

"Good marketing decision," Wyatt says.

"Even when she didn't break the rules, Christie was brilliantly confounding," Amity says. "The best is *The Mirror Crack'd from Side to Side*."

She tells us how in that book, Christie's plot rests on a false assumption made early on by the characters. A famous American actress hosts a party at her home in an English village during the local fete. A young woman, a fan, tells the actress how she'll never forget meeting her years ago, because she had German measles at the time and dragged herself out of her sickbed to meet her idol. Shortly after that conversation with the actress, the young woman is poisoned by a deadly cocktail. But when it is discovered that her cocktail had been accidentally switched with the actress's drink, everyone assumes that the actress was meant to be the target, which makes sense considering the fan was such a nobody.

"The entire investigation, most of the book, really, focuses on Miss Marple trying to figure out why someone would want the actress dead," Amity says, getting up and taking the empty wineglasses into the kitchen. "And there are several plausible suspects. But it turns out that the young woman, the fan, was the target all along. You see, years ago the actress had given birth to a brain-damaged child. And when the young fan told the actress about going to meet her even though she had the German measles, the actress realizes that she had contracted the illness from this young fan and that's why her child was born the way it was. She kills her in revenge."

"Interesting," Wyatt says. He stands up and folds the blankets on the couch. Amity straightens the books on the coffee table.

"It's a great story, but terribly dated," she says. "The actress refers to her child as 'an idiot' and 'an imbecile.' She never says the child's name or if it was a boy or a girl. It's meant to be completely understandable that she immediately shunted the child off to an institution and kept it all a secret."

"Agatha Christie would be canceled for that today," I say.

We move toward the stairs and head up, discussing whether we think Roland Wingford and team have created an old-fashioned, golden age kind of mystery or something more contemporary. We all expect the former.

In my room, I drop myself onto my bed without changing. I lie still, but images are spinning in my mind. The actress in *The Mirror Crack'd from Side to Side* moaning about the misfortune of having an "imbecile child." Poisoned cocktails being moved around like chess pieces. Amity's fictional lovers at improv class, leading every sketch toward a passionate embrace. I shake my head on the pillow to clear my thoughts. I close my eyes and conjure a moment that I want to feel again: Dev's hand in mine, how it was the right size, the right weight, the right warmth. How much I didn't want to let go. I hold on until, finally, I drift off to sleep.

CHAPTER TWENTY-ONE

MONDAY

Are the English a bit loosey-goosey about giving directions or are we Americans feeble about following them? Because we are completely lost. We've emerged from a dense, damp woods and are standing at the edge of a field trying to determine the difference between "bear right," "bear slightly right," and "bear right but pull gradually away." Even if I weren't hungover, I'd be lost.

"It says here we're to head toward a copse of trees," says Amity, looking down at the directions she'd been given by Constable Bucket.

Wyatt points to a row of skinny trees at the bottom of the field. "Is that a copse?"

"Isn't that a strip?" Amity says. "A copse is maybe more like a little grove?"

"Can we rest?" I ask. "Please?"

I sit down on a fallen log. I've finished my water bottle, and, according to the directions for the scenic route that we think we're following, Hadley Hall, the home of Lady Magnolia Blanders, is another mile away. My head is pounding.

"We have to find a copse, cross a meadow, and go through a stile."

"What, pray tell, is a stile?" Wyatt says.

"It's an opening, like a narrow passage or some steps, that we can go through but animals can't," Amity says. "It might even be a wooden turnstile, which I guess is where the name comes from. Or maybe vice versa." She turns back to the directions. "After that we follow a lane that is not a path and traverse a woodland. Which may or may not be the same as a woods."

"Cocktails are dead to me," I say. "I'm never drinking again."

Did I embarrass myself last night?

"Please," Wyatt says. "We've all been there—you, me, and the Bohemian waxwing."

I put a hand to my forehead to shield the sun from my eyes and look up at Wyatt.

"It's a snazzy little bird that tends to overindulge," he says. "When they eat too many fermented berries they get drunk and fly into buildings and fences."

A sharp, high-pitched chirping right above us. And then a quick rat-a-tat-tat that goes directly into my head like a nail gun.

"Please make it stop," I say.

"Great spotted woodpecker," Wyatt says.

Amity puts her hands on her hips. "Onward. Lady Magnolia awaits." She points to some trees in the distance. "I think it's that way."

We cross a meadow and follow the path into the trees, which Amity declares a woodland, where we come upon an astonishing sight. As far as we can see, blanketing the ground and circling the tree trunks, are bright purple-blue flowers that come nearly to our knees. The wind blows, and they bend in unison as gently as seaweed in shallow water.

"How beautiful," I say.

Amity clears her throat and recites:

The Bluebell is the sweetest flower
That waves in summer air:
Its blossoms have the mightiest power
To soothe my spirit's care.

"Who's that?" Wyatt asks.

"Emily Brontë," Amity says.

"The creator of Heathcliff?" I'm astonished. "So by the time she penned that poem, the depression had lifted?"

"Oh, no," Amity says. "It gets much darker."

I take a step off the path so I can be surrounded by this ocean of color. My mother used to tell me a bedtime story, one that went on for years, that took place in a country village surrounded by hills of bluebells that bloomed briefly every spring. All the village children would scamper out to see them before they faded and died, singing a nursery rhyme that was gibberish to me—*bluebells, cockle shells, eevy, ivy, over.*

"Are you okay?" Amity asks.

"The flowers reminded me of something."

I tell them about the country village with the bluebells in my mother's story, and how I never expected to see those flowers in real life.

"Maybe that's why she wanted you to come here," Wyatt says.

"My mother could be flighty, but she would not spend thousands of dollars to show me some flowers, no matter how pretty."

When we come out of the woods, we follow the path across another meadow, this one a cow pasture. The animals ignore us, but their presence is jarring after the peaceful landscape of the bluebells. It's so strange walking through someone's property. I keep expecting a farmer with a rifle to pop out from behind a tree and tell us to get off his damn land. But we're not in America anymore; this is Britain, which Amity says has ninety-one thousand miles of footpaths, often crossing private land, on which the public has the legally protected right to walk and stop briefly to admire the view. There are also bridle paths, where you can ride a horse or a bicycle. The paths go back centuries, I suppose so people could get to the market or church and young women in books could take bracing walks and arrive at their destination with mud on their hems and color in their cheeks.

We cross another field, this one dotted with bored-looking sheep, which seem to be the only kind. My headache starts to dissipate. It feels good to walk the countryside like this, to not only admire the landscape but be part of it. As we traipse through meadows and fields, I start to feel steadier and stronger. I read once that the cure for anything is salt water—sweat, tears, or the sea—and that may be true, but walking is setting me to rights. It's hard to believe I've been here for only three days. There's an ease I feel with Wyatt and Amity that often eludes me with people at home. And this landscape is so soothing, though like nowhere I've ever been. It's a pleasant kind of disorientation. This must be why people travel. Tiny yellow flowers bloom in the grass. The air smells sweet. The breeze is soft, even ticklish. In the distance, a tall church spire rises from the trees.

"The village in my mother's story had a church with a crooked spire," I say. "It was straight until a devil kicked it or something."

"I'm pretty sure there's a church with a crooked spire not far from here," Amity says. "I read about it in a guidebook."

"Engineering wasn't so great, back in the day," I say. "There are probably lots of churches with crooked spires."

Amity takes out her phone. She reads for a bit and then says, "Look at this."

It's a photograph of an old church, with a spire that's twisted like soft ice cream and leaning to one side.

"That's the Church of St. Mary and All Saints in Chesterfield, not far from here," she says. "Otherwise known as the Church with the Crooked Spire. Let's see. The twisting can be explained by the physics, blah blah blah, lead and wood, the sun heating the lead covering on one side, blah blah. But there are also less scientific explanations."

"Such as?" I ask.

"One says that the devil sneezed while holding on to the spire and twisted it in one go. Another is that the devil wrapped his tail around the spire and then tried to fly away with it. And one says that a devil got stung by a bee and it hurt so much that he flung out his leg and kicked the spire."

"This is the same spire?" Wyatt says.

"What?" I don't get what he's talking about.

"That's three things," Wyatt says emphatically. "The Queen's swans, bluebells, and the church with a crooked spire. All things in your mother's stories that have a connection to this area. Don't you find that odd?"

"I mean, maybe? But it's probably just coincidence."

"I don't think so," Wyatt says. "I think your mother knew this area, maybe even Willowthrop itself, and that's why she wanted to come. You need to keep a list—note down anything that links your mother to something here."

I loved my mother's bedtime stories, both because they were fanciful and because they were long. She'd never leave in the middle of a story, and as long as she was talking, I knew she was staying put. I'd ask lots of questions so that she'd go into more detail and conjure more fabulous tales. My favorite part of the village story was about a magical bridge with five arches. The bridge crossed a river, and if you stood on the banks at the right time and lifted your arms up as high as you could, a train would come over the arches and transport you somewhere wonderful—to a fairy village, or an enchanted bakery, or a farm where all the ponies were snow white with gaits as smooth as rocking chairs.

Amity surveys the pasture sloping below us and the woods in the distance.

"There," she says, pointing at four chimneys poking above the treetops. "That must be Hadley Hall. We're heading that way."

At the bottom of the hill is a wooden fence. There's no gate or stile in sight, so we heave ourselves up and climb over, thankful for the placid livestock that don't require barbed wire. We cross the road and find ourselves on a paved path that winds through beech trees. We come upon a sign and an arrow pointing us to Hadley Hall. Amity waves the directions in the air in triumph. I pluck a leaf out of her hair.

The medieval hall looks like one of the blocky sandcastles made by filling rectangular buckets with wet sand and turning them upside down. It's rough around the edges, the kind of place you'd expect to find as a deserted ruin on a stormy coast. There's grass growing between the worn stones of the courtyard and a battered wooden door with an iron knocker. The place looks uninhabited. I imagine Lady Blanders appearing as some kind of a ghost, in a diaphanous nightgown, long gray hair, and overgrown fingernails.

We're stomping our feet to get the mud off our shoes when a shiny black horse canters into the courtyard, its rider a straight-backed woman with flowing dark red hair. The horse's bridle and saddle, which has a brown nylon bag on the back, are so well polished that they gleam in the sunlight. A man comes rushing down the steps and takes the reins.

"Good ride, Your Ladyship?" he says. "The new shoes are sound?" He pats the horse on the leg.

"Seem to be. Have the others been done?" Her manner is clipped and officious.

"Not yet, Your Ladyship. Old Mr. Welch is still at work."

She frowns. "Must he be so slow? See to it that he hurries up." She dismounts and smooths her velvet jacket, turning toward us. There's nothing ghostly about her. She's maybe in her late forties, and striking, with the luxurious flaming hair and green eyes of a heroine from a bodice-ripper romance. She's larger than life, and not only because she's tall and broad-shouldered.

Lady Blanders purses her lips and tilts her head like she's expecting something from us.

Amity says, "Oh," and drops into a deep curtsy.

Wyatt puts one leg straight out in front of him, bends at the waist and flourishes his arm a few times like a court jester.

I nod my head and mumble, "Pleased to meet you, Your Lady-ship."

"Charmed," she says haughtily. The three of us are frozen. I know we're all play-acting here, but the thought of questioning this formidable woman about anything, let alone a fake murder, is intimidating.

And then Lady Blanders throws back her head, slaps her thigh, and lets out a honking laugh.

"Silly Yanks, I'm having you on. Lord knows what they put in the water across the pond, but you're a funny lot."

And with that, she turns and bounds up the stairs, leaving us to gape and follow.

CHAPTER TWENTY-TWO

"Ah, the fire is lit. Delightful."

Lady Blanders ushers us into what she calls "the morning room" but which looks like a place where you'd be informed your land is under siege. Beneath a cathedral ceiling supported by exposed beams, the room is paneled with intricately carved dark wood with one wall nearly completely covered by a tapestry of cavorting animals. The hearth, tall enough to stand inside, makes the wood burning within look as small as Lincoln Logs. On either side of the fireplace are tall windows with wavy leaded glass. Above the mantel is an oil painting of a white bird with a vast wingspan swooping down toward what appears to be a pregnant mouse. The furniture is too small for the room: a gray velvet couch, two matching armchairs, and side tables, each with a few photographs in silver frames. I take pictures of everything.

"The morning room, is this where you do your correspondence?" Amity asks, apparently not registering the lack of a desk.

"Oh, certainly." Lady Blanders gestures for us to sit. "And from where I inform the head housekeeper which sauce to serve with the veal." She peers at us so imperiously that I wiggle farther away from her on the sofa. "Don't be silly. My laptop is on the second floor of the north wing, in my office." She looks toward the door. "Ah, yes, here we are. Thank you, Mrs. Crone."

A pale, angular woman in a white cotton blouse and a black skirt the same color as her sleek bun comes in carrying a tray with a porcelain tea set and a tiered dish of shortbread cookies. She walks stiffly, bowlegged, and bends over slowly to set down the tray. As she straightens up, she glares at me with a look that seems like both enticement and warning, like she's going to bring me upstairs to brush her employer's negligee on my cheek and then hiss at me to flee and never return.

"Milk? Sugar?" Lady Blanders makes a grand show of holding the teapot up and slowly pouring each cup from a great height, either to show off her dexterity with liquids or her jewelry, both of which are impressive. As the teapot rises and falls, the sun catches her rings, one a sparkling diamond, the other platinum with an emerald the size of a domino, and her shiny gold bracelet with three letter charms, *A*, *B*, and *C*.

"What a lovely bracelet," Amity says. "Is there a significance to the letters?"

"It's not apparent?" Lady Blanders says, holding out her wrist.

"The alphabet?" Amity says.

"Obviously, but Ingeborge Svenska," Lady Blanders says.

"The Swedish alphabet?" Wyatt says.

Lady Blanders gives him an icy look. "The Swedish jewelry designer."

"Oh," Amity says.

I turn to Wyatt to see if he has a clue. He shrugs.

Lady Blanders finishes serving us all tea and then, with a cold smile, says, "On to murder. I am at your service."

It's hard not to laugh. She's obviously acting, and I remind myself to play along.

Wyatt flips through the pages of his notebook. "You are believed to be Tracy Penny's last client yesterday, and the last person known to have seen her alive," he says.

"Golly." Lady Blanders brings a hand to her chest. "Does that make me a suspect?" She clears her throat. "Hold on, let me try that again. Golly! Are you suggesting I'm a *suspect*?"

I can't tell if Lady Blanders has been scripted to act snobby one moment and "we're all in on the joke" the next or if she can't help breaking character. It's confusing and also funny.

"At this point, everyone is a suspect," Wyatt says, his voice deeper than usual, his manner suggesting he is fully committed to his role as detective. "If you would, Lady Blanders, what brought you to Tracy Penny's establishment yesterday?"

"Bad luck, I suppose." Lady Blanders crosses one leg over the other. "I had a photographer coming to take my portrait for an upcoming gala at which I'm to be honored for my great integrity. Such a lovely gesture for little old me. I just am what I am, what you see is what you get. Where was I? Oh, yes, my personal hairdresser was detained in London. Something about Camilla, apparently. She's really gotten to be too much since all the brouhaha."

"Since the coronation, you mean?" Amity asks. Her posture is exemplary, like a young lady taught by a governess never to let her spine touch the back of her seat.

"Call it what you will." Lady Blanders waves a hand dismissively. "It was terribly inconvenient. Was I to dry my hair myself? Fortunately, or I suppose *unfortunately*, my maid suggested I go to that little place in town with the silly name, Hair Today, Gone Tomorrow.

"Hairs Looking at You," I say.

"And you." She lifts her teacup and winks. I take a photo, and Wyatt continues jotting down notes.

113

"So you arrived and left at what time?" he asks.

"I got there at four o'clock and I left at four forty-five. I remember because I was already in my car when I got a call from my gardener, who was leaving for the day. He was inquiring if I'd come up with a name for a new rose. It's become such a challenge. We've gone through the whole family, including some of the lesser relatives and the pets. The Rocky Graziano Rose is absolutely stunning."

"Named for the boxer?" I ask.

"Heavens no, our Rocky is a French bulldog. Purebred, of course. Lord Blanders wouldn't have it otherwise. He wouldn't tolerate a pet with imperfections."

"Back to your hair," Wyatt says.

"Anything unusual about your experience at the salon?" Amity asks.

"The result was a little frizzier than I like. More tea?" Her bracelet glitters as she picks up the pot.

"Did you and Tracy talk while she was doing your hair?" Wyatt asks.

"She talked. She's quite the chatterbox. She went on and on about her soon-to-be ex-husband, who sounds rather a bore. Although my maid tells me that Tracy Penny herself wasn't a paragon of fidelity and that she hasn't precisely been on hiatus, carnally speaking, but you didn't hear that from me." She runs her thumb and forefinger over her lips as if to zip them closed. "Tracy Penny also complained about her landlord. How after years of telling her she was the model tenant, he'd taken to badgering her about all sorts of things, as if she was not only being negligent but ruining the building, which, if you ask me, looked like a crime scene even before the murder."

"Did Tracy say he complained about the condition of her flat too?" Wyatt asks.

"I don't believe so," Lady Blanders says.

Amity asks if she knows if Tracy Penny had any enemies.

"I wouldn't have the slightest idea. We don't spend much time here. Digby, I mean Lord Blanders, prefers one of our other homes, Claddington Castle. I come here from time to time to oversee renovations. This place has been in my husband's family for centuries, but it's been quite neglected. I plan to bring it back to life. A legacy for the children."

"How old are your children?" Amity asks.

"I have two sons. Charles and Benedict. Seven and eight years old. At boarding school, of course."

"I've also got only boys," says Amity. "Did you wish for a daughter too?"

Lady Blanders stares coldly. "Why ever would you say that?"

Amity looks deflated. I want to remind her this is all an act, that she shouldn't let herself feel dismissed by someone who isn't real.

I point to one of the framed photographs on the table. It's Lady Blanders, standing in front of another grand home, not as old as Hadley Hall and considerably more inviting. "Is that Claddington Castle?"

"Goodness, no," Lady Blanders says. "That's Sproton House. It belonged to my husband's uncle, Thorton Thorton-Graham, but the poor fellow had a run of bad luck, blackjack in Monte, I believe, and had to pawn it off. Now, it's a luxury spa with a renowned hair salon. Quite an improvement."

"Is it nearby? I'd love to get a massage," Amity says.

"Not too far. In Whitby, a few hours' drive. If you go, you must try their frangipani body wrap. It's brilliant."

"Do you go there often?" I ask.

"I've been going once a month for years."

She stands up. "Will that be all?"

Wyatt and Amity seem as surprised as I am with the abrupt end to the interview. As we stand and start for the door, Wyatt turns and says, "Oh, one more thing." He sounds like a real detective, casually asking an important question on the way out. "Mind telling us where you were Saturday night?"

"Not at all. I was dining with my dear friend Demetra Sissington, at the King George. Eight o'clock reservation. I drove myself there and back, was home at ten fifteen. I'd say you could check with Dissy but she's gone to Mustique. I suppose you could call the maître d'. He seated us himself. I had the snails. Divine. Went right to bed, isn't that right, Mrs. Crone?" She looks to the hall. "Mrs. Crone?"

The maid walks in, wincing with each step. "Yes, Your Ladyship?"

"When was I home from dinner Saturday night?"

"Ten fifteen, Your Ladyship."

"And what did I do?"

"The usual, Your Ladyship. Green juice with cardamom extract, face mask, bed."

"And where were you between eight and ten p.m. that night?" Wyatt asks the maid.

"Here, of course."

"Why 'of course'?" Wyatt says.

"The green juice doesn't make itself," she says.

Lady Blanders turns toward us, waving a hand to dismiss her servant. "Ask any of the other staff, they'll vouch for her. Gladys Crone is absolutely trustworthy. She's been with me forever, since before I was married. Knows me like a favorite book—though, come to think of it, I'm not sure I've ever seen her reading."

She watches the maid move slowly out of the room. "Do something about that walk of yours, Mrs. Crone. Hot soak or something. It won't do."

Lady Blanders turns back toward us. "So, you see, I have an airtight alibi. And even if I didn't, what could my motive be? Why would I possibly want to murder Tracy Penny, a common hairdresser? What is she to me? An utter insignificance."

And with that, Lady Blanders bids us good day and stares at us until there's nothing to do but turn and leave.

CHAPTER TWENTY-THREE

We wait to speak until we're across the courtyard and presumably out of earshot of Lady Blanders and any of her alleged staff. And then we all burst out laughing.

"She has got to be bogus," Wyatt says.

"One million percent," I say. "Roland and Germaine would know that a bunch of Anglophile Americans would be disappointed if we didn't get to encounter a grand lady in a grand home so they created Lady Magnolia Blanders."

"And hats off to her Oscar-worthy mash-up of Queen Elizabeth, Nancy Mitford, and the Dowager Countess What's-her-face from *Downton Abbey*," Wyatt says.

Amity agrees Lady Blanders was playing a part but still thinks she might be the real owner of Hadley Hall. "Did you notice how she said 'home,' like it had two syllables? Just like the Queen in *The Crown*. I think she was genuinely posh. In my town at home, they do house walks to raise money for the local schools, and there's always some fabulously wealthy person who opens up their home, both to show it off and to help make the benefit a success. And it doesn't matter which one is the motivation." She stops and looks back at Hadley Hall, which from this vantage point looks a little creepy. "It was a thrill to be in there, wasn't it? The tea was top-notch."

Amity consults her map and directs us toward a path under some oak trees that look like they've been growing for millennia. It's marked as a bridle path. A little farther on is a small sign that reads, WILLOWTHROP VILLAGE, 1.1 MILES. There was a more direct route all along.

"We have to find a motive for Lady Blanders," Wyatt says. "They would not have made her the last person to see Tracy Penny alive without providing a clue why she *might* have killed Tracy."

I disagree. I argue that Lady Blanders was included for our entertainment, not because she has a role in the murder. She had never met Tracy before Saturday and didn't know anyone in the village. She's an outsider.

Our path winds through a lush forest dotted with deep red rhododendrons and pink azaleas, the kind of bushes people pay good money for back home.

Wyatt starts listing things we learned about Lady Blanders that could be clues: she has a personal hairdresser, a longtime maid, and a gardener; she's being honored by some charity, has two sons and a snobby husband, with whom she doesn't spend much time; and she goes to Sproton House spa every month. She also said that Tracy's husband is a loser and that Tracy is known for having lovers. Oh, and she has a friend named Demetra.

"Who doesn't?" I say.

"Dissy," Amity says. "They always use nicknames."

"We'll have to check her alibi at the King George Inn, but let's go to the stationer's first to question Tracy's landlord, Bert Lott," Wyatt says. "While we're there, we can buy a bulletin board."

"Yes!" Amity says. "And some red string."

"What for?" I say.

"Seriously?" says Wyatt.

"Have you not watched *Sherlock*? *True Detective*?" Amity says.

"A little?"

"*Homeland*?" Wyatt asks.

"Most of it, I think." I remember a wall covered with photographs and newspaper articles and red yarn linking them like Silly String. The whole thing looked like chaos.

"Didn't Carrie Mathison lose the plot?"

"That's not the point," Wyatt says. "We have a lot of details to keep straight, and we need to see them to connect the dots."

We must be close to the village, because we pass by some houses with cultivated gardens and then come to the footpath that runs behind the row of shops along the Willowthrop green. The walkway is quiet and pretty. We pass behind the King George Inn and are nearly behind the hair salon when I trip over what I think is a branch but turns out to be the end of a long black umbrella. I pick it up and am about to rest it against a fence so whoever lost it might reclaim it, but Wyatt says, "Stop right there."

"This could be evidence," he explains. "Edwina said whoever left the salon hid himself with a big black umbrella. Maybe this is it."

Wyatt takes a photograph of the umbrella.

"Our first bona fide clue," Amity says. "This could confirm what Edwina said, that whoever killed Tracy left on foot."

"And must have gone down the alley on the side of the building and picked up the footpath," Wyatt says. "If only we knew where he was heading."

"He might have parked a car somewhere farther away so it wouldn't be noticed near the salon," Amity says.

I put the umbrella back on the ground, and we resume walking.

A squawk, and a plump black-and-white bird flies in front of my face. I jump back.

"What the hell?" I say.

"Magpie," Wyatt says.

"Like the rhyme?" Amity says. "One for sorrow, two for joy?"

"Yup. Member of the crow family."

"You know a lot about birds for someone who doesn't really like them," I say.

"Osmosis," Wyatt says.

"But why do you work at your husband's store if you don't love birds?" Amity asks.

"Because Bernard loves birds and I love Bernard." He stops to pick a daisy, which he puts behind his ear. "And the truth is, I don't know what else I'd do."

"What have you done in the past?" I ask.

"I was a paralegal for a while, which was good money at least. Then there was the law school debacle. Some retail jobs. I was very good at selling cutlery."

"What did you love doing when you were a child?" Amity asks. "That's what I asked myself when my boys grew up and I wanted to get back to work. I loved writing stories when I was a little girl. It was pure joy. So that's what I returned to."

I'm glad Amity didn't ask me what I loved doing as a child. I don't remember wanting much other than to have everyone home all the time. I wanted to know my father, to *have* a father, and to bounce on my grandfather's knee like my grandmother said I used to do. I wanted my mother there too. To have all of them around the table for dinner every day, like families in books.

"When I was a kid?" Wyatt says. "That's easy. I loved performing. I'd put on shows for my family all the time. We had a drama program in middle school, but by eighth grade I was six foot three, had a staggering case of acne, and hair the color of Orangina. I wasn't exactly brimming with confidence. I gathered all my courage and tried

121

out for *The Music Man* and got cast as the understudy for Harold Hill. I never expected to go on, but there was a vicious stomach bug going around, and I had to step in on opening night. And boy, did we have trouble in River City."

"What happened?" I say.

"Early in act one, I hurled."

"You mean you—" Amity stops in her tracks.

"Yup." Wyatt turns to face us. "Projectile vomited all over Marian the Librarian."

"The school librarian?" I say.

"No, Micaela Finkelstein, who played the leading lady."

"Oh my god," I say.

"I was mortified. I rushed offstage to clean up, and while I was back there, Amaryllis and Unnamed Townsman Number Three threw up too. It was a nasty virus, and the show was canceled. After that, I pulled the plug on my acting career."

"Why?" Amity says. "It wasn't your fault."

"Too traumatic. I joined the stage crew. Much safer. I like helping other people shine. Besides, the small stage of retail has its charms."

Wyatt picks up his pace and then says, "Shit!" and lifts one foot. "I've stepped in horse crap." It's a huge pile, right in the middle of the path. I don't know how he didn't see it.

"Oh dear," Amity says. "A hazard of country life." She takes a wet wipe out of her purse and hands it to Wyatt, who's scraping the bottom of his shoe against a rock. "Here you go, friend."

When Wyatt's shoe is clean enough, we continue walking, following the path until we're behind Tracy's building, where we turn down the narrow lane that brings us back to the village green. The stationer's is on the next block. On the way, we pass a fishmonger's with a pile of golden smoked fish, splayed out flat, in the window.

"Those are kippers," I say. "My mother used to love kippers and scrambled eggs."

"I've only encountered them in British literature," Amity says. "In *The Remains of the Day*, the butler serves them to Lord Darlington. For breakfast." She shudders.

"That's four things now." Wyatt's voice rises with excitement. "Swans, bluebells, a crooked spire, and kippers."

"Which were not in my mother's story," I say.

"But they're British, so still significant," Wyatt says. "That settles it. We're getting two bulletin boards. One to solve the fake murder of Tracy Penny—"

"And one to figure out why Cath's mother wanted to bring her to Willowthrop," Amity says.

"Guys, come on, my mother is not why you're here. I promise you, whatever brought her here is not worth the trouble. Let's just focus on the fake murder."

"And leave your story unsolved?" Wyatt says. "Not a chance."

CHAPTER TWENTY-FOUR

Selina and Bix are in the back of the stationer's shop with Bert Lott, who has the build of a former college athlete who's gone soft around the middle. Bix sees us coming down the aisle and, in a loud and stilted voice, says, "That's extremely interesting," like he's trying to make us think we've arrived on the heels of a big reveal.

"What's interesting about plumbing problems at the salon?" Selina says.

"Why would you say that?" Bix says to his wife through clenched teeth. "Are you trying to lose this thing?"

"Cripes," mutters Bert, shaking his head. "Americans. So bloody competitive."

Guilty as charged. We Americans love to win. It probably explains why we're so baffled by the contestants on *The Great British Baking Show*, with their *Oh, Fiona, you'll never crystallize those violet petals in time, let me do some*. I'd help Naomi and Deborah in a pinch, and wouldn't mind teaming up with them, but Selina and Bix make me feel as American as apple pie. I really don't want them to win.

"Any other questions?" Bert asks Selina and Bix.

"Not at the moment," Bix says, "but we may be back."

Bert seems less than thrilled with the prospect of being interrogated again. He says that if we don't mind, he'll continue shelving merchandise while we talk. He answers our questions without offering much embellishment, which makes the charade feel unexpectedly real. Yes, he rents to Tracy. She was a good tenant at first, kept both her flat and the salon in good order.

"And now?" I ask, remembering how Gordon Penny and Lady Blanders each told us that Bert had been complaining about Tracy's upkeep of the salon.

"Recently I've become aware of some troubling practices at the salon." Bert ticks off his complaints: nasty odors, clogged drains, spills on the floor, toxic hair products.

"I thought everything she used was organic," Amity says.

"Pfft." Bert shakes his head. "You believe that claptrap?"

Wyatt asks when he last saw Tracy.

"I don't know, maybe three days ago. I heard her on the phone in the evening. I couldn't make out the words, but on my way upstairs it sounded like she was angry. On my way downstairs a little bit later, it sounded like she was sweet-talking someone. You know, trying to get more bees with honey."

"Did it sound like she was talking to a boyfriend?" Amity asks.

"Maybe," Bert says.

Wyatt asks if Bert has any idea who that might be. Bert shakes his head.

"Probably someone with money though," he says.

"Why do you say that?" I ask.

"There's been a red Tesla Model S parked behind the building on more than a few nights recently."

"Know anyone around here who drives a red Tesla?" I ask.

He shakes his head.

"Can anyone verify your whereabouts on Saturday night?" I say.

"What, like an alibi?" Bert says. "I ate alone, went down to the pub, and was home by nine o'clock for a long talk on the phone with my daughter, Claire.

"And where might we find your daughter?" Wyatt asks.

"She works at Willowthrop Outdoors Outfitters."

"Are you close to her?" I ask. It doesn't seem relevant to the case, but I'm always curious about father-daughter relationships, probably because I never had one.

"I'm trying," Bert says. "Claire was only two when her mum and I split. I didn't stick around, didn't see her much for years. I moved a lot. I wasn't much of a dad, if you want to know the truth. Took me a while to realize what I'd missed. But I'm back home in Willowthrop and giving it a go now."

Amity reaches out and touches his arm. It makes sense to me that she's a fiction writer; she's quick with empathy, even when the object of her concern is bogus. "That must be difficult after all these years," she says.

Bert looks at her with an expression of long-awaited relief, like he either can't believe that someone is finally taking his side or is buying this prepared monologue. "It's all I want in the world, to be her dad again. But it's hard for her to let me, that's what hurts."

In the midst of a faux interrogation, we seem to have fallen into a conversation that feels real. I know nothing about Bert's daughter, or if "Claire" even is a real daughter, but there's something about Bert that makes me want to believe him. Even stranger, I'm envious of his daughter, having a father who, despite the past, is trying to be a dad in such a normal way, not with grand, confusing gestures, but with phone calls and invitations. He probably asks her to meet him at the pub, have a pint. Would be more than happy to drop in, leave her some fresh muffins or maybe some books he thinks she'd like to read. Whatever he did in the past, or more likely, whatever he didn't do, at least he knows now that the best way to make amends is to show up.

CHAPTER TWENTY-FIVE

When we step out of the stationer's, I take a quick glance at Dev's bar. The door is closed, and the lights are off. I'm disappointed in myself for caring. I was drunk, and he was chivalrous, getting me home safely. Period, end of story.

"Next up is Tracy's assistant, Dinda," Amity says. "We need to find out about the argument between Dinda and Tracy that Edwina heard the morning before the murder."

Dinda is outside when we arrive at her place, which is above a garage on the main road on the edge of town. She doesn't ask us in but leads us into the side yard, where there are a few plastic chairs and a kiddie pool filled with murky water.

"It's chilly for wading, isn't it?" Amity asks.

"My baby loves it," Dinda says, plucking a few leaves from the pool. And then she starts asking us questions about our investigation. Are we close to figuring it out, isn't Roland Wingford clever, can you believe he was her schoolteacher when she was ten? "It's so exciting to have a real author in our village. He's a very good writer."

"You liked *Murder Afoot*?" Wyatt asks.

"Murder a-what?" Dinda lights a cigarette.

"Roland's book? About his detective Cuddy Claptrop?" Amity says.

"Ha! Cuddy. That's so clever, don't you think? I never heard of a Cuddy. But no, I haven't read it. Have you?"

She levels a stare at each of us in turn. We shake our heads. I suppose we should buy Roland's book, both because it might give us insight into how he thinks and because it's a nice thing to do.

"Can we get back to the matter at hand?" Wyatt seems annoyed by Dinda, maybe because she's clearly not following whatever script she's supposed to adhere to. I don't blame him. We need her to play her part so we don't feel ridiculous playing ours. "Where were you the night of Tracy's murder?"

"Here, of course. My baby had a cough, so I stayed by her side."

"I understand you had an argument with Tracy on the morning of the murder," Amity says. "Can you tell us what it was about?"

"What else—money." She takes a long drag on her cigarette, juts out her chin as she exhales. "My baby needed alternative therapies for her condition."

"Oh, I'm so sorry," I say, before remembering that this is all fiction.

"I asked Tracy to help me out, and she wrote me a check, put it in a flowered envelope and all. I thought it was the sweetest thing. But turns out it wasn't a gift. It was a loan. And Tracy meant for me to pay it off by working. She reduced my pay by more than half and put the rest toward my debt. As if I wouldn't pay it off eventually."

"That's harsh. Was that in keeping with her character?" Amity says.

"I wouldn't be the first to call her a cheapskate," Dinda says.

"Who else?" I ask.

"The way she made Gordon beg for money each week, it was downright cruel. And she had so much! Right after she kicked Gordon out, Tracy came into some money from a dead relative. And suddenly she was in a mad rush to finalize the divorce and change her will so that nothing would go to Gordon. It was taking longer than she liked, and she used to complain about it all the time."

"How much did she inherit?" Wyatt asks.

"Ten thousand quid," Dinda says.

Amity claps her hands together. "Ten thousand pounds, ''Tis as good as a Lord!'"

"Huh?" says Dinda.

"Mrs. Bennett," Amity says. "*Pride and Prejudice?*"

"Sure, whatever," Dinda says. "It's a lot of money."

"But if Gordon is still in Tracy's will . . . " I say.

"Then the money's his," Wyatt says.

"Which is incriminating," I say.

"Isn't it though?" Dinda says.

"And with Tracy dead," Wyatt says to Dinda, "you no longer have to pay back the money she lent you. Which also gives you a motive."

"It was a gift," Dinda says, stomping her cigarette butt into the dirt. "She changed her mind."

"And you have your own key to the salon," Wyatt says.

"You think I killed Tracy? I'd never."

"And you support yourself?" Amity says. "That must be difficult with a child."

"Who said I have a kid?"

Has she forgotten her lines?

"You did," I say. "A baby who needs some kind of therapy."

Dinda looks at us, speechless, and then starts cackling. She walks over to the garage, climbs the outside stairs, opens the door, and whistles. In a flash, a mangy terrier clammers down the steps, whizzes by us, and leaps into the kiddie pool, yapping and splashing in a chaotic froth. Dinda stops at the bottom of the steps, arms folded.

"Meet the apple of my eye. My baby, Petunia."

CHAPTER TWENTY-SIX

"Was that intentional?" I ask as we head back toward the village center. "Were we supposed to assume that Dinda's baby was human?"

"Could it be a clue?" Amity says. "Maybe Dinda fooled Tracy too, and that's why she demanded the money back? Because the 'baby' was a dog?"

Wyatt puts the kibosh on that idea, convinced that if Dinda had worked for Tracy for a year, Tracy would know Dinda didn't have a human baby. "Also, Dinda doesn't seem smart enough, either as an actor or as herself, to pull off a murder, even one written for her."

"I'm so confused," I say.

"Yeah, we're not really getting anywhere," Wyatt says.

"Let's switch gears," Amity says. "Maybe we need a little break from this case. It's only Monday, and we've got until Thursday evening to figure it out. Let's go talk to Germaine about Cath's mother."

"Let's not," I say. I've liked being distracted by the fake murder; turning back to my mother's secrets is unsettling.

"Germaine is not going to let this go," Wyatt says.

"I think the two of you are not going to let this go," I say.

"We're not, are we, Wyatt?" Amity says.

"Not a chance. And would you look at that, we're already on Crane Street."

I know when I'm defeated.

"Let's get this over with, then," I say.

My spirits lift when I'm standing in front of The Book and Hook, which looks like the kind of place I would visit even if I hadn't been summoned there. The shop sign, which runs the width of the store above the window, is a painting of a young girl with long blond braids, canvas overalls, and tall rubber boots. Her tongue pokes out as she strains against an arched fishing rod to reel in her catch, which is not a fish but a book. I take a picture of the sign, adding to my collection of photographs that I wish I could share with my grandmother. She loved fishing almost as much as she loved reading.

The shop has a sweet, musty scent, a mix of books and old upholstered furniture. It's a comforting smell, reminiscent of home. The walls are lined with floor-to-ceiling built-in shelves. More freestanding shelves fill the two connected rooms. There are also stacks of books on tables, chairs, and the floor.

We find Germaine behind the counter, perched on a stool between a laptop and an old cash register, reading. She doesn't look up from her book until Wyatt clears his throat.

"My favorite trio!" Germaine takes off her reading glasses and rummages around the books and papers on the counter until she finds another pair of glasses and puts them on. "Much better. Now it's the three of you in focus."

"Have you considered progressives?" I ask. "One pair of glasses for both reading and distance?"

"Have I what? Oh, of course. Your mother mentioned that you're an ophthalmologist."

"Optician."

"Precisely. Progressives are not for me. I have no desire to sac-rifice quality for efficiency."

I sense that there's no point in arguing.

Beyond the counter, the back part of the shop is even more cluttered than the front, because along with the plentiful books is fishing gear, old and new. There are reels and nets, baskets, flies, fly cases, clippers, and vests. On the ceiling are fly rods, lying flat across the rafters the way my grandmother used to keep hers in the garage. The name of the shop, The Book and Hook, clicks.

"You're a fisherman," I say.

"A loyal daughter. My father was an avid angler. He opened the shop as The Hook and Book, selling fishing supplies and one book."

"Ah, yes," Wyatt says. "The good book."

"What? Heavens no," Germaine says. "It was *The Compleat Angler* by Izaak Walton. Don't you know it?"

We shake our heads.

"It's a classic, published in 1653. Not much plot—a fisherman, a hunter, and a falconer talk about their preferred sports, and the fisherman prevails. The book is filled with practical advice about fishing. We love it because Walton writes about fishing the River Dove, a trout stream that cuts through the Peak District. Dad sold so many copies that he eventually added more books about fishing. But when I took over, I started shifting the emphasis from hook to book. Changed the name too." She picks up a reel, pushes her finger through the middle, and twirls it around. "But I'd have done better keeping it as it was. There's a better profit margin on fishing supplies than on books."

"Business isn't good?" Wyatt asks.

"Locals favor our very good library, and we don't get many tourists in Willowthrop. The area has too many other villages with more to recommend them."

133

"I think Willowthrop is lovely," Amity says.

"I do too. And as Americans, you probably find it quintessentially English. But we don't have a claim to fame. Not like Bakewell, with its famous tart and the magnificent Chatsworth House, home to the Devonshire family for seventeen generations, or Castleton with its caverns and blue john stone, or charming little Edensor, which was moved lock, stock, and barrel in the 1830s because the Sixth Duke of Devonshire said it blocked his view. Can you imagine? Of such things revolutionaries are made. Though at the new location, the village was rebuilt around a broad green planted with laburnum trees. They have the most exquisite scent, a mix of sweet pea and lilac."

"Ooh, we should go there," Amity says.

"And then there's Ashford in the Water," Germaine continues, "with its medieval bridge, which is not only the most photographed bridge in England but is also, according to the National Tourist Board, the best place in the country to play Poohsticks."

"From Winnie the Pooh?" I say.

"Of course."

My mother and I played that game, dropping branches from the bridge over Ellicott Creek and running to the other side to see whose stick crossed under first. We scrambled through the bushes along the road, racing to get the best sticks, and back to the bridge to play again. This must have been before my mother left for the first time, because the memory carries none of the anxiety that colored my time with her afterward, when I was always worried that she would lose interest or suddenly announce she had to leave.

Germaine is still talking, rattling off the area's other, more notable villages. "And Tideswell is surrounded by limestone mountains, and Eyam, of course, is the plague village."

"That doesn't sound like a draw," Wyatt says.

"Oh, it is. Fascinating history. During the bubonic plague, anyone who could afford it fled London to avoid the disease. But in 1665, the plague found its way to Eyam when an old cloth infested with rat fleas was sent to the local tailor. In no time at all, two-thirds of the village had died. But two clergymen had the unusual foresight to create a quarantine zone around the outskirts of the village that no one was allowed to cross. Outsiders left food and supplies at the edge, which the residents of Eyam paid for by putting coins in troughs of vinegar, which they believed helped kill off the disease. Clever, wouldn't you say? Their methods prevented the plague from spreading to Sheffield and the surrounding area. People like to see where it all happened or perhaps just satisfy their ghoulish curiosity. Either way, it's good for business."

"You thought a fake murder mystery would put Willowthrop on the map?" Amity says.

"That was the idea, and to raise money to save our community pool. You Americans have long loved English-village mysteries, but there was such a boom during the pandemic. Here too. Thinking about murder, I suppose, is less stressful than worrying that you might drop dead because someone coughed on you. Do you know what the big national obsession was during our cholera outbreak in 1854? It was a true-crime case involving a love triangle and a man stabbed to death and stashed beneath a kitchen floor. More than ten thousand Londoners dead from cholera and all anyone wanted to talk about was the Bermondsey Horror. Anyhow, we knew the interest would be there, and when we started planning our murder-mystery week, we had great ambitions. There was talk of a big sponsor—BritBox or British Airways—a larger advertising budget and a big-name author—" Here she hesitates, like she realizes she's said too much. "It was not to be, however, so we corralled some local businesses, rolled up our sleeves, formed a committee, and together with Roland Wingford came up with what I think is a thumping good mystery."

Germaine comes out from behind the counter and sits on the couch by the window. She pats the cushion beside her. "But I didn't ask you here to talk about Willowthrop, Cath. When I told you earlier that I believed your mother was searching for someone, it was more than a hunch. When we first corresponded, when she initially inquired about our mystery adventure, she wanted to know if the town published a phone book. Did she know someone from the area?"

"Beats me," I say. "Maybe she met someone online and wanted to track him down?" That's a nicer way of saying that she sexted with someone for a while, convinced herself they were soulmates, and made plans to cross the ocean to find him.

"She could have been searching for a lost love," Amity says.

They all look so hopeful, I'm sorry to disappoint them.

"Trust me, I knew a *lot* about my mother's lovers. I can't imagine her having a meaningful connection with someone here and not sharing all the details.

"And she'd never been to this area before?" Germaine says.

"Not that I know of."

I give Germaine a quick account of my mother's history, which is not very worldly. She was born in Indiana and raised in a place called McCordsville, where the big excitement was watching the CSX freight train barrel through. After high school, she went to a community college part-time for a while, and when she'd saved enough money, she left home. Her first stop was Buffalo, which ended up being considerably longer than a layover. After leaving me with my paternal grandmother when I was nine, she lived in Vermont, California, New Mexico, New York, and Florida.

"We often went long stretches without being in touch, so I guess she could have come to England, but she probably would have told me," I say. "She wasn't good at keeping secrets."

Germaine looks puzzled.

"Your mother seemed so thrilled to have discovered our mystery week," she says.

"She'd been searching for a fake murder to solve?" Wyatt asks.

"I don't think the mystery mattered to her at all," Germaine says. "She said it was 'a hoot' that she thought you would enjoy."

Did my mother know me at all?

Germaine continues. "She had so many questions. Here, look." She hands me a printout of an email. She's right, it's almost all questions. Was the town very small; were there new buildings or only old ones; who lived there, mostly old people or were there young families too? What was the surrounding countryside like? Was it clean or polluted?

Amity, who's reading over my shoulder, says, "It sounds like she was doing research, almost like she wanted to move here."

"That's not like my mother," I say. "She'd never do research. She'd just get it in her mind to go somewhere and off she'd go."

"Could she have met someone from here who invited her to visit?" Wyatt asks.

"But why wouldn't she have said as much to Germaine?" Amity says.

I'm uncomfortable with the way they're all looking at me, like I should have the answers. I thought I was used to my mother's mercurial ways, but having them exposed like this makes me embarrassed that I know so little about her. What had I missed?

CHAPTER TWENTY-SEVEN

Amity and Wyatt head over to the King George Inn to check on Lady Blanders's alibi, after which they're going back to our cottage to hook up Amity's tiny portable printer so we can have photographs for our evidence board. I hang back at the bookstore to look around. I start at the nearest shelf, where I'm surprised to find a Hardy Boys book, *The Secret of the Lost Tunnel.* I've never read the Hardy Boys, but there's an old set in my attic that belonged to my grandfather.

"Funny to find this here," I say as I flip through the pages.

"Your Hardy Boys had many fans in England," Germaine says. "My brother adored them."

"I guess I shouldn't be surprised. My favorite book as a child was about English girls at boarding school. *More Stories of Melling School.* It was part of a series but I only had that one."

"Is that so?" Germaine bends down and takes a book from the bottom shelf, groaning a little and pressing her lower back as she stands and hands it to me. It's *Summer Term at Melling* by Margaret Biggs. On its cover is a colorful drawing of three girls in identical white blouses and khaki skirts lolling on the grass, reading and talking under an oak tree.

"Well, hello!" I say, recognizing the spunky Blake sisters, whose adventures at a weekly boarding school in 1950s England I adored. I open the book and dip my head down to smell the pages. How I longed to be part of the Blake family and go to a school like Melling, with visits to the village tea shop, and field hockey games, a kind headmistress, and the drama of who would be named head prefect, which I was convinced was a misspelling for *perfect*.

"I still have my Melling School book. It's ancient, already old when my mother got it for me secondhand."

It may seem ironic how much I loved reading about girls away at school, considering how reluctant I was to leave my own home, even for playdates and sleepovers. I wasn't a true homebody; I was just afraid that my mother might show up when I wasn't there. I believed that if I stayed put, she would come. And, of course, sometimes she did, which reinforced my magical thinking that I had made her arrival happen by remaining home. But now I see another reason I might have been so enchanted by stories of Melling School. They were about girls on their own during the week, without mothers or fathers, having a grand time while their parents were home, waiting for them. The girls got to waltz in, waltz out, and have all the fun.

The way Germaine is staring at the book in my hands puzzles me until it occurs to me that she wants to know if I'm going to buy it.

"How much?" I ask.

She tells me, and I ask her to ring it up, and to add a copy of Roland Wingford's first Cuddy Claptrop novel, *Murder Afoot*.

"As you wish," she says, with a look that suggests she's not one of Roland's biggest fans. She steps around to the back of the counter and calculates the cost.

I hand her the money, and she gives me change.

But as she turns to get a bag, she glances outside and gasps. "Crikey!" She thrusts the books at me and dashes out the door.

Dev's mother is standing in the middle of the road in a housedress and slippers handing out wildflowers to passersby. I watch from the front window as Germaine talks to her and eventually takes her hand and guides her inside the store.

"There, there, Penelope, you come here and sit awhile." Germaine settles her friend on the couch by the window.

Germaine takes out her phone and makes a call. "C'mon, Dev. Pick up. Oh, bother!"

"What is this place?" Penelope looks around like she's never been there before.

"It's my shop, love, The Book and Hook." She takes a book from the front table and hands it to Penelope. "Here you go, photographs of beautiful gardens. You sit and have a nice, quiet look." Germaine makes another call, shaking her head as she waits for someone to answer. "For goodness' sake, aren't you young people supposed to be glued to your phones?"

CHAPTER TWENTY-EIGHT

Penelope slowly turns the pages of the garden book. But when a boisterous group of geriatric hikers with walking sticks piles into the store, she pulls her legs up to her chest and wraps her arms around her knees like she's trying to make herself so small that no one will notice her. The hikers, talking and laughing, spread out through the shop, picking up books and asking questions. Does Germaine have a good walking guide, a small laminated map, a first aid book? How about something on geology or the lore and legends of Derbyshire? Germaine pulls out book after book. They want to buy them all and ask if they can pick up some of them later, after their hike.

Penelope watches from the couch, her lips quivering. I try to get Germaine's attention, but she's behind the counter, ringing up sales.

"She'll be a minute," I tell Penelope. "Can I get you another book?"

"Who are these people? They shouldn't be here. They should go away." Her voice is rising. A few of the hikers notice Penelope and shake their heads. One mutters "poor old girl" and then bellows, "Having a lovely day, dear?"

Penelope pulls back like the woman has raised a hand to slap her.

"Please, let her be," I say, positioning myself in front of Penelope to block her view. I crouch down and take her hand. "Do you want to go home?"

She nods.

"Wait right here."

I go to the counter and ask Germaine if Penelope lives nearby. She tells me it's not too far, maybe a ten-minute walk. I get the address and tell Germaine I'm going to walk Penelope home.

As we exit the shop, Penelope's hand hovers over my forearm, barely making contact. She is so slight a brisk wind might make her stumble. My grandmother was seventy-six when she died, but I never thought of her as old. She was hearty, working the garden in spring and summer, raking leaves and shoveling snow in fall and winter. The month before she died, she was on a ladder pulling vines off the garage. I can't imagine her as frail or confused, but if she had become that way, I'd like to think that I'd have cared for her as kindly as Dev does his mother. That I'd be as patient helping my grandmother navigate a narrowing world as she had been raising me.

"We're talking a walk?" Penelope says as we approach the river. "How lovely." At the end of the bridge, she stops. "You've always been so sweet with me. Who are you?"

"I'm Cath," I say. "I'm visiting."

Penelope strokes the back of my hand. "It's been such a long time." She reaches up and touches my hair. The map on my phone directs us to a road that winds up a hill. At the first sharp bend, we stop to rest at a wall along the side of the road. In the distance, children are playing soccer in a field. A boy scores and runs in a circle, his arms out like airplane wings.

"Bravo," Penelope says. "Dev is such a good boy. Is he home from school now?"

"I think you'll see Dev soon."

The houses get bigger as we climb, the narrow ones of the village giving way to stately homes set back from rows of dense bushes. At the top of the hill, I turn back to look at the view. From this height, Willowthrop is a jigsaw puzzle of rooftops and chimneys, sloping down from us, flat for a while, and then climbing the hills on the other side. It occurs to me that I'm now standing inside the view I see from my bedroom at Wisteria Cottage. I'm tempted to wave, in case Wyatt and Amity are looking, but they're probably buckled down trying to figure out why someone wanted Tracy Penny dead. I assume they've set my mother's mystery aside, at least for a little while.

As we start descending the other side of the hill, a tiny green Citroën approaches and stops beside us. Dev hops out. Even disheveled, with splotches of dirt on his work boots, carpenter pants, and T-shirt, he's alarmingly sexy.

"How did—"

Before he can say more, I tell him that Germaine found his mother in the middle of the street and took her into the bookshop, but that it was busy and upset her. Without responding, he takes his mother's hand and settles her in the passenger seat, clips the belt. I'm about to turn away, I think maybe he's embarrassed, when he asks if I want to come with them. "The least I can do is offer you a cup of tea."

I climb into the back seat, which is barely big enough for me. I meet Dev's eyes in the rearview mirror as he turns the car around. He looks troubled. I don't blame him. It's only my third day in Willowthrop and the second time I've come upon Penelope wandering alone. Either no one's looking after her carefully or she's a talented escape artist.

Halfway down the hill, Dev pulls into a driveway of a brick house surrounded by thick hydrangea. I follow him and his mother down a stone path through the bushes. The door opens and a woman rushes out of the house, her cheeks flushed. "Oh my, oh my, I only closed my eyes for a moment, sitting right beside her. Where did she, how did you . . . ?"

Dev introduces Mrs. Carlton, a housekeeper who helps look after his mother. He's perfectly polite but there's a slight edge in his voice that makes me think that Mrs. Carlton's negligence is not a new problem.

"I'll take over now," she says as we walk inside. "We'll have a cuppa and a nice chat, won't we dear?" Penelope follows her out of the room.

"Come," Dev says to me. "Let's go to the cottage. I'll put on the kettle."

CHAPTER TWENTY-NINE

I follow Dev on a path that winds through some bushes before opening onto a garden, at the end of which is a cottage with a single chimney. Dev pushes open a thick wooden door. It's a one-room cottage, with a tiny kitchen in the corner, a square wooden table, an armoire, two armchairs by the fireplace, and a bed covered with an old blanket. There's a neat stack of books and a spiral notebook on the bedside table, shoes lined up in a row behind the door. The place is sparse and tidy but still cozy. Nothing like my house, with my grandmother's things mixed up with my own.

Dev fills the kettle and turns on the stove. He keeps moving, his face always away from me. Is he regretting our moment outside Wisteria Cottage? Maybe he's about to tell me that he's afraid he gave me the wrong idea by walking me home. Maybe I should apologize for giving him the wrong idea, holding on to his hand like that. Why didn't I let go? Why am I still thinking about it? A vacation crush should not be this unsettling.

"Have a seat," he says, still not looking at me.

I sit at the table. He puts mugs out for tea. Takes out tea bags. I don't bother to tell him I don't like tea. At this rate, by the end of the week I'll have acquired the taste. The kettle whistles. He doesn't move.

"Dev? The kettle?"

"What? Oh, right."

He pours the water.

"Are you okay?" I ask.

"Yeah, I'm just worried about my mum." He hands me a mug.

I put down my books and rest my arms on the edge of the table. It's a little sticky. I lift my arm, and Dev pops up, gets a sponge, and wipes off the jam.

"Sorry. I had breakfast in a hurry. I was eager to get some time in the garden today before the rain."

"It's going to rain?"

"It's England. It's always going to rain."

He sits opposite me. We lift our mugs of tea at the same time. His smile seems shy, but his gaze is steady. I look away.

"Tell me again how you came to bring my mum back from the bookshop?" he asks.

I describe the group of noisy tourists, all eager for Germaine's attention.

"You were there shopping too?" He nods toward my books. I pick up the Melling School book.

"A nostalgia purchase. Boarding school in England was one of my earliest fantasies."

"Consider yourself spared."

"I went to the shop because Germaine wanted to talk to me. She's convinced that my mother wanted to come here to find someone."

"And you doubt that?"

I rub my finger on the rim of my mug.

"I think it's unlikely."

"Were you and your mother close?"

He speaks so tenderly that I'm reluctant to disappoint him. He's one of the lucky ones, who was raised well and assumes others were too. I tell him the basics.

"She left when you were nine and never came back?" he asks.

A bird chirps. I turn toward the window as it lifts off, a flash of magenta under a black wing.

"She flitted in now and then, like unexpected sunshine. She'd bring gifts. Dolls, macramé kits, books. It was always a holiday with her, brief and beautiful. I loved it. And then she'd leave." How strange. I don't usually talk about that time. He must be a very good listener. "I started seeing her more three years ago after my grandmother died. But always on her terms and at her place in Florida. I didn't have anyone else. But I can't say we were close."

"That must have been difficult for you."

"It's all I knew."

I've always prided myself on how much I like being alone. Hanging out with friends, having the occasional fling—usually someone who fell into my path, like the guy who fixed my sump pump or the old crush I ran into at my college reunion. Preferably someone who didn't like me too much (no flowers, thank you kindly) or ask a lot in return. But I don't want Dev to think I was a sad, abandoned girl who grew up into a damaged woman.

"My grandmother raised me well. I was loved, and I loved her back."

"I'm glad for that." He leans forward, arms on the table. "And your mother, did she marry again?"

"No, but not for lack of trying," I say. "She was addicted to falling in love. She found her soulmate many times. It never stuck. But she was always ready for another go."

"You say that like it's a character flaw, like there's not something admirable about maintaining hope after defeat."

"What's that definition of insanity, doing the same thing again and again and hoping for a different result?"

"I guess it might be a little crazy, but it's wonderfully optimistic, don't you think?"

I cock my head, like I'm thinking about it, and say, "Nope."

He laughs. He tips back in his chair, balancing it on two legs, like a teenager.

"You're not a searcher like your mother?"

"I'm nothing like my mother," I say quickly, so quickly that I'm a little embarrassed. "Although I am searching for something."

He lets the chair tip back down. "And what's that?"

"A murderer," I whisper.

"Ah, right." He sips his tea, looks right at me. He's smiling. "I have faith that you'll find him."

"Are you assuming that it's a man, or do you know something?"

"*Moi?*" he says in mock alarm. "I know nothing, other than how to make an inordinate number of gin cocktails. There's nothing nefarious about me at all." He wiggles his eyebrows dramatically. "Unless, of course, there is."

"Prove it. Where were you between eight and ten the night Tracy was murdered?"

He bites his lip, an exaggerated expression of nervousness.

"I was helping out at The Lonely Spider, remember?"

"But that was early, and over by eight thirty," I say. "What about your whereabouts afterward?"

"My whereabouts? Is that a technical sleuthing term?"

"Answer the question, please."

"I came home and took a shower."

"Can anyone corroborate that?"

"I should hope not. I generally bathe alone."

"No one was aware that you were showering?"

"Are you implying someone was spying on me?"

"It could happen." I try to sound flippant, but I know I'm blushing. "And after your shower?"

"I went to work."

"You do realize I'm going to have to verify that, right?"

"I'm aware. Now, can I ask *you* a question?" Dev says. "Do you want to take a brief murder vacation?"

"Isn't that what I'm on?"

"No, I mean a vacation from murder. From the mystery. Have you been to Stanage Edge?"

I remember the name from my first Google search about the Peak District, but that's it. Dev tells me it's one of the area's great attractions, a gritstone ridge that runs for four miles.

"It's got stunning views of the moors and the valley. You can't leave the Peak without visiting."

"Is it far?" I ask.

"About a half-hour drive. You can park and climb straight up, takes about five minutes, or you can take the longer, scenic hike from Hathersage that they're now calling the *Jane Eyre* trail."

"*Jane Eyre*? That's one of my favorite books."

My mother and I both loved it, but while she swooned over the happy ending for Jane and Mr. Rochester, I loved Jane's strong sense of her own worth despite being mistreated and dismissed since childhood.

"We can go tomorrow morning if you'd like," Dev says.

"Are you trying to distract me from my sleuthing?"

"I suppose I am."

I watch him waiting for me to answer. He looks hopeful and sincere, like he's made a perfectly friendly offer. And that's all it is. It's not like we're going to start anything. By next weekend, I'll be gone.

"You cannot go back to the States having seen nothing but little Willowthrop. I won't allow it."

He's right. I should see Stanage Edge. It would be silly to refuse an offer to go there.

"Okay. Let's do it."

"Great. Pick you up at ten?"

"It's a date." I regret my choice of words until Dev repeats them.

"It's a date."

CHAPTER THIRTY

Sure enough, it starts raining shortly after I leave Dev's cottage. But the air is still warm, and the moisture feels nice on my face. I jog back into town and take what I think is a shortcut but which takes me to a dead end as the light rain turns into a downpour. I dash into a shop filled with racks of North Face and Patagonia fleece pullovers. This must be the outdoors store where Bert Lott's daughter works. I figure I should try to interview her, though I feel funny about going rogue. Hopefully Amity and Wyatt won't mind. I shake off the rain and walk toward a young woman behind the counter. She has her hair in braids under a knit cap and a tattoo of a carabiner clip on her forearm.

"I'm looking for Claire Lott."

"And who might you be?"

Saying that I'm investigating a murder seems unwise; what if this person is not part of the game or not even aware of it?

"I know her father and wanted to say hello."

"You know Bert?"

"You do too?"

"Well, I should do. He's my dad."

"So you know what I'm up to?"

Claire Lott drains her bottle of kombucha, sets it down, and raises her chin toward me.

"You don't look the type."

"Meaning?"

"You're not an ancient crone."

A guy comes out from the back carrying a stack of shoeboxes, which he puts on the counter.

"Is there somewhere we can talk privately for a few minutes?" I ask.

Claire leads me to the tent displays. She opens the flap of an orange dome tent and crawls in. I follow.

"Okay, let's do this!" she says, now looking like she's up for having some fun.

I tell her what we've learned from Bert, which is that he has been unhappy with Tracy for a while, complaining about the way she keeps her place. "Do you know why he might be so eager to get her out of the building?"

"Out of the whole building or only the salon?"

"The salon."

"That is interesting." She rolls back until her spine touches the floor and bounces up again.

"It's for me," she says. "I told him about my dream to open a vegan café but that I couldn't find a place with affordable rent. He said he might know a place I could definitely afford." She breaks into a sneaky smile.

"He'd give you free rent in the space occupied by Tracy's salon?"

"He'd do anything to make me happy, to be Daddy's little girl again." Claire rocks backward again, this time until she's flat on her back on the floor, arms and legs stretched out like a snow angel. "Bloody hell, am I incriminating my own dad?" She closes her eyes, puts the back of her hand on her forehead. "Cue the smelling salts!"

I think I have what I need and start to crawl out of the tent. But then I remember the most important question. When was the last time Claire spoke to her father on the phone? I don't tell her that Bert has already told us he had a long conversation with her during the time that Tracy was murdered.

"He calls me all the time," Claire says. "But I almost never pick up. Last time I did was probably two weeks ago. If you see him, tell him I'm alive."

Which is more than I can say for Bert's alibi.

CHAPTER THIRTY-ONE

From the front hall, where I'm wiggling my feet out of my wet shoes, I can see that Amity and Wyatt have been busy. The murder bulletin board is well populated. In the middle is a photo of Tracy, from which red string fans out to photos of Gordon Penny, Dinda Roost, Lady Blanders, and Bert Lott. The black question mark, Wyatt informs me before I head upstairs to change into dry clothes, is for the mystery man who may or may not have had a haircut and shave after Lady Blanders left the salon and may or may not be the same person who hid himself behind an umbrella when leaving the scene of the crime.

After changing into dry clothes, I watch from the couch as Wyatt and Amity add more photographs to the bulletin board—the salon chair with the extra-large black robe, the plastic face shield, the appointment calendar, the organic products, and, of course, Tracy herself, sprawled out on the floor as a corpse.

Wyatt tells me that Lady Blanders's alibi checked out. Not only was she at the King George for dinner with her friend, but the maître d' even confirmed that she had snails.

"Apparently, she went to the loo during dinner and was in there for so long that they were all in a panic that the snails had gone off.

He was hugely relieved that she was fine and that they hadn't given food poisoning to the village's most prominent resident."

I tell them what I learned from Bert's daughter.

Wyatt says, "Nice work, Watson," and moves Bert's picture closer to the center of the board. Arms folded, he stares at his handiwork as though if he looks hard enough, the solution is going to make itself known.

"So far we've got three people with possible motives and opportunity," he says. "Gordon Penny is dependent on his ex-wife for money, is apparently still in her will, and stands to come into a nice bundle if she dies."

"And he has a key to the building, as well as a wobbly alibi, being home alone," Amity says.

"Next up," Wyatt continues, "is Bert Lott, who seems to have been trying to evict Tracy in order to give the space to his daughter."

"He's also got a key to her place," Amity says.

"And no alibi," I say. "In fact, he lied, which seems very incriminating."

"And finally, there's Dinda Roost, who also has access to the salon and a motive to kill Tracy," Wyatt says. "We shouldn't eliminate her only because she's not the sharpest tool in the box."

"Right, and then there's Dev," Amity says. "Shouldn't he be on the board too?"

"Yeah, put him on," I say. "I don't know if he has a motive, but he was cagey about his alibi. Said he was showering."

And there I am imagining things again, this time Dev all sudsy in the shower. I've got to stop.

"When were you with Dev?" Wyatt asks.

I tell them about taking Dev's mother home.

"You were in his house?" Amity says.

"We had tea."

"You don't like tea," Wyatt says.

"But she likes Dev," Amity says.

"Anyway, he said he showered and then went to work at the bar," I say. "Which I suppose seems likely."

"He easily could have slipped out of the bar for a little while, couldn't he?" Wyatt says.

I know for a fact that he could. No one seemed bothered when he stepped out to walk me home.

"I can question him further." I tell them about my plans to go with Dev to Stanage Edge the next day.

"Scrummy," Wyatt says.

"This is an excellent subplot," Amity says.

They both look at me, waiting for me to tell them more.

"It's a hike, not a date."

"Get a photo at least," Wyatt says. "We want pinup boy on the board."

Amity reminds me to be back from Hathersage in time for our turn in Tracy's flat. We're the last group to get in, which seems unfair, but Amity is not deterred.

"I'm sure we're going to find answers there," she says. "Unless we've all overlooked something dreadfully obvious, that's where the key to this case is going to be."

I assume we're done for now and get up from the couch to go upstairs. But Wyatt says, "Not so fast, young lady." He flips around a second bulletin board, which was resting against the wall. Smack in the middle is a photograph of me that one of them must have taken on the way to Hadley Hall. It's a bit blurry and not particularly flattering. My hair is swooping up behind me on a gust of wind and I look tired and hungover. Maybe because of the unusual angle, I see my mother in my face, which is rare. Unlike me, she was fair and petite. But in this picture, I can see our wide-set eyes,

short straight nose, and what I like to think of as our "gentle chin."
The unexpected resemblance lets me imagine her walking through
this countryside with her quick strides, following a footpath across
a meadow and striking up conversations with farmers and other
walkers. If she were here, she'd ask so many questions in her usual
quest to charm everyone that she'd probably solve the fake crime
without even trying.

Wyatt takes out a pile of index cards.

"Now what was in the story your mother used to tell you?"

Amity speaks up before I can answer. "Swans. Bluebells. Church
with a crooked spire. Kippers."

"Again, kippers were not in the story," I say.

"Again, they're English, so they stay," Amity says.

She writes each thing on a card and tacks them all onto the
board. She adds another that says "Searching for someone. Male?
Female?" And she tacks on photographs of Gordon Penny and Bert
Lott. When she sees my face, she shrugs and says, "We have to
consider everything."

"It's not much," Wyatt says. "Is there anything else here that's
reminded you of your mother?"

I think back over the day.

"It's not really about my mother, but I bought an old book."
I show them *Summer Term at Melling* and explain why I purchased it.

"Your mother gave you an English book?" Wyatt says.

"She gave me old books all the time."

"Nevertheless." Wyatt writes "Melling School Book" and tacks
it to the board. All the cards make this quest seem important, like
we're going to figure it out, but they add up to so little that it's hard
to take it seriously.

It's still raining hard, so we decide to stay in for dinner and order pizza, which we agree is the best kind of savory pie. We drink a bottle of wine and come up with elaborate scenarios for Amity's next romance novel.

"A beautiful bird-watcher leading a campaign to ban hunting in her country town goes head-to-head with the area's best marksman, who turns out to be a soulful and bookish artist who's been hunting since he was a kid and only kills what he's going to eat," Wyatt says. "Can she love an animal killer?"

"Soulful hunter sounds like an oxymoron," Amity says.

"How about this," I say. "A lonely female optician pines for the shy, distracted manager of the pet shop next door, whose only friend is the ancient boa constrictor that no one wants to buy. But when he realizes he needs glasses, he gets them from the optician next door. When he puts on his spectacles, he really sees the optician for the first time and falls madly in love."

Amity laughs. "And he abandons the boa? That could be problematic. Animal lovers will cry foul, and everyone else will be creeped out by a protagonist with a snake fetish."

"Do you ever write things from your own life?" I ask.

"Not really," Amity says. "Whenever I write something real, it ends up sounding like bad fiction. The first time I wrote a romance, I tried using Douglas's marriage proposal. Total flop."

"It was a bad proposal?" I say.

"Not at all, it was very good."

"Go on," Wyatt says. "Please?"

Amity laughs.

"We were in Florida visiting Doug's parents, and we fled to a Publix supermarket for some space and to escape the heat. We were in the cereal aisle having a silly conversation about which of the eight billion cereals to choose. There were so many things to consider: *Does the bran in Raisin Bran make up for the excessive sugar around the raisins? Why isn't Lucky Charms in the candy aisle? What's so special about K?"* Amity touches the base of her neck like she's fiddling with a necklace that used to be there. "I was prattling on when Douglas took my hand and said he knew which one he wanted. 'Say Grape-Nuts,' I told him, 'and you'll break my heart.' And he said, 'I want only you, Amity, for all time.' He pretended to slip a ring on my finger and there we were, kissing and crying in aisle five."

"Wow," I say.

"Golly," Wyatt says.

"But that," Amity says, "was a long time ago."

We sit in silence for a few moments, and then Wyatt says, "I think Douglas is a wanker."

Amity puts a hand to her mouth, like she can't believe what Wyatt said. But then she giggles and says, "Complete and total wanker."

When I finally go upstairs to bed, I'm too wired to sleep. I consider downloading one of Amity's novels, but I've never been drawn to reading straight-up romance. I've always figured they offer a false sense of what's possible. Also, they're supposed to be an escape, but what about the letdown when you close the book and come back to reality?

I toss and turn and listen to the rain on the roof. I wonder if it sounds the same from inside Dev's cottage. I can't deny it, I liked being in his kitchen and talking to him. Who knew a conversation could feel easy, sincere, and sexy at the same time? I hope I didn't overdo it, blabbing on about my mother. But he wasn't judgy at all, either of her for leaving or me for having been left. I'm usually not drawn to people who seem entirely well-adjusted and stable, but there's nothing boring about Dev, nothing at all.

I still can't sleep, so I pick up my phone. There's an email from Kim from our office account:

Cheerio, Cath, I hope all is well in merry England. First things first, the display cases were installed and they don't look crowded at all. More important, I couldn't bring myself to make lentil soup (it's so gross) so I cooked up a batch of spicy Thai shrimp soup for Mr. G. He was skeptical but said it was very interesting. So that's good, right?

There's also an email from Mr. Groberg.

Dearest Cath, I hope all is well and that the week will fly by, not only because that will be an indication that you are having fun (time flies when, you know) but because it will mean you'll be home soon. I don't think I can survive another of Kim's meals. Thai soup for an old man? My mouth is still aflame. Kim is entertaining (so much energy), but maybe not wise? In other words, you are missed. And not only for your cooking.

I write them back, giving each a brief account of the murder and everyone I've met. It's so many people, after only three days. It makes me realize how small my circle is at home and how little happens in a typical day.

I flip through the Melling School book, which is comfortably nostalgic, but I'm not in the mood to read about girls away at school. Finally, I turn to *Murder Afoot*.

The first chapter begins with Cuddy Claptrop, "stooped of back, bent of finger, and sly of expression" in his blacksmith shop, tidying his tools after his latest disaster of an apprentice left behind a mess. Cuddy, muttering about the "indolent youth" who is more trouble than he's worth, begins to put his things away. This gives Roland Wingford an apparently irresistible opportunity to display the results of his extensive research into the art of forging. Tools are named and described in excruciating detail. Ball-peen hammers for spreading rivet heads, splitting punches for making swelled holes, flatters, and anvils. Each has a purpose and a place. The effect is undeniably dull, but also pleasantly numbing. As I read about chisels and drifts, I start to feel drowsy. *Murder Afoot* may not be a page-turner, but it's as good as a Xanax.

CHAPTER THIRTY-TWO

D ev gets out of his tiny car surprisingly quickly considering his size. He's smiling as he comes around to open the passenger door for me. But then he pauses.

"You look skeptical. Everything okay?"

"Nope, all good." That's a lie. I'm wary of the matchbox car and disconcerted by the extremely good dream I had about Dev last night. I remember only that we were naked and wrapped in a dark green velour blanket. It was so embarrassingly lovey-dovey, it almost made me want to cancel our hike, but when I floated the idea at breakfast, Wyatt wouldn't hear of it.

"He's smoking hot and obviously likes you," Wyatt had said. "Go forth and frolic."

I can frolic. No biggie, I tell myself. Chill out. I'll have a lovely day with Dev walking the *Jane Eyre* trail, climbing up to Stanage Edge, and seeing actual moors, which I've only read about in books. I hope they're wind-swept and boggy and depressing in a kind of mesmerizing way.

Once we're out of the village, Dev turns onto a two-lane highway and speeds up, going too fast for someone driving on the wrong side of the road. I crack the window for fresh air and pray I don't get carsick. When we come to a fork in the road, Dev bears right, toward Hathersage.

."Tell me something about Stanage Edge," I say. "Is it famous for anything other than being beautiful?"

"Robin Hood hid from the Sheriff of Nottingham there, in a place called Robin Hood's Cave."

"Funny coincidence, Robin Hood finding a cave named after himself."

"Isn't it though?"

I love the way Dev smiles at me.

"There's a churchyard in Hathersage with an unusually long grave that's said to contain the remains of Robin Hood's gargantuan henchman, Little John."

"He was real?"

"Probably not. But do you want to visit his grave anyway?"

I can't wait to tell Amity about this.

Hathersage has many of the obligatory features of a charming English village: an old stone church with a tall steeple, an inn that looks like it probably has mutton on the menu, adorable shops, and inviting pubs. There are also three large outdoor stores, which Dev tells me cater to the hikers, rock climbers, and hang gliders drawn to Stanage Edge.

"It's got a thousand different climbing routes," he says.

We park outside of a tearoom and walk down to a narrow lane that brings us to a stile. We pass through and follow the footpath across a meadow. Sheep watch us with their dull eyes as we climb the gentle slope. I pick a golden buttercup and hold it under my chin as we walk, remembering how my mother used to do that to me. She said if my chin glowed yellow, which it always did, it meant that I loved butter. It was true, I adored butter. How did the flower know? My mother said it was magic, and I believed her. I drop the buttercup.

The path flattens out and Dev says, "This may seem bizarre, but you wouldn't want to run a little, would you?"

It's an odd request, but I'm wearing sneakers and running might be just what I need to dispel some of my nervous energy.

"Actually, I would."

I start at a quick pace, which I think surprises Dev, because it takes him a few seconds to catch up. As the path climbs, we both go faster, hopping over stones and tree roots. I haven't run in a while, and it feels good to move like this, to get my heart working. Dev passes me, letting out a little whoop when he jumps over a log in the path, which makes me laugh. Moving like this, not for exercise but just for fun, makes me feel free.

"Race you to that tree," I say, and speed up.

My thighs are burning as I pull even with Dev. The path is too narrow for both of us. Dev takes the lead again, and I strain to catch up. I get close, and I imagine grabbing his torso and tackling him, rolling down the hill together. But he pulls away and is several lengths ahead of me. I push hard, but my legs lag with heaviness and I'm gasping for air. Dev reaches the tree first. He bends over, hands on his knees, breathing hard. When I reach him, I collapse onto the grass on the side of the path.

"That was glorious, until it wasn't," I say.

"Agreed."

"I'm not ready to get up," I say.

"I'll join you, then."

We're both on our backs on the grass, looking up at the enormous oak tree.

"I didn't expect you'd want to run, let alone race," he says.

"I'm feeling exceptionally free. I am off duty. And this"—I lift an arm up, toward the oak tree and its branches stretching out, the leaves and the blue beyond—"this is an excellent place to be on vacation. Do you know I haven't had a real vacation in more than four years? The last one was with my grandmother. We drove to Maine for a week. We swam every day in frigid water, picked blueberries, and ate an obscene amount of chowder and clam strips."

"Four years?" Dev says. "I'll never understand Americans."

A bird swoops above, perches on a limb. Bobs its head this way and that and flies off. The oak branches form a canopy that shades us.

"How old do you think this tree is?" I say.

"I don't know. Three hundred, four hundred years old?"

"Wow."

"How old are you?" Dev says.

I turn to look at him.

"I'm thirty-four."

"Fancy that, I'm thirty-four too," he says.

We're lying very close to each other. Not on a bed of moss, but still. A gust of wind rustles the leaves above us. I sit up. After a moment, Dev pops up and brushes off the back of his pants. He puts out a hand to help me stand. We continue following the path, which winds through narrow tree trunks. The silence is starting to feel awkward, but then Dev tells me he wasn't keen on the murder-mystery week when he first heard about it.

"I didn't see how it would be good for Willowthrop to promote itself as something fake, ye olde murder village," he says. "But Germaine won me over. I'm all for saving the community pool. And it's certainly bringing new business to my bar."

He explains that Willowthrop, like country villages throughout England, experienced a real estate boom during the pandemic, with city people snapping up holiday properties at exorbitant prices. It

165

made the housing situation even worse; people who grew up in the village can't afford to stay. Now that people can travel anywhere again, the appeal of a local vacation in the Peak has dropped off. But the housing is still unavailable. Many of the newly purchased properties in Willowthrop sit empty.

"If my mum didn't have a house with a separate cottage, I probably wouldn't be living here either."

"You wouldn't live in the house with her?" It looked big enough.

"I don't know. I'm not sure I'm *that* good a son."

Ahead of us is an old stone house, solid and grand, almost like a castle. It's three stories high, with mullioned windows, several chimneys, and battlements around the top. Dev takes out his phone and reads aloud.

"This is North Lees Hall, which is said to be the inspiration for Thornfield Hall in *Jane Eyre*," Dev says.

"Said to be?" I tell him about the Rutland Arms Hotel and the Jane Austen myth and why the phrase makes me suspicious. But looking up at the house, I can see it. Jane Eyre standing right there on the second floor, looking as plain and simple as so many wrongly assumed her to be and gazing out the windows wishing for more than life as a neglected governess.

Dev turns back to his phone. "This might be more than just a legend. It says here that Charlotte Brontë visited her friend Ellen Nussey in Hathersage in 1845, during which she paid two or three visits to North Lees Hall. And this is interesting, 'a persistent local legend' has it that the first mistress of the hall, Agnes Ashurst, was confined to a padded room and died in a fire."

"You're telling me Mr. Rochester's madwoman in the attic was inspired by a real person? No way!"

"Does it matter if it was?" Dev asks. "Either way, it's a good story, right?"

"Of course it is," I say. I'm tempted to commend Dev for having read Charlotte Brontë—back home, it's the rare guy who wouldn't mix up Jane Eyre and Jane Austen—but maybe this kind of thing is common knowledge in England.

The path brings us to a road, which we cross before picking up a new trail. It twists and turns and slowly ascends. The rocks in and around the path give way to larger and larger boulders. Soon I can see Stanage Edge in the distance—it's not a mountain, as I'd imagined, but more like a ledge or a cliff made of piles and piles of enormous boulders. We come upon some rock climbers, sitting on a flat rock having a snack, their ropes hanging from the ledge above them. One of them raises a hand.

"Oy, Dev. Taking the easy route up today?"

"No shame in it," Dev says. "I'll join you chaps tomorrow, yeah?"

"You didn't say you were a climber," I say, as we continue up the path.

"You didn't ask."

We keep climbing, and then I see what looks like a flock of prehistoric birds flying in the distance. Hang gliders. I count fifteen of them.

"Are you a glider too?" I ask.

"Nah, I like having my feet on the ground."

The path gets steeper, winding between rocks. In some places, the rocks are like steps; in others, it's more of a scramble, and I use my hands to make my way up. At the top, there's a wide, flat path running the length of the ledge. The landscape is extraordinary, like experiencing two levels of the earth at once. In one direction, the higher level, are dark moors, acres of low, bushy heather in hues of deep auburn, brown, and green that blend like the colors of a vast ocean. On the other side are the boulders, some as big as cars, some in stacks with flat tops you can walk or sit on. They make a ledge of rocky outcrops that drop off steeply, down to the valley and pastures below. In the distance, the rooftops and church spires look tiny, nestled by trees. The fields are crisscrossed by long hedges and stone walls.

Looking behind me to the marshy moors and ahead to this pastoral vista, I have the strangest feeling. Like I know this place, like I've already sensed how the moors seem to roll toward the rocks at the top of the cliff that holds them back.

"This feels familiar," I say.

"It's very famous," Dev says. "It's used in a lot of films." He turns back to the moors. "Ruth Wilson wept over there as a distraught Jane Eyre." Then he turns and points to a large, flat rock jutting like a wide diving platform out over the edge of the cliff. "And that's where Keira Knightley had her best windswept moment in *Pride and Prejudice*."

"Of course, with the jutting chin. But it's not that. It's more than that."

"Like you were here in another life?" Dev says.

"Do you believe that stuff?"

"Not in the slightest," he says.

That's a relief.

"Neither do I."

We walk over to a smooth stone and sit, our legs hanging down. The drop below is at least fifty feet. Dev takes a bag of nuts and raisins from his backpack, pours some into my cupped hand.

"No Scampi Snacks?"

"Scampi Fries, which are to be consumed only when drunk."

"That's the custom?"

"That's a law."

The wind lifts my hair, which flies in a tangle of strands in front of my face and in my mouth. I push my hair away, and the gusts send it back into the air, chaotic, and not in a Keira Knightley kind of way. I angle my face against the wind. In the distance, I see tiny figures walking a path across a pasture.

"This place is magic," I say.

Dev smiles.

"I know, I probably sound like everyone who comes here for the first time."

"I wish."

"What do you mean?" I say.

"When my mum first got sick, I was living in London. I started coming up on weekends to see her. My girlfriend would come with me from time to time. Lucy was great with Mum, but she found Willowthrop, the whole Peak, deadly dull. I took her all over trying to win her over. It was hopeless."

"What happened?"

"We didn't want the same things. As Mum got worse, I started coming more often and staying longer. Lucy stayed behind in London. She started to resent my time here. I think she thought I was only here out of obligation, that as soon as I arranged a carer for my mum, I'd come back to London. But the more I was here, the more it felt like I was meant to be here. I wasn't unhappy in London, but the freedom I felt here was transporting. Exciting and calming all at once. That probably sounds illogical."

As of this moment, it makes perfect sense to me.

"I get that. Totally."

We're sitting so close our thighs are touching.

From up above us in the sky, a deep voice calls, "Go for it, mate!"

We look up to the glider, where the man is giving us a thumbs-up.

"That was presumptuous," I say.

"Childish."

"Ballsy."

"But not entirely outlandish." Dev puts out his palm, flat, like he's displaying something. I open my palm and touch it to his, lightly tapping against it a few times, watching only our hands. And then he wraps his hand, large and warm, around mine and holds on. This time, I don't turn it into a handshake. I look at him through the strands of hair dancing across my face.

I know so little about this man. But up here on the top of the world, I'm willing to leap, and not only because I know I'll never see him again after the weekend. It's something else, something undefinable and unfamiliar. I move my face barely an inch toward him and sense he has done the same. Or is it the wind? And then with two fingers, he pushes my hair to the side.

"May I . . . " he whispers.

I nod so slightly it's almost a quiver and, slowly, he brings his lips to mine. It's a light kiss, but the sense of him runs through my every vein. We pull away, then let our foreheads touch. We kiss again, and it's not just a good kiss but a happy kiss. We are kissing and smiling. We are smile-kissing, which I didn't even know was a thing.

"This makes no sense," I whisper.

"None whatsoever." Dev's hand is on my neck, his fingers in my hair.

I lean in again and close my eyes. Above, I sense gliders drifting across the sky, banking away from the moors in unison, like swallows.

CHAPTER THIRTY-THREE

When Dev drops me off, he asks if I'll come by the bar tonight. "For another Hanky Panky?" I am ridiculous.

"If that's your fancy, but I do make other cocktails too," he says, twirling a strand of my hair around his finger and pulling me gently toward him.

Oh my. It could be his accent, but when he says things like this, I think he's clever and sexy and not using a well-worn line. It doesn't seem rote, or slick, or sleazy. It feels honest. It doesn't really matter though. Whether we share a few kisses or a few nights, in less than a week there will be a very big ocean between us. Which is probably why I'm leaning into it so easily.

"I have to go. I told my cottage mates I'd be back around three. I'd hate to disappoint them."

"You hardly know them."

"I hardly know you."

"Excellent point."

"I should go."

"Right." He pushes my hair back over my shoulder.

"We're going to visit Tracy's flat," I say. "To search for clues."

"Okay, Sherlock, off you go."

"Off I go." I turn to unlatch the door, but then turn back. "Can we—"

But before I ask, he's kissed me again.

I stop at the cottage door to catch my breath. Inside, Amity and Wyatt are at the kitchen table. The minute Amity looks at me, I can tell that her romance radar is up.

"Looks like it was a strenuous hike," she says, smiling. "You're quite flushed."

"Quite radiant." Wyatt is grinning too.

"Do you know when Brits say 'quite' something, they mean the opposite?" A deft change of topic. "I had no idea until Dev filled me in on the way to Hathersage. I happened to mention that our pub lunch yesterday was 'quite good' and he said, 'That bad?' Turns out a lot of what they say does not mean what we think it does. If you give a Brit a piece of helpful advice and they say, 'I'll bear it in mind,' they pretty much mean there's no effing way they're doing that. 'Very interesting'? They mean 'What a total bore.' It's quite confusing—and I mean that in the American way."

"How extraordinary," Amity says, still looking at me like I've got the proverbial lipstick on my collar. "It's like every day is opposite day."

"So when Germaine said that Roland Wingford was 'quite instrumental' in developing the story for this mystery, what did she really mean?" Wyatt asks.

"Probably that he didn't contribute at all," I say.

"Then who created the mystery?" Amity says.

"That's obvious," Wyatt says. "I'm quite confident—make that *damned* confident—that when we crack this case, and we will crack it, we're going to find Germaine Postlethwaite's fingerprints all over it. Roland may be the published author, but she's the brains behind this operation."

Amity and Wyatt have the murder bulletin board on the table.

I pick up the much sparser board devoted to my mother's mystery. If Germaine is so smart, might she figure out what my mother was hiding too? I lean the board against the wall and take an index card from the pile on the kitchen table. On it I write "Stanage Edge," though I'm not sure if I should add it to the board.

Amity asks what it means. I try to describe what it was like to be there.

"Was it from your mother's bedtime story?" she asks.

"It might have been. It must have been. I don't know."

"I believe that sometimes, against all logic and reason, people know the answers to the mysteries that perplex them," Amity says. "They know it viscerally, in their bodies, if not intellectually. Are you sure there's nothing else?"

When I don't respond, she pats my hand, the way my grandmother used to.

"Not to worry. We'll keep trying."

My throat constricts, a familiar feeling from childhood, when I was trying to hold back tears, because it wasn't the right time, because I was at a friend's house, or at school, not in my room at home. Why am I suddenly so sad? I don't realize that my lips are trembling until I notice the way Amity is looking at me. She comes over and puts an arm around me.

"Let's sit," she says, guiding me to the couch.

I start to speak but can't find the words. For a few hours, I'd forgotten about my mother, and how she bolted and reappeared and never explained herself. I'd forgotten what brought me here. I let myself kiss Dev and enjoy the moment without overthinking. It's like I let down my guard out of happiness, and now sadness is rushing in. That glorious feeling of being up there on Stanage Edge has dislodged everything I've been holding back.

I have an overwhelming desire to call my mother. To ask her

what I'm doing here. To demand answers. All my life, I've wanted answers from her. Why did she go? Why did she return, only to leave again? Why didn't she miss me the way I missed her? Why was it so difficult for me to be apart from her even after she'd left me again and again? She was so disappointing. How can I miss her so much? My eyes sting. The first tears since my mother died.

"I'm sorry, I don't know what's come over me."

"Don't you?" Amity says, handing me a tissue. "I think I do."

I blow my nose, looking up at her and waiting for her to clue me in.

"This, my dear, is grief."

CHAPTER THIRTY-FOUR

I tell Amity I need to shower before we go to Tracy's flat. Under the rush of water, I let the tears come. I don't like crying like this, but I can't help myself, overwhelmed by memories.

I must have been eleven, maybe twelve, and my mother and I were walking in a park near my grandmother's house. When my mother stopped to talk to a man carrying a baby on his shoulders, I ran ahead and climbed into the hollow of an old sycamore tree. The trunk was huge but scooped out like a cave with two openings. I think it had been hit by lightning. I crouched into a little ball in the darkest space, between the openings, hidden from view. My mother didn't notice that I was gone and kept chatting with the man. I waited without moving for what seemed like an eternity. Finally, she started calling my name. She sounded playful at first, but then her tone changed. I could tell she was annoyed and, after a few more minutes, angry and afraid. I'm ashamed to remember how long I stayed there, silent, giving my mother a real scare. The truth was, I liked hearing how frantic she sounded. From inside the tree, I had my mother's undivided attention. I felt sure of her love. For once, I was the one who'd disappeared and she was left thinking about me.

Back downstairs, I'm too tired to talk. Amity and Wyatt want to stop by Bert's store on the way to Tracy's flat so we can question him about his alibi. I'm fine with following their lead.

Bert's outside having a cigarette when we walk up to the store.

"We talked to your daughter," Wyatt says. "She says she hasn't spoken to you in weeks."

Bert drops his cigarette onto the pavement and grinds it with his foot.

"All right. I was at the pub in the next town over, meeting someone."

"Anyone in particular?" Wyatt says.

"Sassygirl442."

"Pardon?" Amity says.

"I met her online. It was our first IRL. In real life."

Men his age shouldn't try to keep up with the times, I think, until I remember that he's talking according to a script.

"Why did you lie about this?" Amity's voice is so soothing. She would make an excellent therapist.

"I didn't want anyone to know I'm doing this kind of dating. Like I'm some kind of loser who can't meet women any other way."

"Have you gone on many online dates?" Amity motions for me to take out my phone, whispers to me to open a picture of my mother.

"A few," Bert. "What's that got to do with the case?"

"Nothing, honestly," Amity says sweetly. "This is another matter entirely."

She holds out my phone to him, displaying a picture I took during my last visit to my mother in Gainesville. She's in a string bikini, her hair swept into a ponytail, standing by the Ichetucknee River. She made me take a lot of pictures that day, probably because she knew she looked good.

"Bert, if your real name is Bert, have you encountered this woman online?"

"Did something happen to her?" Bert asks.

"You recognize her?" Amity says.

I don't dare tell him the truth.

"I feel like I might have seen her," Bert says. "Do you have any other photos?"

I take the phone and look through my photos until I find another one, the kind my mom might pick for a dating profile. Here's one she sent me from a fundraiser to save the manatees. Her hair looks lush, and her lips are bright red. Her smile is appealingly mischievous.

"Oh yeah, I FaceTimed with her for a while."

"You did? When was this?" I ask.

If he says last month, we'll know it's a mistake.

"It's been a while, maybe it was last summer. She was funny and very curious. Had a lot of questions. Wanted my whole life story. She said she was thinking of coming to England."

Bert is not a bad-looking guy, and he's about my mother's age. But would she come all the way to Willowthrop to meet him? It seems like a stretch. Maybe she was just looking for information about the village. But again, why?

"What happened?" Amity asks.

"Never heard from her again. What do the young people say? She ghosted me."

CHAPTER THIRTY-FIVE

Tracy's place is above the salon, a one-bedroom flat with a living room that includes a corner kitchen and table for two. The decor is pretty, if a little frilly, and surprisingly disheveled. The windows have lace curtains, though a few of the hems are undone and dip down on the dusty sills. There's a glass vase of white calla lilies on a table, the petals beginning to brown and the water cloudy. The coatrack by the door looks like it's about to topple over from the weight of coats and jackets piled onto it.

We're only allotted fifteen minutes to investigate the flat, so we decide to take lots of photographs so we can continue going over the evidence later. There are a few things that might be significant: a paper on the glass coffee table that's headed "A legal notice of forfeiture issued to Tracy Penny, sole proprietor of Hairs Looking at You," and which details a timeline, starting the following week, for an eviction procedure, and a pink Filofax calendar, which is open to the page two days after Tracy's murder, where someone—presumably Tracy—has written in all capital letters "TELL PIPPA!" I flip through the previous days and see only things that seem ordinary—a volunteer commitment at Whitby Stables, a delivery date for a new salon chair, and a reminder to watch *The Big Blow Out* on Channel 4.

On the table is also a copy of *Hair Magazine*, dog-eared at articles for Barbiecore Hair and TikTok Hair Trends, both of which I photograph for no logical reason. I feel guilty snooping around Tracy's apartment and have to remind myself that it might not even be hers and, even if it is, at the moment it's a stage set.

Wyatt pulls a tiny white card from the wastepaper basket and hands it to me. The top of the card reads "Willowthrop Florist" and the message scribbled below says, "Forever Yours." I take a picture of that too.

Tracy's bed is unmade, the pink sheets rumpled and slightly depressed as if someone had been lying there not too long ago. On the floor by the closet is a silky black negligee, the kind put on to be taken off. I hope Amity has plenty of paper for printing photos.

The kitchen counters are clean, but there are dishes in the sink. The refrigerator is nearly empty. Just a bowl of roasted almonds, a container of nonfat Greek yogurt, a large package of salad greens, and a ready-made macaroni and cheese from someplace called Tesco. The freezer contains only double-chocolate ice cream, full-fat.

"I have deduced that the deceased was conflicted about food," I say, hoping to get a laugh from Wyatt and Amity, but there's no response. They are standing by the little dining table, their backs to me. I wedge myself between them to see what they are looking at. On the table is a bottle of gin and two glasses. The bottle has a familiar blue label.

"That's Dev's gin," I say. "Good for him. Nice to see he's getting some business."

"Hmm," Amity says.

"I'm not sure this one was purchased." Wyatt picks up a note card that is sitting on the table next to one of the glasses and hands it to me. It reads, "Trace—thanks for, well, all of it. XO, Dev."

"He's got thick dark hair," Wyatt says.

"And he's tall," Amity says.

"So?" I don't know what they're getting at.

"The nosy neighbor said the man who visited Tracy on Monday afternoons, when the salon was closed, was tall and had a thick head of dark hair," Amity says.

"Dev's bar doesn't open until eight o'clock," Wyatt says. "It could have been him."

Was Dev playing me? He was part of this all along?

"Why would he have been here?" I say. "What would be the motive?"

Amity glances back to the bedroom. I follow her gaze to the negligee on the floor.

"You think Dev was sleeping with Tracy?" I say.

"Not in real life," Amity says. "It's pretend, remember?"

"He might be our man," Wyatt says.

At his cottage, Dev *did* say the murderer was a man. I go over my encounters with him—at the village green, the opening-night dinner, in his cottage, on the drive, at Stanage Edge. Did he say anything that could have revealed a plausible motive for him to kill Tracy? He didn't mention Tracy or the mystery at all, except to say he was initially a skeptic.

"The dashing distiller has some questions to answer," Wyatt says.

"Yes, he does," I say. I can't deny it. I'm excited by the thought of putting the squeeze on Dev. "I'll drop by his bar and question him later."

"We'll *all* go," Amity says.

"Are you worried that my investigative abilities might be compromised by my—"

"Libido?" Wyatt says.

"The word I was going to use was 'friendship,'" I say.

From Tracy's we head to the village's sole Indian restaurant. Over curry, we review the evidence we saw at the flat.

"The eviction notice on the table seems to be enough to rule out Bert Lott," Wyatt says.

"But doesn't it confirm what we already know—that he wanted Tracy out of the salon?" I say.

"Yes, but if he was taking legal action to evict her and had a court date set for a month after the murder, it makes no sense that he would kill her," Amity says.

"Okay, no more Bert Lott."

It feels like we're making progress. We look at the photos on our phones to see if there are other clues. There's one of the card we found in the wastebasket from whoever sent Tracy flowers. But it's too late to call the Willowthrop Florist, so we put that off for tomorrow. We also agree we need to ask around about the "Pippa" mentioned in Tracy's Filofax. She'd written "TELL PIPPA" and underlined it with such force that the page was nearly torn. What was she going to tell her? Did it have anything to do with why Tracy was murdered?

CHAPTER THIRTY-SIX

Dev's bar is packed. The Tampa book club women are sitting at a big round table, raising glasses and toasting with Naomi and Deborah. As soon as she spots us, Deborah jumps up and rushes over.

"It's the three mush-keteers!" she slurs.

Naomi is on her heels. "We went to another bar first. Bad intel but good drinks. I'm afraid my sister overindulged."

"Isn't this place marvelous?" Deborah says. "I want to move to Willowthrop and come to this charming establishment every night. It will be my Cheers. My Cheerio!"

Naomi sighs and shakes her head. "I am *so* sorry."

"Not to worry," Amity says, patting Naomi on the arm. "You are not your sister's keeper."

"I kind of am," Naomi says.

Deborah steps close to us, peers up at Wyatt. "I do not for one moment believe that Dev could be the murderer. Is he a devil with the cocktails? Yes, yes, he is. Might he have slept with Tracy? Yes, yes, he might. But a killer? Impossible."

"Come, let's grab a table," Naomi says. "I've had enough of the Tampa girls. Can you believe that's actually what they call themselves—girls. It's worse than ladies."

Wyatt promises we'll join them after we question Dev. We seat ourselves at the bar. Dev is working fast, taking orders, making drinks, wiping down the counter. He's not aware of us yet, which gives me a good chance to watch him. He brushes his forehead with the back of his hand, holding up the drinks to the light before he places them on the counter with a barely visible but charmingly self-satisfied smile. It must be something to love what you do. Finally, he notices us.

"Welcome to Moss," he says to Amity and Wyatt. And to me, a quiet hi, which travels all the way down to my toes. "What can I get you?"

"Answers," Wyatt says.

"Do I need a solicitor?" Dev says.

"Not yet," Wyatt says.

"Okay, go on, then."

"You need to tell us more about your shower," I blurt out.

"Whoa," says Wyatt.

Amity laughs.

"My shower?" Dev says, grinning at me. "I lathered. I rinsed. I repeated."

"So you're squeaky clean?" I can't help myself.

"Maybe still a little dirty." Dev winks at me.

"And what precisely are we talking about now?" Amity says.

"His alibi," I say, trying not to laugh. "If you showered and then you came here, how do you explain the bottle of gin, dirty highball glasses, and note signed from you that were on the table in Tracy's flat?"

"I was there earlier on Saturday."

"What for?" Wyatt says.

"A friendly chat," Dev says.

"How friendly?" I lean onto the bar. "Black-lingerie friendly?"

"That's not a term I'm familiar with," Dev says, stepping closer to me. "But I'd love to know more about it."

Oh Lord.

"What did you and Tracy 'chat about'?" Wyatt says.

"If you must know, it was my hair."

"You went there for a haircut?" Amity says.

"No," Dev says. "She's been cutting my hair for free for the past year."

"Is that so?" I ask. "And what does she get in return?"

"I keep her in gin," he says. "I stopped by Tracy's flat at about five o'clock to give her a fresh bottle and thank her."

"And where were you later that evening, specifically from eight o'clock to ten o'clock?" Amity says.

"I helped out at The Lonely Spider until 8:30, went home and took a quick shower, and was here by nine." Dev raises his arm, calls over one of the waiters, who corroborates his alibi.

"We were slammed," the waiter says. "Best night ever. We could barely stop to take a breather."

"Now, what can I get you?" Dev says.

Wyatt and Amity get red wine and join Naomi and Deborah. I hop off the stool and jerk my head toward the back room.

"I've got questions," I say.

The door swings behind us, and we're kissing again. I kiss his beautiful lips, press my body against his. "This gin-bartering business. Who else are you trading favors with?"

His lips are on my neck, my collarbone. "What makes you think I'm so easy?"

"You're not exactly playing hard to get."

"I'm very discriminating," he says, nibbling on my ear.

"You're driving me crazy," I say.

"Yeah? That's good."

Why can't I stop kissing this man?

"I should get back," he says.

His mouth is on mine again.

"Me too. I'm on the trail of a murderer."

"Are you sure you don't need to question me some more?"

"I probably should. I mean, to be thorough."

"Let's take this interrogation home, to my place."

I pull back, look him in the eye. "For real?"

He puts a finger under my chin and tips it up. "No joke." He kisses me lightly. "What do you say?"

Instead of answering, I kiss him back. And why not? It's a foreign fling, all in good fun, nothing more.

CHAPTER THIRTY-SEVEN

On a quest to try all the pubs in Willowthrop, Naomi and Deborah convince Wyatt and Amity to join them at the Goat and Spur down by the river. I hang back at Moss, nursing my second Hanky Panky. By the time Dev's closing up, I've had only half. I'm not completely sober but not buzzed enough that I'm not nervous about going back to his place. Was I jittery like this with that cute engineer I met at Kim's New Year's Eve party? I remember laughing a lot and having a few good nights. I must have felt skittish then too and just don't remember it because the whole thing was over so quickly.

Neither of us says a word on the short drive. The full moon makes a mosaic of shadows throughout the garden as we walk to the cottage. I'm worried our earlier ease has vanished forever and that this is going to be awkward. But as soon as Dev latches the cottage door behind us, he turns and takes me in his arms.

"Now I've got you where I want you." His lips are on my neck. Is he kidding?

"That's a classic villain line." It's ridiculous how much the pretend danger turns me on.

"Is it?" Dev whispers. His lips move up behind my ear. "It's also what's said by a bloke who's been thinking about this since the moment he met you."

Between my fingers, his hair is thick and smooth.

"On the village green? When I thought your mother was a fraud?"

"You were so sure of yourself." He runs his hands down to my waist and pulls me closer. "I couldn't believe I was attracted to such a brash American."

"That's the best kind." I press my forehead to his, my lips nearly touching his. "Our cockiness gives you stuffy Brits permission to let loose and do wild things like say what you mean."

"Stop talking," he whispers.

"See, you're learning already."

And now we're kissing in earnest, like there's no time or need for banter. I slip my hands under his T-shirt. His back is strong and warm, I want to touch every part of it. We move toward his bed, still kissing. We kick off our shoes. We both have trouble with our jeans. Laughing, I finally manage to fling mine off my shins. Dev attempts the same but loses his balance and falls onto the bed. I push him gently back and climb on top of him. There's enough moonlight coming in the window for me to see him smile like he can't believe his good fortune. It's what I'm feeling too. Usually when I'm with someone new, I'm the first to close my eyes, the last to open them. But I want to see Dev. I want to see him looking at me.

I bend down and kiss him, my hair falling like curtains around our faces.

"We don't have to rush," I say, and realize that I'm talking to myself. There is no end goal here, no getting off and moving on, there is only this, and I want it to last forever. We kiss until we're breathless. I roll over and pull him onto me, reveling in the weight of him. And then I push and flip him over again, so I can look down on him, but I'm not aware of where we are and his head thumps, hard, against the headboard.

"Ow!"

"Oh my god, are you okay? I'm so sorry." I turn on the light.

He touches the top of his head and winces.

"Is there a bump?"

"No."

"Please don't just say that. Do you need some ice?" I can't believe I've hurt him.

"No, I'm okay. I mean, I will be in a minute."

I flop down on my back beside him.

"I feel like such an idiot," I say.

"You are the opposite of an idiot."

I take a deep breath, wait for my heartbeat to settle. I can sense that Dev is looking up at the ceiling as I am. And then, like a whisper, his fingers brush mine.

"I really fancy you, Cath."

"I really like you too."

Our fingers intertwine. We stay like that for a few minutes until Dev turns onto his side, toward me, and I do the same. We kiss lightly now, tentatively, like we're beginning again, not trying to hide our unease. I take off my shirt and bra. We explore each other, fingers trembling, until they are not. We let them roam up our bodies, and down. Dev's touch is a revelation, here and here, and oh yes, there, and let me show you precisely where, like this, and now I don't want to slow down, and I tell him not to stop. And I love how he watches me. And I keep my eyes open so I can map his pleasure on his face, his beautiful, kind face, and when he says Cath and even calls me Cathy, I don't mind at all.

CHAPTER THIRTY-EIGHT

WEDNESDAY

I'm awakened by the scents of cinnamon and coffee. I stretch under the comforter, bare legs on cool sheets, and can sense without looking that I'm alone in the bed. When I open my eyes, a white curtain is floating above me, the breeze pushing it up and up, until it sighs down. There's a pastry on a napkin atop the stack of books on Dev's night table. And a note: "Yesterday's cinnamon roll, but still good. There's a clean towel on the chair, hot water if your shower's quick. Coffee on the stove. I'm in the garden."

I grab my shirt off the floor, put it on, and tiptoe over to the front window. Dev is at the other side of the garden, by his mother's house, pushing a shovel into the ground with his foot. I wonder how long he's been out there. After a typical hookup, I'm out of bed first, making coffee, ready to start the day, on my own. I tap on the window, and Dev looks my way, a hand over his brow. He smiles and spears his shovel into the ground. He spreads out his arms as if to present his garden on this sunny day. I splay my palms against the window—ten minutes.

Hair twisted up in a knot, I take a quick shower. Despite the lack of sleep last night, I'm already, or still, buzzing. I get dressed, down some coffee, have a few bites of the cinnamon roll. It's surprisingly bright outside, the warmest day we've had yet. The plants are still damp with dew, and some flowers already open to the sun. I know only a few of them—iris, peonies, some tulips on their last days.

I ask Dev for a tour of the garden, and he takes my hand like it's the most natural thing in the world. He's cultivated every patch of land. There are rows of seedlings just starting to come up and dirt beds with no signs of growth, their names written on plastic tags in Dev's neat, slanted handwriting. There will be tomatoes, garlic, carrots, peas, and rocket, which I think is arugula. Sorrel, rhubarb, and fennel, and a whole section of herbs—rosemary, coriander, dill, and oregano. Climbing up a trellis behind the herb garden is another plant I recognize, hollyhock, though it hasn't flowered yet.

"That was my mother's favorite," I say. "She told me once she almost named me Holly, but my father, who was Jewish, thought it sounded too Christmassy. So she turned to *Wuthering Heights* instead."

"You're named for Catherine Earnshaw?"

Ten points for Dev for knowing another Brontë.

"Don't remind me," I say. "She was ghastly."

"She was wild with emotion," he says.

"Exactly."

He laughs. "I meant it as a good thing."

We move through the rows, Dev bending down from time to time to pull out a weed. He disentangles a delicate stem from a bushy plant as tenderly as a mother pushing an errant curl off her baby's forehead. He picks up a tray of tiny seedlings. "These are ready to plant."

"Can I help?"

Dev hands me the seedlings and points to an empty patch of

ground. He tells me how deep to dig and how far apart. I kneel in the dirt and start to scoop away soil with my hands. Dev asks if I want a spade, but I like the feel of the damp earth.

"Full disclosure," I tell him. "I have the opposite of a green thumb."

"It's not rocket science. It's water plus sun, a bit of manual labor, and patience."

"Is that all?"

"And faith."

"Ah, there's the rub," I say.

"Let me show you." Dev gets down next to me, takes a seedling out, tips it from its plastic pot. "Pull out the root strings gently like this." He teases them out, holds the whole thing in one hand while he moves more dirt away with the other. He sets the plant down and pushes dirt around it and pats it down.

I'm extra careful as I take one of the seedlings and repeat what Dev did, conscious of him standing above me and watching. But then he moves on and I lose myself in the task, tipping and scooping and patting. The breeze moves through my hair. I wipe a fly from my face. At the other edge of the garden, Dev resumes digging. Birds chirp, and the wind sashays through the bushes. A dog barks; a car shifts gears as it climbs the hill.

When all the seedlings are in the ground, I stand and brush the dirt from my hands and jeans. Dev pulls a hose from the side of the house and hands it to me. I put my thumb on the nozzle and spray the ground where I planted.

"I think they'll do fine," Dev says.

I imagine it will take weeks, if not months, for these plants to grow and bear fruit. The sun will rise and set and rise and set, rain will sprinkle down, and the seedlings will push their way into plants, stems thickening until they are sturdy and strong. And one morning, perhaps as sunny as today, there will be tiny buds, little vegetables beginning their journey. I see it with astonishing clarity: I'm walking through the garden with a wicker basket, filling it with tomatoes, and green peas, and thick bunches of chard. I hoist the basket on my hip like I'm carrying a toddler and bring it inside the cottage to Dev.

A gust of wind brings me back. It's sudden and strong, like a rogue wave, prodding me to attention, if not like an electric shock, then like a spark. *Wake up.* I look around the garden. It all looks the same. And yet, something is different and unsettling. The wind picks up again and now I hear her voice. *This, this is it, Cath. This will be perfect!*

A coo of a bird, a morning dove, and the breeze pushes the plants, makes them bow. I can see her too, eyes shining with excitement, talking about fate, and stars aligning, and divine justice, and even jiggery-pokery, putting right on my path, among all these villagers and dowdy tourists, a man like Dev. My mother may as well be squeezing my hand. *This is what you must run toward. Leave everything for this. It is everything.*

I don't realize my hand is trembling until I see the hose shake. I drop it, watch it flip on the ground like a wounded snake. The iciness in my gut spreads to my chest, my hands.

"I don't feel well," I say.

"What's wrong?" Dev says.

"I have to go."

The water from the hose is making a puddle.

"Do you want some water? Some tea?"

"I don't like tea." It comes out too loud, emphatic. "I have to go."

"I'll drive you home," Dev says, brushing the dirt off his hands.

"No, you garden, I can walk."

I rush inside, pick up my bag.

"Cath, what's going on? You're acting odd." He's not stupid; he knows this is not a sudden illness. He scribbles down his number on a paper and hands it to me. "Call me later and let me know how you are."

I rush through the garden and out the gate.

CHAPTER THIRTY-NINE

I barely notice the houses, or anything at all, as I head down the hill, away from the village. I don't know where I'm going, but this is countryside, not wilderness. There are paths everywhere. I'll find my way, use my phone if I need to. At the bottom of the hill, I go through a stile and onto a footpath, which takes me across a pasture, pale green in the morning light. I dodge cow pats, pass through splotches of dandelions bobbing in the breeze. It was cowardly the way I ran off, but I wasn't lying. I didn't feel well.

The path takes me into the woods, where it's cooler and damp. I keep my eyes down to watch for rocks and tree roots so I don't trip. Walking like this requires a welcome kind of focus, which pushes everything else out. But then there's my mother talking to me again. *I said rush in, Cath, not run the other way.* She had no idea how hard I've tried to resist her pattern. I'll be damned if I'm going to fall into it now.

As the path slopes downward, the forest starts to thin. I catch glints of water as I descend until I'm on flat ground, at the edge of a broad green meadow. The path is barely visible in the tall grass. I let my fingers brush the tips as I walk toward the river. It's wider than I expected and shallow. The water is clear; tiny fish, jumpy and indecisive, dart this way and that above smooth, speckled rocks. It's calming to walk along the river and follow its wide, gentle bends. But after one sharper arc, I stop. Way up high in front of me, crossing the valley from one peak to another, is an enormous stately bridge, supported by a row of high arches. It looks like an aqueduct or, more likely, a railroad bridge, the kind you see in action movies where a steam engine bullets out of a mountain tunnel to reveal men brawling on its roof, nearly pitching off the edge as the train crosses high above the river.

"It's something, isn't it?"

An elderly man in a fly-fishing vest and waders is sitting by the river's edge, an open thermos beside him.

"It certainly is," I say, looking up at the bridge.

The fisherman puts the top back on the thermos. He gets up and rambles toward me. "That's the viaduct. Built in 1863 as part of the railway connecting London and Manchester."

"It's impressive."

"Limestone. The highest of those arches is seventy feet."

"It's quite beautiful," I say. "Very beautiful."

"'The valley is gone, and the Gods with it; and now, every fool in Buxton can be in Bakewell in half an hour, and every fool in Bakewell at Buxton.' That's what John Ruskin said, he did. Called it good for nothing but an exchange of fools. And now there's no more train. It stopped running in 1968. What might Ruskin say about that? A big structure cutting across this beautiful valley for cycling and walking. It's called the Monsal Trail now. Lovely view of the valley from up there, I'll give it that. You're visiting from?"

"America. New York."

"Crikey, that far?"

I take a photograph of the viaduct, but realize if I get myself in the picture it will give a better sense of how tall it is. I feel silly taking a selfie, so I ask the man to take a photo of me with the viaduct in the background.

"There you go, a nice souvenir for you to bring home." He hands back the phone. "Tell your Yankee mates about our magical arches."

"Pardon?"

He chuckles. "Not magic, I suppose. Engineering, but like you said, beautiful."

I look up at the bridge. There are five arches. The river below is shallow and calm with a path running along it. On one side, trees grow right to the bank, their boughs bending over the water. On the other, a meadow and a trail. All that's missing is a low, stone house with a single chimney.

I turn back to the fisherman, but he's already on his way. I know it's impossible, but I can't help thinking about the story my mother used to tell me. The one with the old house and the path along the river to the bridge. A bridge with five tall arches that were a portal to adventure via the little train that ran above. This is crazy, but I feel like I'm in her story. This is exactly how I pictured all of it. I saw it this way because this is how my mother described it. But that's impossible. I look back at the bridge, the river, the path snaking along it. What is happening? First I hear my mother in Dev's garden, and now I'm seeing her stories? All of this defies logic. Is this part of grief, a swirl of emotion that has gotten me all mixed up? But I know this place, like I've mapped it out in a dream. I can't pretend I don't. It's a story, but it's real. Impossible to believe, impossible to dismiss.

I walk toward the viaduct. The closer I get, the higher it seems. When I'm directly beneath an arch, I lift up my arms, tip back my head, and close my eyes, just the way I imagined doing it when my mother spun the story. There is a gentle breeze, and I can feel the rumble as the little train approaches. I can hear the gears groan as the train stops above me and the doors slide open, ready for me to enter and go on a journey to a place where I am safe, where I am not seeking answers and not waiting for anyone, because everything I want to know and everyone I love is already there.

CHAPTER FORTY

Amity is rolling up a yoga mat in the living room when I walk in. Wyatt, still in his pajamas and robe, sits on the couch. He has the bleary face and rumpled hair of a just-roused toddler.

"Rough night last night?" I say, trying to sound normal.

"Don't ask," he says. "Who knew trivia was a drinking game?"

"You played trivia?"

Amity hands Wyatt her water bottle and says, "Drink."

"How'd you do?" I ask.

"Let's see." Wyatt stretches his legs onto the coffee table. "We'd never heard of the game of conkers, so we had zero chance of knowing how many strikes per turn are allowed. I'm not really up on the proclivities of Henry the Eighth, and it went downhill from there. Plus, Amity and I each had a moment of personal humiliation."

"The shame!" Amity says, moving into the kitchen. "How could I not have known that the person on the back of the ten-pound note is Jane Austen?"

"How was I the jackass who didn't know which bird is called the laughing jackass?" Wyatt says. "I mean, kookaburra, obviously. What else could it have been?"

Amity comes back, somehow holding three mugs. It's coffee, and it's good and strong.

"Deborah and Naomi were brilliant," she says. "They have an extraordinary amount of useless knowledge. They knew that Prince Harry proposed to Meghan Markle over a meal of roast chicken, that Greece has one hundred and fifty-eight verses in its national anthem, and that the collective noun for a group of unicorns is a blessing."

"And now you do too, Amity," Wyatt says.

Amity smiles. "I suppose I do."

She looks at me expectantly, obviously wanting to know everything. And then she frowns.

"Are you okay?"

"We missed you," Wyatt says with a wink. "Good night?"

"Yes," I say. "It was fun." That's it, keep it light. A romp. Fun. "But the strangest thing happened on the walk home."

Wyatt cradles his coffee. "Do tell."

"This might sound completely deluded." I take a seat and tell them about the viaduct, the arches, the river, and how it was exactly as my mother had described it in the story she used to tell me. I almost wish they'd laugh and brush it off, tell me I'm being foolish, but they don't.

"There's no doubt about it, your mother knew this area." Amity picks up the bulletin board and puts it down on the table. "Swans, bluebells, the church with the crooked spire, Stanage Edge, and now the bridge with five tall arches."

"She'd been here before," Wyatt says. "That's got to be it."

"I know my mother, and it doesn't make sense," I say.

"Maybe you don't know her as well as you think," Amity says. "We never know what's going on inside another person's mind, no matter how close we think we are. Trust me, I know."

"How am I ever going to figure this out?"

"You mean how are *we* going to figure this out," Amity says.

"We're going to keep asking questions," Wyatt says. "We're going to be good sleuthhounds and ask everyone not only about Tracy Penny but also about Skye Little. And you must keep noting any associations that come to mind. You might remember something significant."

The doorbell rings, and for a split second I think it's someone coming to tell me the answer, to clear up the mystery once and for all. But Amity returns with a manila envelope that she says was delivered by Germaine's assistant, the one with the clipboard. She was supposed to give us the autopsy results yesterday at Tracy's flat but forgot.

Amity slides the page out and puts it on the table so we can all read the results at the same time. There's a lot of gibberish medical stuff that sounds legit, not that we'd know otherwise. Then we come to the significant part. Not surprisingly, the cause of Tracy's "death" was loss of blood due to the wounds on her head. The weapon was an "as yet unidentified object, perhaps like a hammer, but smooth with sharp edges and with the inflicting end in a square shape of approximately $2\,^3/_8$ inches."

"Square?" Amity says. "Maybe a meat tenderizer?"

Wyatt shakes his head. "Those are bumpy, not smooth."

He takes an index card and draws a square object with a long handle as we imagine it to be, but it doesn't look like anything we've ever seen. This case seems to get harder the further along we get. We're four days into our investigation with only a day and half remaining before the deadline to submit our solution. And all we know so far is that it was someone, possibly a tall man with good hair, in the salon with something that resembles but is not a meat tenderizer.

CHAPTER FORTY-ONE

We reconvene in the living room when Amity and Wyatt have showered and dressed. Wyatt seems ready for action. He stands in front of the bulletin board like a general mapping out an attack. He lists the most pressing questions:

1. Who sent flowers to Tracy?
2. Who is Pippa, and what was Tracy planning to tell her the day after her murder?
3. For whom did Tracy don and doff the black negligee? Was it the driver of the red Tesla that Bert had seen parked behind the building?

Wyatt suggests we start with the low-hanging fruit—the flowers.

"We know they came from Willowthrop Florist, so let's give them a call."

Amity calls on speakerphone. Making her voice sound gruff and businesslike, she introduces herself as "DS Clark," which I think stands for detective superior or maybe department superintendent? Whatever, Amity is clearly amused with her ruse. She says she's pursuing a murder investigation and that the public good would be

served by knowing who recently ordered a bouquet of white calla lilies to be delivered to Tracy Penny.

"Oh, yes, of course, you're following up." The woman sounds excited, maybe a little nervous. "I mean, oh, how surprising. Let's see, the white calla lilies. Let me see if I remember. Hmm, white calla lilies." She's the first genuinely bad actress we've encountered yet, which makes me appreciate how good everyone else has been. "Here we are. Oh, how interesting. I remember it well, because he didn't call as so many do these days. He came into the store himself and paid in cash, including some loose change from his pockets. He was a few pence short, but I let it slide. He seemed so desperate."

"Did you get his name?" Amity asks.

"I'm afraid not."

"Do you remember what he looked like?" Amity asks.

"He had excellent posture."

"Dark hair?"

"I suppose you could call it dark, what's left of it anyway. Only a few strands and worn that sad way some men do. A comb-over, I think? I'm sorry I can't be of more help. He knew exactly what he wanted though, despite the price. I suggested carnations, much less expensive, but he said no, it had to be calla lilies, nothing else would do. I hope she enjoyed them before she, well, you know."

"I'm sure she did." Amity hangs up.

"Not very illuminating," I say.

"On the contrary," Amity says. "I don't know why I didn't think of it sooner. The flowers were calla lilies, the same flowers that Tracy held as a wedding bouquet in the portrait on the wall. That's why they were sent to her. The person with the comb-over and the good posture who sent them and wrote 'Forever Yours' on the note was Gordon Penny."

"Why would Gordon send flowers to Tracy?" I ask.

"Because, Watson, he's still hopelessly in love with her," Wyatt says.

"Why hopelessly?" I ask. "Maybe they were going to get back together."

Amity gives me an indulgent look, like I'm an adorable child but not very bright.

"The note was in the garbage," she says.

Wyatt picks up a red Sharpie, walks over to the bulletin board, and puts a large *X* over Gordon Penny's photograph.

"We have eliminated a suspect," he says. "Gordon didn't want Tracy's money. He wanted to win her back."

CHAPTER FORTY-TWO

" I t's time to visit the vicar," Amity says. "He's bound to know
something useful."

Walking to St. Anne's Church, she and Wyatt debate which
archetype they expect to encounter: a young dreamboat like Sidney
Chambers in *Grantchester*, an unassuming priest with extraordinary
insight like Father Brown, or a suspicious clergyman whose manner
hints at a nefarious past. I'm hoping that Dev is still in his garden
and not in town. I am not ready to see him.

At the entrance to the churchyard, we meet a tall woman, even
taller than me, probably in her fifties and with bright blue eyes and
straight gray hair cut at a slanted angle by her chin. She's wearing the obligatory white collar over a black button-down shirt and
black slacks. But on her feet, she's wearing electric-blue rubber-toe
shoes, the kind that runners wear because they think they'll ward
off plantar fasciitis.

"Good morning! I'm Sally, the vicar here," she says, opening the
gate. Her handshake is firm. "Shall we walk?" She sets out into the
churchyard without waiting for a response. Her strides are longer
than Wyatt's.

"I didn't know there were female vicars." Amity is nearly skipping to keep up.

"The ordination of women as priests goes back to 1994." The vicar speaks to us over her shoulder. "My path to the clergy started ten years after that, upon the occasion of a midlife awakening. In my past life, I was an accountant. One day, I found myself contemplating a ledger of numbers and yearning for them to tell me something more important than whether the company that employed me was in the red or the black. I could have tried kabbalah, I suppose, but I was raised in the church. And to the church I returned."

We have reached the stone wall that separates the churchyard from the surrounding fields. She turns around to face us and leans back against the wall.

"Tell me, are you ordinary tourists come to see a medieval church or pilgrims in search of spiritual succor? Or are you hot on the trail of an imaginary crime?"

"The latter, I'm afraid," Wyatt says.

"Delightful," she says, and resumes walking.

It seems we're making laps around the graveyard.

"In full disclosure, I'm neither a real or pretend murderer or a real or pretend gossip. I never lie, but I don't always tell the whole truth, as a matter of ethics. I do my best to be available to my parishioners twenty-three hours a day, seven days a week. because I leave one half hour a day for running." She stops, lifts a foot, and wiggles her toes. "And a half hour for silent meditation. I put on my oxygen first, so to speak."

She turns her attention to me with a look of concern. "You've lost someone recently? Someone dear to you?"

"How can you tell?" I say.

"It's the way you're not looking at the headstones."

I don't know what to say. It feels intrusive how she's guessed at something so personal. Amity and Wyatt take a step away, suddenly interested in reading the inscriptions on the old graves. Arms folded, the vicar waits, like she has all the time in the world.

"My mother died," I say, with an unfamiliar pang of sadness.

"Yes." Sally takes my hands. Hers are cold. Did Germaine tell her about my situation too? "Anything I can do, I am here. I will not say that suffering brings great enlightenment, but it often does. May the Lord comfort you."

Even more unexpected than a blessing from a vicar is the lump in my throat. I don't know what to say, so I turn away.

The gravestones are old, many with moss covering their inscriptions. When I was in middle school, I used to ride my bicycle to the cemetery where my father was buried. His grave was on the edge, near a grove of birch trees. I'd sit there and try to talk to him, like people do in movies. But I had never known him. Was I supposed to introduce myself? Tell him I was good at spelling and volleyball? Or should I confess something, like the time I took my mother's favorite earrings because I thought she might come back for them? I had so many questions, and I wanted answers. To know what he was like, what my mother had been like when he was alive. If he hadn't died, would she have stayed?

"You can ask me anything," the vicar says, as if she's been reading my mind. "Anything else you'd like to know about death?"

Of course. She's reminding us that we're there not to inquire about a real tragedy but a fake one.

"Amity, Wyatt, any questions?" I say.

"What can you tell us about Tracy," Amity says. "Did you know her well? Was she a churchgoer?"

"As I said, I will not pass along idle talk, but I can share observations of existing facts. It's conveyance of information, not gossip. Agreed?"

"Agreed," we say in unison.

"Tracy came to Sunday services regularly. It was impossible to miss her because every week she'd have a new elaborate hairdo. They were spectacular, often high up enough on her head to cause a stir. She loved them, but my parishioners did not. More than once, I had to ask her to sit in the back, on the far outside edge of the pews, so as not to block anyone's view. But wherever Tracy sat, she would gaze attentively in one direction."

"At the pulpit?" Amity asks.

Sally lets out a big laugh.

"Of course not. She would stare at Stanley Grange."

"Who's Stanley Grange?" Wyatt asks.

"Why was she staring at him?" Amity says.

"Who wouldn't? He's a beautiful man. Chiseled features, bold jawline, always glowing like he was freshly exfoliated. Tall, with a head of lustrous dark hair. That would have appealed to Tracy, as a hair professional, don't you think? He's a successful businessman and very well-dressed. Posh clothes to go with his expensive car. A red Tesla in Willowthrop. Fancy that!"

"Let me get this straight," Wyatt says. "Tracy came to church alone every Sunday, all dolled up, and stared at handsome Stanley Grange, who also came to church alone every Sunday in his red Tesla?"

"Who said Stanley came alone? Au contraire. He was always with his beautiful wife, Pippa."

"Pippa?" Amity says.

"Yes, Pippa Grange," Vicar Sally says. "Do you know her?"

I open my phone and find the photos of Tracy's flat. The wilted flowers, the legal notice, and finally her to-do list on the calendar in the Filofax. And there it is, a note to herself to "TELL PIPPA!" I show it to Amity and Wyatt.

"What was Tracy going to tell Pippa?" I say.

"That she was having an affair with Stanley Grange," Wyatt says. "It was his red Tesla that Bert saw parked behind the salon at night. And he's tall with thick dark hair. Just like the man Edwina saw visiting Tracy on Mondays when the salon was closed."

"And Edwina said the man leaving Tracy's salon the night she was killed was tall," Amity says.

"Are you saying that Stanley killed Tracy to stop her from telling his wife about their affair?" I say.

Wyatt looks bug-eyed, like we're on to something big.

"I'm saying it gives him a very good motive."

CHAPTER FORTY-THREE

We get Stanley and Pippa's address from the vicar and talk through a possible scenario in the taxi to their house. Assuming that Stanley and Tracy were having an affair, it's possible that Tracy was pressuring Stanley to tell his wife about them and to declare that he was leaving her for Tracy. But maybe Stanley had been putting it off. Maybe he had no intention of ending his marriage and that, finally, Tracy called his bluff and gave him an ultimatum: either tell Pippa everything or Tracy would do it herself. She even gave him a deadline. He had to do it by the day noted in her Filofax, otherwise she would tell Pippa. In this case, it would have been Stanley who went to the salon that night, bashed in Tracy's head, and shielded his departure from the salon with an umbrella.

The taxi stops in front of an imposing brick home with a conservatory on one side. The lawn is flat and wide, its grass as neat as a fresh crew cut. It's a bland estate, with none of the charm of the village cottages, but it might be the kind of place Tracy had dreamed of moving into once Pippa was out of the way.

The doorbell echoes through what sounds like a sparsely furnished home. Indeed, the door opens to an abundance of glare—from the marble floors and sweeping staircase, a garish gold-and-glass chandelier in the foyer, and tall windows looking out over the back lawn.

Wyatt tells the maid we'd like to have a word with Mr. Grange. The maid nods and escorts us into the living room, which looks like a gallery of contemporary art, with abstract paintings on white walls and flat, black leather benches without backs or armrests. There is a single stone coffee table with nothing on it.

Stanley enters the room with long, confident strides. He is slick and polished, his dark hair combed back in the wet look, a handkerchief in his jacket pocket, and slip-on leather shoes that look like they've never been worn outside. He offers a hand to Wyatt, a firm shake by the way Wyatt winces, and nods at Amity and me.

"Stanley Grange," he says. "What's this all about?"

He doesn't sit, and neither do we.

"It's about Tracy Penny," Wyatt says.

Stanley glances quickly toward the foyer.

"Terrible shame. Ugly thing. Murder."

"We may as well cut to the chase," Wyatt says. "You were seen entering Tracy's salon several times. On Mondays."

That's a leap. We don't know for sure that Stanley was the man Edwina had said she'd seen on Mondays.

"Seen? Me? Mondays? Uh, yes. Haircuts. You know. Neat. Trim. Fastidious."

"The salon was closed on Mondays," Amity says.

"Closed? Right. Indeed. Funny, that."

He looks to the foyer again, like he wants to finish this conversation before anyone comes in. I appreciate how well he is staying in character, but it's an odd performance.

"Your car—a red Tesla, I believe—was also spotted behind Tracy's building," Wyatt says. "At night."

Stanley paces back and forth. "Tesla. Yes. Brilliant car."

"Mr. Grange, we believe you were having an affair with Tracy Penny." Wyatt's eyes are shining.

Stanley sighs. "Ethical lapse, yes. Crime, no. A mistake. Terrible mistake."

Amity looks at me wide-eyed, like we may be on the brink of nabbing our man. I give her a thumbs-up.

"Did you promise Tracy you'd tell your wife about your affair?"

Stanley slumps, sinks down onto a couch-bench.

"Yes, yes. Many times. But did I? No. Couldn't do. Terrible thing."

Wyatt has a glint in his eye like he's moving in for the kill.

"But then Tracy threatened to tell your wife herself, didn't she?"

"Threatened? Yes, yes. She did."

"And you believed she would go through with it."

"Formidable woman that Tracy. A tiger." For a moment he looks like he's forgotten his shame and is remembering more exciting times with Tracy. Black-negligee times. "Argh," he roars, bares his teeth, and laughs. "A wild woman."

"And you had to stop her," Wyatt says.

Amity is standing beside me now, I can feel how excited she is. We're about to get a confession. We're going to win this thing!

"That's right. I had to stop her." He looks up, almost pleading, like he wants us to understand why he did it.

"And how did you do that?" Wyatt asks softly. This is the last thing we need. We know whodunit. We know whydunit. And now Stanley Grange is going to tell us howdunit.

"I woke her up."

"Yes?" Amity says.

"Middle of the night."

"Go on," Wyatt says.

"And I told her how terrible I felt." Stanley sits on the leather bench, puts his head in his hands.

"Yes," Wyatt says, sitting beside him. "You felt bad about what you were about to do, but you couldn't stop."

"No, I couldn't stop. Once I had started, I just . . . "

"You struck her?"

Stanley looks up. "Why would I strike her?"

"To protect your secret," Wyatt says.

"No, I, I felt so wretched," Stanley says. "I told her everything. I told her about Tracy and me."

"Told who?" Amity says.

"What?" I say.

Stanley stands.

"Pippa."

"I'm confused," I say.

"I told Pippa everything."

"Wait, weren't you at Tracy's salon?"

"Why would I be at Tracy's salon? I was upstairs, in our bedroom."

Wyatt gets up and asks Stanley to explain again.

"In complete sentences, tell us what happened," he says.

"I was so scared. She's a very frightening woman, you have no idea," Stanley says.

"Who, Tracy?" I ask.

"No, Pippa. I was so afraid for her to know. But I had to tell her. I had to do it before Tracy got to her. I couldn't take the risk. I decided to just tell her everything."

"When was this?" Wyatt says.

"It was on Friday evening."

"So, the day before Tracy was murdered?"

"Well, I didn't know Tracy was going to be murdered. All I knew was that if I didn't speak to Pippa before Monday, Tracy would get to her."

"So you confessed everything?" Amity says.

"Yes, and I promised to end my affair with Tracy."

"Damn straight, he did."

None of us have noticed Pippa in the doorway. She's in a perfectly pressed white pants suit and high heels. "Told me what he'd done, the fool. With a hairdresser, of all people! So tacky. He promised to make it up to me. And I made him start straightaway. Booked us the royal suite at Clitheridge Spa for two nights, where I kept him on a tight leash. Couples massage, yoga, steam room, the works. He was at my beck and call twenty-four hours a day. He still is, aren't you, darling?"

Stanley doesn't look handsome now, more like a punished puppy. "Yes, dear."

"We returned the day after Tracy Penny's body was discovered." She waves some papers in the air. "Here are our receipts, and a schedule of our meals and spa activities so you can see precisely what we were doing when Tracy Penny met her maker. My husband may be an egotistical, cheating bastard, but he is not your murderer."

CHAPTER FORTY-FOUR

W e're too disappointed to talk much during the taxi ride back to the village.

"I thought we had it," Amity says.

"I did too. But maybe that was too simple a solution," Wyatt says.

I don't tell them that I'm relieved that Dev was not Tracy's dark-haired mystery lover. It shouldn't matter, as it's all fiction, but it does.

Back in the village, we buy some sausage rolls and walk down to the river, where we sit on a bench to eat. Two pairs of ducks swim in circles near the bridge, steering clear of two haughty swans closer to shore. At the next bench over, a hunchbacked woman scatters seeds on the ground for the pigeons. She clucks at the birds like she knows them, mumbling what sound like pet names. "Here you go, Ollie. Come now, Violet." I hope they're not her only companions.

The food seems to revive Amity.

"Pippa was impressive, all that anger, don't you think?" she says. "She was wronged, but did she crawl in a hole with shame? She did not."

"Go on," I say, unsure where Amity is going with this.

"That's all." Amity sighs. "I thought she was formidable."

"If it's formidable to force your sorry-ass cheating husband to stay with you," Wyatt says. "Who wants someone who doesn't want them?"

"Stanley did not seem happy about how things turned out," I say.

"Exactly!" Amity says. "And serves him right too. Why should he be happy?"

Has Amity forgotten the whole thing was an act? She stands up and wipes the crumbs from her lap. "That was a perfect lunch. Are we ready to proceed? What's next?"

Wyatt thinks we might get "more bang for our buck" if we use some of our limited time left in Willowthrop to focus on my mother. But how? Should we return to Bert Lott and ask to see his messages with her? Maybe they reveal something about her knowledge of this place. I'm thinking of calling my mother's friend Aurora to see what she might know when Wyatt slaps himself on the thigh and says, "Of course! Edwina!"

"The nosy neighbor?" Amity says.

"She might be an actor," I say.

Wyatt is convinced that Edwina received us in her real home, which he reminds us was decorated with lots of old photographs, a mix of family portraits and scenes of Willowthrop.

"Edwina Flasher may be pretending to be a nosy neighbor, but I bet she's lived in Willowthrop for a long time, maybe even her whole life, and will know something useful."

Edwina comes to the door right away.

"More questions? How lovely."

I get the feeling she hasn't been visited recently by any of our competition. "Make yourselves at home. I'll just put on the kettle."

While she's clanging around the kitchen, we look at the photographs on the walls, which show Willowthrop through the years. There's even a black-and-white picture of the viaduct.

"Are you closing in on the culprit?" Edwina sets down a tray on the coffee table and drops herself into her easy chair. She waves a hand for us to help ourselves to tea and Jaffa Cakes.

"Actually, no. We're not here about that at all," I say. "Can we go off the record?

"Are you a journalist?"

"Definitely not. We'd like to talk simply as visiting Americans conversing with a long-time resident of Willowthrop."

"Isn't that what we are?"

This is going to be trickier than I thought.

"We don't want you to make up any answers," Amity says.

"This has absolutely nothing to do with the murder mystery?" Edwina says. "I'd hate to give you an unfair advantage. Germaine would never forgive me. She worked so hard, you know."

"Totally unrelated," Wyatt says.

"I suppose that should be all right."

"Do you know of anyone by the name of Skye Little?" I ask.

"Is that a woman's name?"

"Yes, an American woman." I show her a picture of my mother on my phone. "This woman."

"I'm sorry, but no."

"Have there been many Americans passing through here?" Amity asks. "Tour groups?"

"I'm afraid not. Willowthrop is a tad off the beaten path. Tourists usually go to Bakewell, what with its famous tart—frangipani and raspberry jam, so scrummy—and the *Pride and Prejudice* connection with Chatsworth House."

"Which Austen never visited, you know," Amity says. Good on her for trying to rein in the runaway myth.

"Of course not," Edwina says. "She never came to Derbyshire at all. A whole lot of nonsense."

"Finally, a voice of reason," Amity says. "Thank you."

"I'm afraid I'm not much help," Edwina says. "Terribly sorry."

"Please, don't apologize," I say. I'm embarrassed we've even troubled her. "It's not your fault. We're on a ridiculous quest." I get up and walk over to the photograph of the viaduct. "I took a walk and ended up here, below the viaduct, and it was all exactly as my mother had described in a story when I was little, and it makes no sense, but I was convinced my mother had been here." I'm babbling, but I can't stop. "It's so stupid, but I felt something under those arches, like the whole place was special, that I was there for a magical reason."

"That would be highly unlikely," Edwina says. "The place isn't special at all; it's rather cursed. There was a terrible fire there a long time ago. George Crowley lived there with his wife and child. He was a blacksmith, though not particularly good with horses. Rumor is that he passed out drunk, smoking a cigarette, which started the fire. He got out, of course, as did his poor wife, Ann, but then she went back in because she couldn't find the little girl, Susan. They say that Ann Crowley was frantic, running around the property, calling for her only child. She was convinced the girl was still inside the house and ran back to find her, but a beam fell on her head, and, well, may she rest in peace."

"How awful. Did the little girl die too?" Amity asks.

"No. She hadn't even been inside. She'd been up late reading in the loo in the empty tub, cheeky thing, and when everyone started yelling fire, she tried to leave the room, but the door was jammed. She jumped out the window and ran off along the river all the way up to the viaduct."

"Why did she go there?" I ask.

"Instinct, maybe? To run from danger? Poor thing. Comes back to discover she's lost her lovely mum in a fire started by her dad. And that her mum died going back into the fire to look for her. How do you live with that? She was such a slip of a thing too, only nine years old, and small for her age. Poor little Sukie."

"Sukie? Who's Sukie?" Amity says.

"That's what they called her. It was her nickname."

"How do you spell Sukie?" My hands have gone cold and clammy.

"S-U-K-I-E," Edwina says.

I know that name. I can see the letters written in bubble font at the top of the inside cover of my Melling School book, each letter carefully shaded in with a different colored pencil. I remember being shocked that someone had been so naughty, drawing inside a book, especially a good hardcover book about kind and spunky sisters at boarding school. But it can't be the same Sukie, can it?

"What happened to Sukie and her father?" I say.

Edwina takes a sip of tea, sets down her cup, her actions painfully slow.

"George Crowley was never too well-liked and after the fire, I'm sure he didn't want to show his face. Falling asleep smoking like that, drunk. The shame. Moved away for years. Came back eventually, but I haven't a clue where he is now."

I try to remember what else was written in the book, a last name or an address. Or maybe I'm remembering it wrong. Maybe it wasn't Sukie at all. Maybe it was Suzy or Sally. My mind might be playing tricks on me, making connections that aren't there. I ask if I can use the bathroom.

I sit on the pink, fluffy cover on the toilet and take out my phone. It's almost 1:00 p.m., about eight in the morning at home. Kim should be at my house, probably done meditating. I message her that I have an urgent favor. I ask her to go into my bedroom and look on the bottom shelf of the bookcase. The Melling School book is on the right side. I tell her I need to know what it says inside the covers.

When I step back into the living room, my phone dings. Kim has sent a photograph. It's the inside cover of the book. There are the bubble letters, just as I remembered, spelling SUKIE. At the bottom of the page are drawings of daisies and unicorns, foxes and rabbits. I turn my phone around.

"This is in an English book my mother gave me. I always thought she bought it secondhand."

Another ding. A photograph of the back inside cover. A drawing of a horse with a long mane. And at the bottom, three letters that I don't remember at all, also in colored pencil. SMC.

"What's SMC?" Amity asks.

"I don't know."

"They could be initials," she says. "Edwina, did Sukie Crowley have a middle name?"

"I think she was Susan Marie? Yes, that's it, Susan Marie Crowley."

Wyatt and Amity trade a look.

"Where is Sukie Crowley now?" Wyatt asks. "Did anyone stay in touch with her after she moved away?"

"My friend Polly did for a while," Edwina says. "She used to look after Sukie. But that was many, many years ago."

"Could I talk to Polly?" I say. "Maybe she knows something that might help."

Edwina sighs. "I'm afraid Polly's not with us anymore."

"I'm so sorry." It must be hard to outlive your friends one by one.

"You're not going to find answers here anyway," Edwina says.

"Why not?" I ask.

"Didn't I already say? After the fire, Sukie Crowley was sent to live with relatives in America."

"In America?" Amity asks. "Where?"

"In the Midwest, I think. Yes, that's it. Indiana."

"Oh. My. God." Wyatt stands up.

"I don't know if she's dead or alive, but Polly told me years ago that the relatives who took her in over there in Indiana adopted her and gave her their own last name. She wasn't a Crowley anymore."

"What was her new last name?" Amity asks. "Maybe we could google her."

"I'm so sorry, but I don't remember." Edwina says.

Is that it, then? The source of my mother's stories was a girl named Sukie that she met in Indiana? Sukie gave her the Melling School book and told her stories about Willowthrop and the Peak District, a place she'd been torn away from after losing her mother? She must have wanted to keep the place alive by talking about it, sharing all the beautiful details—the bluebells, the swans in the river, the church with the crooked spire, the marshy moors, the grandeur of Stanage Edge. And my mother told the stories to me. But why did she hide all of this?

"Sanders!" Edwina shouts. "That's the name. Sukie became Sukie Sanders."

"That can't be," I say. "That's not possible."

"No, I'm sure that was it," Edwina says, tapping her temple.

"Are you okay?" Wyatt asks me. "You've gone pale."

"What is it?" Amity says.

"My mother's maiden name was Sanders," I say.

"Her family adopted Sukie Crowley?" Amity says.

"No," I say. "I would have known about such a thing. My mother was an only child."

"Did you have aunts or uncles? Cousins?" Amity says.

I shake my head, feeling like the answer is hovering around me, but I can't grasp it.

"Why didn't anyone ever tell me about Sukie?"

Wyatt crosses the room and crouches beside me. "Because, Watson," he says gently. "Your mother wasn't looking for Sukie Crowley. She was Sukie Crowley."

CHAPTER FORTY-FIVE

"We must call Germaine," Edwina says. "She'll know how to find out more."

Edwina dials the black rotary phone, which turns out to be real, and tells Germaine what we think we've figured out, though I still can't believe it. We can hear Germaine's voice, quickening and rising in pitch and volume.

"She's going to close the shop and come right over," Edwina says.

It doesn't feel real. My mother has disappointed me so many times, but could she really have kept something like this from me? This isn't just a white lie; it's a lifelong betrayal. When was she going to tell me the truth? Before we left for England? On the plane somewhere over the Atlantic? Or was she going to wait until we were immersed in solving a fake murder that had nothing to do with why she'd wanted to come here?

"We've got to be right," Wyatt says. "Susan Marie Crowley, nine-year-old Sukie, became Sukie Sanders."

"Who took the name Skye?" Amity says. "It is close to Sukie."

"My grandmother always thought it was a stupid name," I say. "I never asked."

"The magic arches, the crooked spire, the bluebells, the way your mother must have told you about Stanage Edge, they weren't a story, they were memories," Wyatt says.

Edwina takes a bottle of sherry from a cupboard and pours four little glasses.

"Are we celebrating?" Amity says.

"I'm not up for that," I say.

"This is medicinal." Edwina hands me a glass. "You've had a shock."

I down the sherry like it's a shot of tequila.

"My mother used to call the bathroom 'the loo.' I thought she was being pretentious."

"There were no other signs?" Amity asks.

When my mother and I visited Indiana when I was little, I'd sleep in her childhood bedroom, in her old twin bed with the pine headboard and nubby chenille spread. There was a heavy old maple dresser, and on the wall above it, a framed drawing of a unicorn. Like the one doodled on the inside back cover of the Melling School book.

"Did you ever see photographs of your mother as a baby?" Amity asks.

"Maybe? I was only eight the last time I was in Indiana. I don't remember much. Grampa Hal smelled like black licorice, and Granny Lou's hugs lasted too long. She served chicken and noodles over mashed potatoes."

The Indiana house was nothing like our house in Buffalo, which had so many mementos from my father's past—his baby book filled with photographs and notes about the first time he rolled over or ate solid food, the white wicker bassinet he slept in as an infant, his first shoes, preschool photos against a painted backdrop of fir trees, the library card he got in kindergarten. The Indiana house was sparse, with little decoration other than lace doilies on the tables and some framed photographs of my mother and her parents.

I take out my phone to look at the photos of the book that Kim sent. I wish I had the Melling School book with me. If my mother really was Sukie, did she get this book after the fire? Or was it saved from the fire? If this is the book she'd been reading in the bathtub when the fire started, then I'd had a link to my mother's past all along.

"I knew it! I knew your mother had an extraordinary story!" Germaine bursts into the cottage holding some papers. "She was one of us. You're one of us! She was bringing you home."

She spreads her papers on the coffee table. They're newspaper articles she found online and printed out before coming over. Most offer the same details about the fire that we've already learned. A few of them include a photograph, dark and grainy, of the remains of the house, stone wall stumps and what looks like half a chimney. One has a picture of the exhausted fire brigade that fought the blaze. Another shows a fire truck and a canvas hose, depleted, on the ground. Off to the side is a thin, fair-haired girl in a long cotton nightgown and bare feet. A wool blanket is wrapped around her narrow shoulders. Her head is tipped up toward the ruins of the house. Her profile, with a prominent forehead, delicately tilted nose, and what's often called a weak chin, is as familiar as my own.

CHAPTER FORTY-SIX

Germaine wants to take us along the Monsal Trail to the top of the viaduct so she can point out where the old stone house was in relation to the river and the bridge. Then we'll walk down to where the house stood.

Wyatt and Germaine lead the way, first over the bridge to the other side of the river. We walk in silence until we're climbing the steep road that will intersect with the old railway.

"Are you okay?" Amity asks.

I shake my head. I'm too angry to speak.

"It's a lot to take in. You must be overwhelmed."

"I could kill her."

Amity stops and rests a hand on my arm. "It's awful to be lied to. Believe me, I know."

And then I'm crying. Heaving, gasping, ugly sobs.

"She never told me anything." It sounds so petulant and childish, but I can't help myself.

Amity doesn't say anything. She stays by me and lets me cry.

"I'm sorry," I say, rubbing my eyes. When I look up at her, she's wiping a tear away too.

We follow Germaine and Wyatt to the top of the hill, where

225

they walk around an old station house and onto the trail. It's wide and flat hard-packed gravel. On either side are thick bushes and trees. Germaine turns left, either toward Bakewell or Buxton, I have no idea which. We pass a trio of toddlers spinning in circles while their mother or babysitter talks on her phone. A bell dings behind us. We step to the side and an old man on a bicycle doffs his cap as he rides by.

"Didn't I deserve the truth?" I say.

"Of course you did."

"All she did was lie. I don't even know if she told my father. And my grandmother couldn't have known; there's no way she would have kept that from me."

"Maybe it was too painful for your mother to think about," Amity says. "Maybe that's how she survived."

Maybe this, maybe that. Why this, why that? I am so tired of trying to understand my mother.

"She had so many opportunities to tell me."

"The longer one lies, the harder it becomes to reveal the truth. Or so I've been told."

It wasn't until my freshman year of college that it occurred to me to ask my mother why she had left me. By then I had just accepted it, that my mother was flighty and left me to be raised by my grandmother, a very good mother indeed. But freshman year was all about getting to know new people, and there were so many questions. My friends complained their mothers were too involved in their lives, micromanaging and fretting over everything, their grades, and summer plans, and romances. Their mothers even commented on their Facebook posts. *You look so pretty! Why aren't you wearing a bicycle helmet? Love you, sweetie!* They couldn't believe my mother was barely aware of what I was up to. I was shocked when she showed up to parents' weekend, though of course she wasn't interested in any of the official activities. It was a beautiful October day, so we walked along the trail by the Willimantic River. I must have thought about how to ask the question for half a mile before I finally spoke.

"Why did you leave me?" I asked.

It made her stop in her tracks, which made me nervous. Maybe I didn't want to know. But her answer was anticlimactic.

"It wasn't you, of course," she'd said, like I'd be absurd to think that being abandoned had anything to do with me. "I was too young. Married, a mother, and a widow by the age of twenty-four. A child on my own, in Buffalo? I wasn't ready."

What I didn't say: *Neither was I.*

And then she took my hand in hers and said, "Why dwell on the past? Nothing comes from that. I'm here now. You're here now. Isn't that enough?"

I couldn't bring myself to say, *No, it's not enough.*

Amity and I continue walking. From the other direction, two girls rush by, their heads bent and thumbs tapping out texts. A golden retriever, straining against its leash, bounds up to us, pulling a young woman in yoga pants.

"I'm so sorry, he's *beastly*," she says.

We come to an old train tunnel that's so long that the light winking at the end looks like a tiny bulb. Inside, the tunnel is dank and cool. A whoop ahead of us; Wyatt is trying out the echo. He and Germaine are almost out.

"You've described your mother as extremely charming, always taking an interest in everyone, which makes perfect sense," Amity says.

"How so?"

Above us, a bare bulb flickers and buzzes.

"People deal with trauma in unexpected ways," Amity says.

"It's like grief; everyone experiences it differently and on their own schedule. There's no norm. Maybe your mother's charm and curiosity and passion gave her the privacy she needed. Maybe it kept other feelings at bay."

That and bolting.

We come to the end of the tunnel. The light is dappled through the bushes. And then the vegetation falls away, and we see the valley ahead of us, vast and green and rolling. The sun is almost too bright. We are on the bridge. The viaduct. We join Wyatt and Germaine, who have stopped about halfway across and are leaning on the ledge.

"It's beautiful," Amity says.

Below, the river ribbons its way through the valley. I see the narrow path where I met the fisherman. I follow it back toward the village. Somewhere between here and there a stone house once stood and then burned to the ground. I imagine a thin girl with wispy blond hair and narrow shoulders, running at night, the hem of her nightgown damp and dirty, her feet cold and scratched, her small heart thumping in her pale chest and delicate throat, pounding in her ears. Does she even know why she's running, where she's going? She must be so afraid. My anger starts to dissipate. Tears slide down my cheeks, but now I'm not crying for myself but for a nine-year-old girl whose life went up in flames, who lost everything and was shipped across an ocean to be raised by strangers. My heart is breaking for poor little Sukie Crowley, my mom. I wish I could hug the child she was and hold the woman she became, the mother who never shared her heartbreak or hinted at her enormous loss but kept running.

Germaine leads us down a rocky path to the riverbank and onto the path. We follow it back toward Willowthrop until Germaine steps off the trail and through the tall grass. "I think it was here." We follow her away from the river to the edge of the forest. And there they are, stones, toppled and neglected, too big to have been washed up by the river. A piece of a wall, and then another chunk of remains, maybe part of the foundation, grass and weeds nearly concealing it. I put my palm on another stretch of wall, what was once part of my mother's home, and try to imagine the rest. A child growing up here, a family. A life before the fire. I want to mark this place and my presence here. I pick up a few small rocks and place them on the wall like I used to do on my father's gravestone. It's a Jewish tradition, and I wonder if I should explain to the others, but before I say anything, I sense Amity beside me, and then Wyatt, and Germaine. Each of them places a rock on the wall too. I want to remember this, to etch it into my mind. This is where my mother's childhood ended. And where Ann Crowley died. My grandmother, found and lost in a single swoop.

CHAPTER FORTY-SEVEN

Germaine takes us back to town a different way, on a footpath through a forest and then across a pasture. The landscape hasn't changed, but it feels different now. I can't pass any of it, the tufted yellow tops of dandelions, the pale trunks of birch trees, or the clumps of fanned out ferns, without imagining my mother here too, skipping across the field, her little fingers brushing the tips of the tall grass. It's disorienting, like I haven't been here before. But when we pass through a stile that takes us onto a road, I know where we are. We're at the bottom of the hill where Dev and his mother live. Germaine looks up toward their house and says, "I should stop in. See how Polly's doing."

"Polly?" I say.

"My friend," Germaine says. "The one you walked home."

"Penelope."

"Whose nickname is Polly."

"Edwina's friend Polly?" I'm not sure what I'm grasping at.

"Same Polly. Same Penelope."

"But Edwina said Polly was dead."

"Why would she say that?" Germaine says. "Polly lives right up that hill. You've met her yourself."

Did I hear wrong? I think back to our conversation. Edwina said that her friend Polly stayed in touch with Sukie for a while. When I asked if I could talk to Polly, Edwina said Polly wasn't with us anymore. *Because she has dementia.*

"The Polly who knew your mother is the Penelope who's Dev's mother?" Amity says.

"That makes you and Dev practically cousins," Wyatt says.

"It does not," Amity and I say at the same time.

Maybe Dev's mother will have a moment of lucidity and can tell me more. I want to see her and I want to see her alone.

"Let me go check on her," I say. "Please. You guys go on back." Before anyone can stop me, I'm running up the hill to the brick house. I ring the bell and the door opens, and it's not Mrs. Carlton. It's Dev. The morning comes back to me, and I know I should say something about running out so abruptly, but I can't.

"Are you okay?" Dev says. "Come in."

I step inside the front hall. The house is too warm. He takes me into the living room and sits me down on the couch.

"Let me get you some water."

Everything is paisley, the couch and chairs, an ottoman, the curtains. There's a deck of cards on the coffee table. Someone was playing gin rummy. Does Dev play cards with his mother? He hands me a glass of water and sits beside me. I set down the glass without drinking any.

"Everyone lied to me, my whole life. Even my grandparents, who aren't even my grandparents. Why didn't they tell me the truth? My mother's life was a lie. It makes me feel like mine is too."

I tell him everything in a rush, a run-on sentence about a girl and a fire, a death, a journey to Indiana, an adoption, a new name. A big fat secret concealed for decades that no one thought I deserved to know.

"The fire down by the viaduct, that was your mother's house?" Dev says.

Of course he would have heard about it. Willowthrop is tiny.

"That was my mother's family. Her *real* family."

"I'm so sorry, Cath."

There's pressure in my chest, a lump in my throat. I bite my lip to stop it from trembling. Dev turns away for a moment—this must be too much for him, he's afraid I'm going to start bawling—but then he's facing me again and handing me a tissue.

I sniffle, wipe away the tears that I can't hold back.

"And my mom knew your mom."

"What?"

"Edwina said Penelope used to babysit Sukie. That's my mom. That *was* my mom's name. Not when I knew her. Not that I ever knew her."

"Edwina Flasher?"

"That's why I came here. I need to know what else your mom remembers. She might be my only link to my mother's childhood."

"She's taking a nap right now," Dev says. "I hate to wake her. She's at her most confused after sleeping. I usually give her some time before talking with her about anything important."

My mother was selfish, flighty, an infuriating puzzle. She's gone, and she's still messing with me. I feel anger bubbling up. My neck is tight, my shoulders so stiff they hurt. My head is pounding.

"Do you know why I ran out this morning? It wasn't because I felt sick, it was because I heard my mother's voice telling me to stay, that you were someone special, that what I felt for you, and with you, was rare and precious and I should jump in, and hold on and I wanted to, I really, really wanted to, and that scared the hell out of me. All my life, I've refused to be like my mother. She'd have pushed me toward you: *Stay in England, forget Buffalo, move in with this man, get some goats, make cheese.* She was always running off to something, a shinier future, a better chance she wanted to grab, something or someone to be infatuated with. I swore I'd never rush in the way she did, I'd never get my hopes up, to want something from someone, because it doesn't work. People leave you; people let you down; they die. It's not worth it."

I stop to take a breath, and it hits me what I've just said. What is wrong with me? I wouldn't blame Dev for wanting to be the one to bolt now.

But he puts out his hand, face up, the way he did on Stanage Edge. My hand is trembling as I put it on top of his, and we sit like that, palm to palm.

"It doesn't always have to be that way," he says.

"What do I do with all of this?" It comes out as barely a whisper.

"I don't know. Maybe you need to give yourself some time."

"Will that help?"

"It might."

My mind is too full to think.

"I'm just so, so tired by all of it," I say. "It's too much."

He lets his fingers slip between mine. A gentle squeeze.

"Come," he says. "I'll drive you home."

CHAPTER FORTY-EIGHT

All night, my dreams cross territories, with Lady Blanders running around a burning house looking for her children and Gordon Penny doing the cha-cha with my mother in my living room at home.

"Look how we dance, one, two, three," my mother shouted. "We're never going to stop, one, two, three."

I wake up exhausted, still half in the dream. Dancing is the perfect metaphor for how my mother lived her life. Don't stay in any one place long enough to feel pain or remember how life has slapped you. Just keep dancing.

I'm amazed to see I've slept late; it's already almost eleven. I wonder if Amity and Wyatt are still here. I think about my family as I pull on some clothes. I've always taken for granted that I'm descended from good people. Grandma Raya was my everything, and I've heard only good stories about my grandfather. In Indiana, Granny Lou and Grampa Hal were quiet and kind and always sent cards on my birthday and Valentine's Day with a dollar inside for "something sweet." I was sad when Granny Lou passed away when

234

I was eight and Grampa Hal a year later. Now I have a grandmother who died in a fire caused by a grandfather who doesn't sound like someone I'd like to know, let alone be related to. It pains me to think about him, which probably should make me understand why my mother buried her past.

Downstairs, Amity and Wyatt are at the kitchen table, all their notes laid out in front of them. Since the revelations about my mother, I haven't given the fake mystery a thought.

"Tea?" Amity says. "I just made a fresh pot. We're having a lazy morning."

"Cath doesn't like tea." Wyatt pushes the French press toward me.

But I move the coffee away and take the teapot instead. I fill a mug halfway and pour in milk. I add two heaping teaspoons of sugar.

"I'm half English. Shouldn't I try?"

It's good to laugh.

"You're a Derbyshire girl, the granddaughter of a blacksmith," Amity says. "It sounds like a story from a book."

"But definitely not a fairy tale," I say. "My grandfather George Crowley sounds like a bad man. Maybe my mother was better off in Indiana."

"Don't you want to know where George Crowley is now?" Wyatt asks.

"He'd be so old," I say. "You think he's still alive?"

"I have no idea," Wyatt says.

"I'm not sure I want to know," I say. "I mean, I want to know, but I'm not sure I want to meet him."

"You can decide that later," Amity says.

"How would we find him?" I ask. "If Edwina and Germaine don't know anything about him, I can't imagine anyone else would."

"There's got to be someone in the village who remembers him. Who went to school with him or worked with him," Amity says.

"We know he was a blacksmith, so let's start there. Let's talk to the oldest blacksmith in town."

She gets up and starts opening kitchen cabinets. "Bingo," she says. She drops a phone book on the table, sits down, and starts flipping through pages. "Here we go, there are quite a few in the area. R. W. Martin, Master Farrier; Thomas Max Farriers; Davis Troy and Sons Farriers; Joseph B. Welch, Farrier; Oliver—"

"Stop," Wyatt says. "Joseph Welch. We've heard that name."

"We have?" I say.

Amity looks as confused as I am.

Wyatt picks up his notebook and starts thumbling through the pages.

"I don't remember meeting anyone by that name," Amity says.

"Hold on," Wyatt says. "Aha! I knew that name was familiar. Lady Blanders's horse servant mentioned him."

"Horse servant?" Amity says.

"Hoof man?" Wyatt says.

"I think he's called a stable hand," I say. "Or a groom."

"Okay, the stable hand asked Lady Blanders about the new shoes and she asked if the others were done. The other horses. And here it is, I wrote it down—my god, I'm good at this—he told her that, and I quote, old Mr. Welch was still at work."

"Mr. Welch is a blacksmith?" Amity says.

"Mr. Welch is an *old* blacksmith," Wyatt says. "The stable hand called him 'Old Mr. Welch,' remember? And he may be our best shot at finding out something about Cath's grandfather. Wouldn't one old blacksmith know another?"

CHAPTER FORTY-NINE

'm still not sure I want to meet George Crowley, but I agree to go along to talk to Mr. Welch. His forge is off the main road, less than a mile from our cottage. A thick man in a long leather apron steps into the dusty courtyard to greet us.

"Well, well, it's high time. Come on in, and I'll answer all your questions."

"You know why we're here?" Amity gives us a look.

Did Edwina or Germaine call ahead?

"Of course not, why would I know that?" He looks like he's having a hard time keeping a straight face. "You look like you're here for a lesson. Just the type. Plenty of folk want to learn blacksmithing these days, all the old ways. Don't want to buy things, want to make them. Like it's easy-peasy."

"You're Joseph Welch?"

"That I am."

"We wanted to ask you about a George Crowley," Wyatt says.

"A who what now?"

"He was a blacksmith. He lived near the viaduct a long time ago. His house burned down."

"Forty-six years ago," I say.

Mr. Welch rubs a hand over his mouth.

"What has that to do with—?" He looks around, like someone is going to appear in his courtyard and come to his rescue, get him out of this pickle.

"We're trying to locate him," I say.

"This isn't what I was—"

"She's his granddaughter," Amity says, giving me a little nudge forward.

"George Crowley, your granddad?" He scowls and spits onto the dirt.

"I know what he did, so don't worry about hurting my feelings. I've never met him."

He nods, chewing his lip, and sits down on a tree stump in the yard. He gestures for us to sit on the wooden bench opposite.

"I remember him all right. He went away after the fire, as well he should. Nothing was proved, but we all knew what he'd done. Didn't know anything about his whereabouts for years, but I figured he was traveling around, betting the horses, losing. Years later, I heard he had a stroke of luck, he did. Had a friend who was worse off than he was, and Crowley won his friend's cottage in a bet. Not much of a place, but not a bad spot, out toward Bakewell. He lived there alone, like a hermit, for a while. But maybe eight years ago, I heard he moved into a care home."

We ask a few more questions but have exhausted Mr. Welch's knowledge about George Crowley. He has no idea which care home and doesn't know if George is still alive. Nor does he know anyone who might. Wyatt seems disappointed, but I'm relieved. We thank Mr. Welch and say goodbye. As we're leaving the yard, Wyatt turns back.

"Why did you seem to be expecting us?"

"Thought you were with those crazy Americans playing at being detectives." He leans forward and whispers. "I've got myself a key role in the murder. Not in the killing, mind you, I wouldn't step up for that. My role is to pretend I was at Hadley Hall, looking after their horses. How about that?"

Wyatt turns to Amity and me, eyes wide, mouth agape.

"Is this fair?" Amity whispers. "Isn't coincidence one of Roland's no-no's?"

"This isn't coincidence, it's serendipity," Wyatt says.

"Oh dear." Mr. Welch seems to realize what he's done. "You're—?"

"Yes," I say. "We are some of those crazy Americans."

"And as long as we're here . . . " Wyatt sits back down on the bench.

Before Mr. Welch can object, Amity asks him to confirm that he shod Lady Blanders's horses.

"Yes, that I did." He's all puffed up, like he's relieved to get to play the role he practiced. "I was working at her stable for several days."

"Did you talk to Lady Blanders?" Amity says.

"Didn't even see her."

"You worked alone? No one else was around?" Wyatt asks.

"The stable lad was in and out, and on my last afternoon one of the maids was hanging about my van and chatting him up."

"Do you remember which one?" I ask.

"Maybe Lady Blanders's maid, but I'm not sure."

"Gladys Crone?" Amity says. I'm amazed that she remembers her name. "Pale face, severe expression, dark hair slicked down in a bun?"

"That's the one."

Scowling Mrs. Crone was friendly with the groom? I didn't see that coming.

"Anything else out of the ordinary while you were there?" Wyatt asks.

"No, everything was fine when I was *there*," Mr. Welch says.

"And after you left?" Amity says.

"It wasn't until I was all finished and back here that I noticed that one of my tools was missing from my van."

Amity gasps and whispers, "Murder weapon."

Wyatt flips through his notebook.

"Was it a square metal tool with a long handle?" he says.

Before Mr. Welch answers, I jump up from the bench, unable to contain my excitement.

"I know what you were missing," I say.

"You do?" Amity says.

It's amazing what you can retain even from reading when you're only half awake.

"It was a flatter," I say.

"That's exactly right." Mr. Welch looks impressed.

"Granddaughter of a blacksmith." I wink.

"What's a flatter?" Amity asks.

"It's like a hammer, but it's square, with a smooth surface and sharp edges," I say.

"On the nose," the blacksmith says. "It's struck with a hammer and used to smooth out bumps and marks."

"Where did you learn about a flatter?" Amity asks me.

"From Roland Wingford's crime-solving farrier, Cuddy Claptrop. Who else?"

CHAPTER FIFTY

W e're too excited by what we've learned from Mr. Welch for a sit-down lunch, so we get fish and chips to go and return to the cottage. We prop our evidence board against the wall above the kitchen table so we can work while we eat.

"If the murder weapon was stolen when the blacksmith was at Hadley Hall, then Lady Blanders could be the murderer," Wyatt says, dousing his fish with salt and vinegar.

"Or Gladys Crone," I say. "She was hanging around the stable. Couldn't she have taken the flatter?"

"But wasn't one of Roland's rules that the culprit couldn't be a servant?" Amity squeezes lemon on her fish.

"That's right," Wyatt says. "But she could have been an accomplice."

We agree to focus on Lady Blanders and to try and figure out why she might want to kill Tracy Penny. After all the emotional drama of my mother's story, it's a welcome relief to be doing something silly again.

Wyatt starts moving photographs from our visit with Lady Blanders to the top of the bulletin board: Lady Blanders on horseback, a close-up of her new boots, the morning room, the creepy painting over the fireplace, the picture of Sproton House, Lady Blanders's hand lifting the teapot extra high, her bracelet dangling off her wrist.

"Let's look at photos from the salon again," Wyatt says. "There has to be a connection."

We sift through the photos, this time removing those related to suspects we've eliminated. We toss pictures of the calla lilies and the card from Gordon, the eviction notice, and the Filofax with its scribbled "TELL PIPPA!" On the board we put up snapshots of Tracy's empty refrigerator, unmade bed, and the framed pictures on the salon walls.

"Could it have to do with Sproton House, the place that Lady Blanders visits every month?" Amity says. "Did Tracy work at the salon there?"

"Why would she drive all the way to Whitby to cut hair when she has her own salon here?" Wyatt says.

Amity puts down her fork.

"Hold on. Sproton House is in Whitby?"

"That's right," Wyatt says, tapping on his notebook.

"Isn't that where Tracy used to work and still sometimes volunteered?" Amity says. "Whitby Stables?"

We all react like it's a light bulb moment, but we can't figure out a connection.

"We have to think beyond the obvious," Amity says. "We can't make the same mistake they made in Agatha Christie's *The Mirror Crack'd from Side to Side* by assuming there couldn't be anything connecting a glamorous American movie star and a provincial English fan. We have to find the baby."

"What baby?" I say.

"I'm speaking metaphorically," Amity says. "By 'baby,' I mean the hidden connection between Lady Blanders and Tracy Penny."

Wyatt brings his hands to his cheeks.

"Amity, you're brilliant!" He picks up his notebook and flips the pages back and forth, reviewing his notes. "Oh my god, why didn't we see it?"

He starts ripping pages from his notebook and tacking them to the board. The names of Lady Blanders's sons, Charles and Benedict. Some scribbles about Lord Blanders and his awful snobbery. And then he takes the photograph of the magazine article with the picture of Tracy at the horse stable with little Ambrosia in the saddle. He stares at it for a moment and then tacks it to the center of the bulletin board.

"Look at her hair," he says.

"Must we?" Amity says. "The perm is so unfortunate."

"Not Tracy's hair. Ambrosia's hair."

"What about it?" I say.

"It's red," he says.

"Oh my god, that face," Amity says. "Do you think? Are you saying?"

I'm not following. "What is he saying? What does he think?"

Wyatt is frantically thumbing through his notebook.

"But if that's the why, what's the how?" he mumbles.

"Is he talking to himself?" I ask Amity.

"Seems like it."

"Can you fill us in, Wyatt?" I ask.

"Do we have a map of Willowthrop?" He's like a man possessed.

Amity takes her map from her purse. Wyatt unfolds it, puts it on the table. He runs his finger from the King George Inn to Hair's Looking at You salon and back again.

"Bear with me here. If I'm right, I know where we'll find the murder weapon." He's by the door, slipping on his sneakers and grabbing his blazer. "Get your shoes. We don't have much time. Follow me!"

And he's out the door.

CHAPTER FIFTY-ONE

Amity and I have to run to keep up. We follow Wyatt to the King George Inn, where, instead of going inside, he goes around to the back, to the footpath that runs behind the shops.

"Look carefully in the bushes on both sides of the path," he says. "We have to follow this all the way back to the salon."

I pick up a stick and use it to swat at and poke the branches, which are lush with flowers and leaves. "This would be much easier in the winter."

"Make sure you look deep," Wyatt says. "The weapon could have been flung quite a distance."

Trying not to get scratched, I wade into the shrubbery. I hope they don't have ticks here. I think I see something, but it turns out to be an empty can of Jaipur IPA. If only England weren't a horticultural paradise. These bushes grow like they've been watered with steroids.

We're about halfway to Tracy's salon when Wyatt tells us to slow down.

"It has to be here." He's sounding a little desperate.

We come to the public footpath sign where the trail branches off and goes down to Tracy's parking lot. The windows are open in Tracy's flat, and I can hear the television from inside. I hope she's celebrating being undead by watching something good on Netflix and polishing off her double-chocolate ice cream.

I'm almost ready to give up when Amity shouts, "Bingo!"

And there it is, on the ground beneath a scraggly bush. How had we missed it before? We stand over the flatter, which looks just as Roland described it in his book.

"Should we take it?" Amity says.

"Is that allowed?" I say. "It's evidence."

"But we're the detectives," Wyatt says.

"The sleuthhounds," Amity says.

"Is this cheating?" I say.

"There's nothing in the rules about not taking evidence," Wyatt says.

"What about the others?" I say.

"Finders keepers?" Amity says.

I remind them of the motto of the Detection Club, which Roland Wingford told us was "Play Fair."

"That means the authors have to reveal enough clues that observant readers could solve the crime," Amity says. "It has nothing to do with what we're doing here."

"Right," Wyatt says. "This is a competition."

"And it *is* nearly over," I say.

The question is clear: Do we play this American-style, because we're Americans? Or British-style, because we're in England? Do we act like contestants in *The Great British Baking Show*, who would gather their fellow contestants and lead them to the murder weapon, or do we follow our natural, cutthroat, new-world instincts?

In the end, it's no choice at all. We're American. We take the weapon.

CHAPTER FIFTY-TWO

By the time we're back at the cottage we have three hours and forty minutes before the deadline to turn in our written solution at the parish hall. We kick off our shoes and settle in around the coffee table to map out the case. Amity volunteers to write it all down. She makes herself a pot of tea and sits at the kitchen table scribbling, handing pages to us as she goes. The more she writes, the faster she seems to get. From time to time, she emits a loud "Ha!" or shakes with laughter. I've never known writing to look like so much fun.

We go over what she's written to make sure all the details are there and that she's covered the who, the why, and the how. We go through all our photos and notes again to make sure we haven't missed anything.

By six forty, we're done.

"There's just one thing," Wyatt says. "I'd like to play Poirot— that is, if we win."

"You mean you want to take the stage?" I say. "Fine with me."

"Absolutely," Amity says. "You're overdue for a comeback."

Wyatt wants to stay home and practice how he'll spin the tale. Amity and I head down to the parish hall to drop off our solution, after which we go directly to the Goat and Spur, where we settle at a table near the entrance. Amity looks at the painting on the wall above us, four men in knickers and argyle sweater-vests playing golf.

"Golf," Amity sneers. "Douglas loved golf. He called it his 'me time.' I never minded. He'd do sixteen or eighteen holes or whatever, and I'd have the entire day at home alone to write. It was a win-win, or so I thought. When he told me he'd met someone on the golf course and was in love, he kept saying, 'It's not you, it's me,' which I figured was just a line to soften the blow." She takes a big swallow of beer. "But maybe it was about him. Maybe he bought into all the things I wrote about—the thrill of plummeting. He was willing to give up on me and our family to chase excitement again."

"I don't think you invented the midlife crisis," I say.

"But maybe I should have put epilogues on my stories. You know, like in the movies when they update you on all the characters before the credits roll? *Elaine and Alan continued to desire each other, but over the years with less frequency and intensity and sometimes in the exact same sequence and position as the week before. On occasion, they fell asleep binge-watching shows, now and then on different televisions in different rooms. But they loved each other and stayed true.*"

"Or maybe it's time to give up romance," I say.

She looks at me like I'm missing the point.

"Give up romance? That's not what I want. I still want love and lust, but not *only* that. You know why? Because I'm sad and I'm angry. Why not write about grief and rage too? Yesterday, when I saw how angry you were, something opened up in me. You're right. It's terrible being lied to. It's awful being abandoned. It's infuriating and it's not fair. Douglas chose a do-over, and the boys and I were collateral damage."

Amity leans in closer.

"Do you know what I was hoping?" she whispers. "I was hoping that Pippa was the murderer. That she took all that rage and righteous anger at stupid, stupid Stanley and sought revenge. Wouldn't that have been fun—to see a sassy, gorgeous older woman let her fury fly and do something ghastly? That's what I should write, something deadly and cathartic. What I need now is to pick up my pen and kill someone!"

Amity's cheeks are pink. She's beaming with energy and beauty. I raise my glass.

"Okay, then," I say. "To murder!"

She clinks her glass with mine.

"To bloody murder!"

We throw back the rest of our beers. We're still smiling at one another when the Tampa book club ladies spill noisily into the pub. They're so amped up they appear to be celebrating, but one of them sees us and says, "We've completely failed! We haven't a clue!" She's smiling like it couldn't please her more.

Selina and Bix walk in too. They come right to us.

"Drowning your sorrows or toasting your success?" Bix doesn't seem sarcastic. "Our solution is inelegant, to say the least, and most likely wrong."

Selina, right behind him, gives a devil-may-care smile. "We're not as good at this as we thought. It's been confusing, don't you think?"

"Absolutely," I say at the same time that Amity says, "Not really."

"You think you've got it?" Bix says.

"We've definitely figured some things out," Amity says, and winks at me. "I think we've got it."

"Impressive." Bix nods.

"Bravo," says Selina. "What are you drinking? The next round is on us."

This week is full of surprises.

CHAPTER FIFTY-THREE

FRIDAY

The dining room of the King George Inn is plush and glittery, like the inside of a jewelry box. The guests are suitably bedazzled. Germaine, standing by the door, is nearly unrecognizable in a long, sleeveless black velvet dress and a gold art deco choker. Roland Wingford, who's sticking close to Germaine, has retired his tweed ensemble in favor of white-tie—a black tailcoat and white bow tie that make him look very old Hollywood. Constable Bucket, still in uniform and still perspiring, has adorned his black jacket with ribboned military metals that look surprisingly real. The Americans are no less glamorous. There are sparkly dresses and sequins, high heels, suits with cuff links, and hair so sleekly coiffed that I wouldn't be surprised to hear that Tracy revived herself to open for business.

Wyatt looks dashing, not boyish like he did that first day, but more confident and elegant, in a slim-fitting suit, a narrow tie, a linen handkerchief in his breast pocket, and buttery leather shoes. Amity is all smiles, her flowery silk dress a happy match to her mood, which is impressively perky for someone who spent most of the day thinking up vicious scenarios for her thriller-in-progress. I've made an effort too. After a long run on the Monsal Trail this afternoon, I took a bubble bath and then a shower, washing and conditioning my hair so I could wear it down without looking like I put my finger in an electrical socket. I think it worked, because Wyatt and Amity both whistled when I came downstairs, and that was before I fancied up my black wrap dress with some of Amity's jewelry. I'm also wearing heels, "leaning into my height" as my grandmother used to advise. I don't, however, feel as sleek as my dress. I'm overloaded on revelations and plot twists, both fictional and real. When Amity brings me a gin and tonic, I down it quickly, even though I've barely eaten today. I hope it calms my nerves so I can enjoy the silly and fun finale to this mind-boggling week.

A microphone squeaks. Germaine, Constable Bucket, and Roland Wingford are at the front of the room.

"Good evening, ladies and gentlemen," Germaine begins. "We have spent the day going over your solutions, which have been exceedingly entertaining and, dare I say, creative. Your many hours in front of the telly and reading our golden age classics have paid off grandly. You sought out the obvious suspects, and most of you added to your lists the usual archetypes—the vicar, the nosy neighbor, and the village doctor."

Wyatt and Amity and I exchange astonished looks.

"How did we miss the village doctor?" Wyatt whispers.

"Other than dead Tracy sneezing, no one was sick," I answer.

"Let's hope it doesn't matter," Amity says, but she looks troubled.

"In the end, however, only one team figured out the entire scheme," Germaine says. "In so doing, they utilized all the reasoning suggested—observation, careful questioning, and most of all, a keen eye for *every detail*. They did such a good job that I've already told Constable Bucket that if Willowthrop ever experiences a real murder, which I sincerely hope it does not, he should call in this team. And so, without further ado, I'd like to invite to the microphone three people who not only have never worked together to solve a real or a fake murder, but until arriving in Willowthrop a week ago had never met."

The three of us exchange delighted looks. Amity squeezes my hand.

"They have become a formidable trio and, I hope, good friends. The winners of the First Annual Willowthrop Fake-Murder Week, ladies and gentlemen, are the residents of Wisteria Cottage—Amity Clarke, Wyatt Green, and Cath Little."

A burst of applause and cheers. Wyatt grabs us each by the hand and pulls us to the front of the room. As we take our bows, the kitchen door swings open and Dev steps out and joins the applause. I want to find him later to ask if his mother remembered anything. And I need to say goodbye, though I'm not sure how I can or why the thought of never seeing him again makes me so sad.

Germaine steps toward Wyatt.

"It is now my pleasure to hand the microphone to Wyatt Green, who will explain this devious crime to us. First, however, I'd like to say a special thanks to Wyatt, Amity, and Cath for sparing us the embarrassment of being accused of not playing fair. We were concerned that the crime we devised might be too tricky, but we refused to dumb it down. A mystery that's easy to solve, after all, is not worthy of the name. Wyatt, the floor is yours."

CHAPTER FIFTY-FOUR

Wyatt waits until the crowd is completely quiet before opening his arms like a benevolent minister greeting his flock. If he's nervous about being in the spotlight, he's hiding it well.

"Ladies and gentlemen, as Jane Marple said about an English village, 'turn over a stone and you have no idea what will crawl out.' Willowthrop, in this regard, is no exception. The pleasant facade of your quiet village hides dark secrets and forbidden passions. This evening, I will explain how and why your own Tracy Penny was murdered and by whom. You will not be surprised to know that the murderer is in this room at this moment. Allow me, however, to reassure you, or perhaps warn you, there is no escape. The doors are locked."

Laughter and light applause as everyone looks around and tries to spot the guilty party.

Wyatt starts to pace. As he nears the kitchen, I see someone peeking out the door. I catch only a glimpse, but I think it's Tracy Penny herself, who I imagine is eager for justice.

"Tracy Penny was well known in Willowthrop, not just as a talented hairstylist, but as a woman of many passions and complicated relations," Wyatt says, moving smoothly through the crowd as he speaks. "She was not without enemies or people who have reason to want her dead. The first, and most obvious, suspect is her ex-husband, Gordon Penny."

"Not ex," shouts Gordon, loud enough to suggest he's not entirely sober. "Separated, not divorced."

"Yes, Gordon and Tracy were still married," Wyatt says. "And Gordon remains in Tracy's will, thereby standing to inherit the sum of ten thousand pounds upon her death."

Suitable oohs and aahs from the assembled.

"In addition to needing money for his dance studio and probably to repay debts from his gambling habit, Gordon had to suffer the humiliation of seeking a weekly allowance from his more successful, estranged wife. Obviously, her death would not only bring him into substantial money but also spare him this indignity. Gordon Penny had the motive to kill Tracy Penny and, still in possession of a key to the building, he had the means."

Wyatt lets that sit for a moment, a sly smile on his face as people start whispering and looking at Gordon like he's the culprit.

"But there is one simple reason why Gordon Penny would not murder Tracy." Here, Wyatt demonstrates the power of a good pause. We wait, until people start glancing at one another to see if anyone else has noticed that Wyatt is still silent. Only after a few more beats, as the rustling among the guests suggests restlessness, does he continue. "And that reason is that Gordon was still in love with his soon-to-be ex-wife."

"Now how'd you know that?" Bix says. Oddly, Bix is the only man not in a suit or a jacket. He's wearing stretchy yoga pants and a fleece vest. I guess that counts as cocktail wear in Silicon Valley.

Wyatt explains about the calla lilies that Gordon sent to Tracy, the same flowers that were in her wedding bouquet, and describes the note that accompanied them, in which he pledged his eternal love for Tracy and which was cruelly tossed in the waste bin.

"Gordon Penny," Wyatt says, "you are guilty, not of murder but of unrequited love. You as much as admitted it yourself when you told us that you bet on a horse called Hopeless Romantic and you lost. My condolences, but you are not our man."

More laughter and an elegant ballet dancer's bow from Gordon. When the audience quiets down, Wyatt walks to the center of the room, turning slowly as if he's delivering a soliloquy in a theater in the round.

"If the next of kin is not guilty, then the next most obvious person would be the last person known to have seen Tracy on the evening of her death. And that is you, Lady Magnolia Blanders."

She looks stunning, her red hair flowing over a dark green silk dress, and appears pained to be among such a plebeian crowd.

"You came to Hair's Looking at You salon for the first time ever on the last day of Tracy Penny's life. You had your hair blown out, and you departed. You have spent little time in Willowthrop and know no one here. You have no obvious motive to have killed Tracy. Your involvement, it seems, was a classic red herring and an amusement. Even detectives like the opportunity to nose around a grand home, and Hadley Hall was not a disappointment."

Lady Magnolia steps toward the door, waving to Mrs. Crone, still in her white blouse and black skirt, to follow, but Wyatt says, "Not so fast, Your Ladyship. We're not done with you yet.

"Who else had access to Tracy's salon and also a reason to want her dead?" Wyatt asks. "Bert Lott, you were desperate to get Tracy out of the salon."

Bert, leaning against a back wall with his arms folded, cleans up nicely. He's wearing a navy suit and looks good enough that it's entirely possible that my mother matched with him on her dating app in hopes of setting up a rendezvous during our visit.

"You created complaints—about the plumbing, and the toxic fumes, and hair in the drains," Wyatt says. "But the salon was in tip-top shape. Why were you trying to build a case against your tenant? Because you wanted to win back the love of your daughter, Claire. You were prepared to give her the salon space for free so she could open the vegan café of her dreams. Would you kill for Claire? You might. But did you? Alas, you did not. You were pursuing legal proceedings and had made a court date, as evidenced by the legal notice among Tracy's papers. A court date during the week *after* the murder. You're no fool, Bert Lott. You knew that a potential murder charge was not the way to get your daughter back. However dishonestly, you opted for legal recourse. Claire Lott, to you I say, note your father's love and abandon your business plan. Willowthrop may lack some of the fame of its neighbors, but it will not be vegan cheesecake that puts this village on the map."

More laughter. Claire, who has taken out her braids but is still in hiking boots, throws her arms around Bert and plants a kiss on his cheek. I hadn't noticed the resemblance before, but I think they may be father and daughter in real life.

"Now we turn to someone who spent a great deal of time with Tracy Penny and had good reason to resent her. Dinda Roost, as Tracy's assistant, you had access to the salon. And you owed her money, money that you thought Tracy bestowed as a gift only to discover she meant it as a loan. Even worse, the money was for much-needed alternative therapies for someone near and dear to your heart, your beloved pooch, Petunia. This is what Edwina Flasher, the nosy neighbor, overheard you and Tracy arguing about the morning before the murder. You wanted to keep the money, and Tracy wanted it paid back."

Dinda curtsies, but nearly falls over, no doubt because bundled in her arms is her date for the evening, her dog.

"Yes, Dinda, you were in a financial bind because of Tracy. But you didn't kill her, because a dead Tracy would be worse for your finances than a living Tracy. True, you wouldn't have to pay back the loan, but you would have no job and no income. You've tried several jobs in Willowthrop, none of which have worked out. This job was your last resort, and you had to keep it."

"It's true," Dinda says over the yapping of Petunia. "I'm no murderer."

Wyatt brings his palms together, bows his head, and waits for silence. Clearly, he's loving the attention. He starts up again, speaking so quietly that everyone leans in.

"What do we know about the night of Tracy's murder?" Wyatt says. "Who might have visited the salon? Perhaps it was Tracy's 'Monday lover,' as observed by Edwina Flasher from across the street."

Edwina is in fine form, in a gray jacket and skirt, sensible shoes, and a feathered hat that looks like it was designed by the same milliner who made my bedside lamp. She peers dramatically at the crowd through her opera glasses.

"Who's that?" Selina asks.

"The nosy neighbor," Naomi says. "She was our favorite."

I'm glad to know that Naomi and Deborah eventually found their way to Edwina.

Wyatt continues.

"Edwina described Tracy's Monday visitor as a tall, dark-haired man in well-cut clothes. One man who fits that description is Dev, who owns a bar called Moss and makes his own gin. You may recall that on the table in Tracy's flat were a bottle of gin, two used glasses, and a thank-you note from Dev to Tracy, all of which suggest a cozy rendezvous between the gin distiller and the hairdresser. But alas, it was not Dev's thick head of hair that attracted Tracy Penny but the luxurious mane of another man, a man who occasionally parked a red Tesla roadster behind Tracy's building at night. Tracy herself led us to the identity of her lover by making a note in her datebook, left open on the coffee table in her flat. The note, in all caps, said 'Tell Pippa!' Thanks to Sally, the vicar, who, for the record, is *not* a gossip, we learned about a dashing man named Stanley Grange, who came every Sunday to church services, where he often drew Tracy's lustful glances. The vicar told us that Stanley, a tall man with lustrous dark hair, drove to church in a red Tesla with his wife, Pippa. From this fact, it was easy to surmise that Stanley Grange was having an affair with Tracy, visiting her on Mondays and often at night, when he would park his Tesla behind the salon."

Oohs and aahs from the crowd.

Pippa, in a red dress with a plunging neckline, thrusts back her shoulders, grabs Stanley's arm, and puts it around her. Stanley sticks his nose back in his drink. Still in character, they look like a truly miserable couple.

"Tracy had threatened to tell Pippa everything, which surely would give Stanley a reason to want her dead," Wyatt says. "She had even set a deadline, after which if he didn't confess everything to his wife, she would tell her herself. But before Tracy got the chance, Stanley admitted everything to Pippa. In penance, he took her away to Clitheridge Spa for the weekend, where they were the night that Tracy was killed."

Pippa looks around the room with smug satisfaction. She kicks Stanley, who looks up from his drink for a moment and then downs the rest of it in one go.

"This leaves us with the least obvious person of all, the person without an apparent motive to kill Tracy Penny." Wyatt is walking back toward Lady Blanders. "Lady Magnolia Blanders did not plan to have her hair done by Tracy Penny. She had never been to Hairs Looking at You and only went there because of a fashion emergency. Like many of you, when Lady Blanders entered the salon, she would have seen the photographs on the walls. But the one that caught her eye, and alarmed her, was a framed magazine article about a riding school that included a full-page photograph of Tracy holding the bridle of a pony on which sat a small child with red hair. A girl, according to the caption, named Ambrosia. When Lady Blanders saw this photograph, she knew she had to act. It was because of this child that Lady Blanders made monthly visits to Sproton House in Whitby—not for spa treatments as she'd claimed, but to see the child she had hidden away in an institution after meeting Lord Blanders."

The audience breaks into exclamations of shock and confusion.

"Yes, that is the sad story. Lady Blanders had put her first child, born with a disability, into a home for children, the same home that took its residents for equine therapy at Whitby Stables, where Tracy Penny had worked. In terror that Tracy would remember seeing her at the stable, where she often went to visit her daughter, Lady Blanders came up with a plan."

"I had no choice, I was in a panic," Lady Blanders says. "Tracy kept saying I looked familiar. I couldn't risk it. You don't know my husband. He annulled his first marriage because his wife couldn't produce an heir. He wouldn't have married me if he'd known about Ambrosia. It was him or her, and I chose him. And now I was trapped. If he found out I'd been lying all these years, he'd leave me and he'd take our boys. I couldn't let that happen."

"Ah, thank you for the confession, Your Ladyship," Wyatt says. "It adds to the convincing proof we already have gathered."

"How'd you figure it out?" Bix asks.

"Listen to the story," Amity says serenely. "All will be revealed."

"The first clue," Wyatt says, "was Lady Blanders's bracelet. She poured tea for all those who questioned her, did she not? And she poured magnificently, lifting her arm, making sure that her bracelet caught the light. Her bracelet with letter charms—A, B, and C. At first, we thought them meaningless, just an indulgence, the work of a Swedish designer who Lady Blanders admired. But then Lady Blanders mentioned her sons, Benedict and Charles. Together, they account for the B and C on the bracelet. But what about the A? When asked about children, Lady Blanders said only that she had two sons. She said nothing about a third child, because that was her deepest, darkest secret. The third child was the daughter sent to a children's home in Whitby. A little redheaded girl who looked strikingly like Magnolia Blanders. Ambrosia. The missing A."

The crowd bursts into applause. When it quiets down, Wyatt turns toward Lady Blanders. "Your Ladyship, would you like to tell us how you killed Tracy Penny?"

"I would prefer to consult with a solicitor."

"Then I will proceed," Wyatt says. "First, she made sure she had a solid alibi, dinner here at the King George Inn with her dear friend Demetra Sissington."

"Dissy," Lady Blanders says.

"She also had an accomplice, her devoted maid, Gladys Crone, who had been with her for years, since before the marriage to Lord Blanders. Gladys was there when the daughter was born and sent off to the institution. She was loyal to her employer and wanted to protect her reputation. She would do anything for her. Even get on a horse."

"Of course!" shouts Naomi.

"Lady Blanders went to dinner by car, as she said, to meet Sissy," Wyatt says.

"Dissy!" several people shout.

"She dined on snails, also as she said," Wyatt continues. "But during dinner, according to the maître d', she excused herself to go to the loo. A normal enough occurrence, except for the fact that she was there for quite some time. Long enough for the maître d' to worry that the restaurant might have given her food poisoning. Thankfully, Lady Blanders returned to the table, not looking pale at all. She even looked quite flushed. By which I mean, very flushed." Wyatt gives me a wink. He weaves through the crowd and stops inches from Lady Blanders, who, other than a delicately raised eyebrow, doesn't flinch. Wyatt continues.

"It's not surprising that Lady Blanders was flushed, because she had not been in the lavatory but had gone on an adventure. She had slipped out the back of the restaurant, where she met her devoted maid, who had come from Hadley Hall on horseback, with the murder weapon in the saddlebag. The maid got off the horse, and Lady Blanders got on. She rode along the footpath that goes behind the shops to Tracy's building. There, she banged on the back door for Tracy to open up. Inside, Lady Blanders hit Tracy once, knocking her unconscious. Then, to protect herself from spattered blood, she donned a plastic face shield, also brought in the saddlebag and smuggled into the salon, and one of the black nylon robes, and bludgeoned Tracy Penny to death. She then manipulated the crime scene to make it look like a man had been at the salon after her that afternoon. She left an extra-large robe on the back of the chair, and on the counter left a bowl of shaving foam and a brush. She washed the plastic face shield in the sink and put the robe in the washing machine and turned it on."

"How about that, a toff like her knowing how to do the wash," Dinda says with a smirk.

"Oh, Lady Blanders was very clever," Wyatt says. "Almost clever enough. When she was set to leave the salon, she bolted the back door from the inside and took one of the large black umbrellas that

Tracy kept for clients who didn't want their new hairdos ruined by the rain. She opened the umbrella and let it shield her from view as she left via the front door, no doubt unaware that she had been spotted from across the street by Edwina Flasher, who assumed that the tall person hiding behind the big umbrella was a man. It was a stroke of luck for Lady Blanders that Edwina Flasher, who had been sitting in her living room, had left her glasses upstairs and was too nearsighted to realize that the tall person behind the umbrella was a woman. Lady Blanders walked down the alley to the back of the building, got on her horse, and galloped back on the footpath to the restaurant. At the King George, Lady Blanders dismounted, and Gladys got on the horse and rode back to Hadley Hall, which explains the maid's noticeably stiff, bowlegged walk on the following days."

"I thought she had a dodgy hip like me," Naomi says. "It never occurred to me that it was a clue."

"And it never occurred to Lady Blanders that she had left behind several clues," Wyatt says. "First, Lady Blanders put the black nylon robe in the washing machine to ensure that there would be no traces of blood on it. But the fact that the next day there was only one robe in the machine was suspicious, as surely the practice would have been to wash all the robes at the same time. She also left the plastic face shield in the sink, no doubt assuming that since it was clean it wouldn't raise suspicion. Which might make sense if Tracy was known to use face shields, which she was not. Lady Blanders also failed to adequately hide either the umbrella that had shielded her upon her exit from the salon or the murder weapon, both of which she tossed in the bushes along the path. And there was one crucial clue that was an unfortunate act of nature. No doubt unbeknownst to Lady Blanders, her horse deposited a pile of manure on the path, which was immediately suspicious to the careful observer given that the path in question was clearly marked as a footpath, not a bridle path."

"Damn horse," hisses Lady Blanders.

"Impressive," Bix says, holding up his arms and clapping loudly. "Bravo!"

"Very smart indeed," says Selina, looking dumbfounded.

"We're not done yet," Wyatt says. "We still need a murder weapon to clinch this case. And for that, I would like to thank Cath Little and Roland Wingford."

Roland, who had been nodding off on the side of the room, perks up and smooths his tweed jacket.

"As you know, the autopsy results described but did not identify the murder weapon. But Cath's careful reading of Roland Wingford's detective novel *Murder Afoot* pointed her in the right direction."

General surprise, with none looking more delighted than Roland Wingford himself, who turns red in the cheeks, either from pride or the realization that he might be a few pounds closer to earning a royalty on his book.

"By reading about the hero of the book, Cuddy Claptrop, Cath learned about a blacksmithing tool called a flatter that is shaped precisely as the mysterious murder weapon described in the autopsy report. A flatter may seem like an unlikely weapon for Lady Blanders to secure, unless you recall the conversation between Lady Blanders and her groom after her daily ride. He inquired about 'the new shoes.' He was referring, of course, to new horseshoes. Lady Blanders said they were fine and asked if Mr. Welch was finished 'with the others.' He was not; he still had other horses to shoe. Remembering this unusual detail, we visited the blacksmith, Mr. Welch."

This version is not accurate, of course, but I appreciate Wyatt not bringing in my personal story and the truth of what led us to the blacksmith.

"Lo and behold," Wyatt continues. "Mr. Welch was missing a flatter. And he revealed that none other than Gladys Crone, Lady Blanders's devoted maid, had been hanging around his van in the late afternoon on the day of the murder. A quick search in the bushes behind the salon and, voilà!" Wyatt nods to Amity, who steps forward with a tote bag. Wyatt takes the bag and, using his handkerchief, pulls out the tool. As the crowd exclaims and applauds, he hands the murder weapon to Germaine, who takes it between two fingers as if she's holding a dead mouse.

When the room is quiet, Wyatt says, "I'm quite sure that, upon testing, the traces of blood on the flatter will prove to be a match for the blood of Tracy Penny."

Everyone is clapping and hooting, even Lady Magnolia Blanders and Mrs. Crone. Wyatt takes a bow. He is beaming and laughing and might even be a little teary. Amity hugs me tight. If I hadn't cried so much in the past two days, I might be crying too.

Wyatt can't stop smiling. He looks so proud and happy and like he's just had the most fun of his life. I'm impressed with how he put it all together. And he was clearly born for the stage.

Lady Blanders asks to have a word. She goes up and takes the microphone. "I am guilty, as charged," she says, apparently back in character. "What was I to do? I was crazed with fear that I would be exposed and would lose everything. I had to act quickly. Tracy was a hairdresser, for god's sake. She would gossip. I couldn't take the risk. I had no choice but to protect my reputation, my marriage, and my children."

This elicits much laughter and applause and shouts of "Boo!" from the crowd, at which point Lady Magnolia Blanders curtsies slowly, all the way to the floor. When she comes up, she is laughing too.

CHAPTER FIFTY-FIVE

Selina and Bix are doing shots with the women from the Tampa book club, and Deborah and Naomi can't seem to stop hugging Wyatt. The waiters bring out dessert, the promised sticky toffee pudding, which is so delectable that I don't understand why it hasn't already made Willowthrop famous.

Germaine comes over to the three of us. She wants to know how we made the connection to Ambrosia.

"It was Amity, talking about *The Mirror Crack'd from Side to Side*," Wyatt says.

"Agatha Christie helped you solve the case?" Germaine says.

Wyatt laughs. "Yes, she did."

He explains how Amity had not only been impressed with the plot twist in Christie's mystery but had remembered it vividly because she'd been so offended at the way Christie's character referred to her child as an "imbecile" and how strange it was that everyone in the story seemed to accept without question that the child would be institutionalized.

"Suddenly, it all fell together. Details we had overlooked were key. Lady Blanders's bracelet, her odd reaction to being asked if she'd wanted a daughter, the photograph of Sproton House, the magazine article on Tracy's wall with the photograph of the redheaded girl on the pony and the girl's name, Ambrosia, in the caption."

Germaine looks so delighted that I suspect she did considerably more than assist Roland Wingford in developing the story.

"I never did like *The Mirror Crack'd* for that very reason," she says. "All children deserve love and family and a name. I hated how Christie allowed her character to be ashamed of and banish her own child."

She returns to the microphone and announces that she'd like to introduce the cast. Finally, we'll know who was acting and who was playing themselves. Germaine starts with Gordon Penny, who she tells us is Gordon Greensleeve and has never been married to Tracy Penny, though they dated briefly as teenagers and are still friends. Gordon runs the dance studio, which he named himself. He participated in the murder mystery in hopes that the publicity might help get him onto a show like *Strictly Come Dancing*.

Tracy Penny, real name, is a reputable hairstylist whose clients include many people in the village and the surrounding area. She hasn't cut the hair of anyone with a title, but she did act as a backup stylist for a television commercial shot in neighboring Bakewell last year in which a Kate Middleton look-alike was advertising vitamins.

"I am particularly chuffed to introduce the genius behind the character of Lady Magnolia Blanders," Germaine says. This prompts an exaggerated frown from Amity, who had very much wanted Lady Magnolia to be the real deal. "Ladies and gentleman, meet my niece, the Canadian stage actress Imogen Postlethwaite."

"I knew I recognized her!" Selina Granby grabs her husband's arm. "She played the crazed lover in that musical version of *Fatal Attraction*!"

Lady Blanders/Imogen wraps her arms around Germaine. I see the resemblance, especially now that Imogen has dropped the haughty expression and posture. "In addition to being a great actor, my niece has also been honored for her support and work on behalf of disability rights in Canada," Germaine says. "The child at the center of this mystery, Ambrosia, does not exist. The photograph in the magazine was a result of some clever photoshopping in which we put a picture of Imogen as a child on horseback with a photograph of Tracy when she had a perm. Sproton House and the Whitby Children's Home are also fabrications. Whitby Stables, however, not only is real but also has a wonderful equine therapy program for children throughout England. It was our pleasure to use some of the proceeds of this event to make a donation."

Germaine waits for the applause to subside and then expresses her gratitude to her dear friend Lady Cressida Sterling, who is the real owner of Hadley Hall, for giving them use of the estate.

"Lady Cressida, unfortunately, could not be with us tonight, but she invites you all to return to Willowthrop next summer when renovations are complete and Hadley Hall will be open to the public," Germaine says.

"I'm coming back for that," Amity tells me. "Maybe it will overlap with the swan census."

Holding the microphone, Germaine flits around the room introducing the others. Dinda Roost works for Tracy but does not owe her money. Petunia, Dinda's terrier, does not need therapy of any kind and is in perfect health. Edwina Flasher has lived in Willowthrop her entire life and is known as a bona fide busybody, though she prefers to call herself the unofficial village historian. Bert Lott is the local stationer. He has never acted before and doesn't plan to do so again. His daughter, Claire, who is neither estranged from her father nor interested in opening a vegan café, is one of the area's most accomplished hang gliders. Sally, the vicar, is the vicar. Stanley and Pippa Grange, real names, are husband and wife, dinner theater actors who believe that playing turbulently married couples keeps their own marriage alive. The village doctor is the village chiropractor. And Gladys Crone is not and has never been a maid; her real name is Alice Sweet, and she's a pastry chef.

"What about Dev?" shouts one of the Tampa book club women.

Germaine looks toward the kitchen door, beside which Dev is leaning against the wall.

"And this is Dev Sharma, who is everything he's told you he is. He owns Moss, a marvelous bar, and he makes top-notch artisanal gin."

The kitchen door swings open, and the light from within pools around Dev. He glows with warmth and kindness as he looks around the room. I will him to find me in the crowd. When his eyes finally meet mine, I put my hand to my heart and he does the same. I can't look away.

"There is one person I have saved for last," Germaine continues. "She volunteered for the most thankless part, a starring role that was at the center of this mystery but that did not require learning a single line. Ladies and gentleman, I give you our victim, a veritable wunderkind of playing dead, Tracy Penny."

The kitchen door opens again, and Tracy Penny rushes to the center of the room like a ballerina flitting to the spotlight. She's done her hair into an elaborate updo with perfect tendrils spiraling down to her bare shoulders. The sequins in her long, slinky dress sparkle in the light as she twirls and blows kisses and strikes poses. And then she throws her arms up in the air and her voice rings out strong and clear.

"It's bloody brilliant to be alive!"

CHAPTER FIFTY-SIX

The party is in full swing now. Someone has turned on music, and there are some funny pairings on the dance floor: Gordon is trying to teach Naomi, Deborah, and Edwina Flasher the Cha-Cha Slide, and Pippa Grange is dancing cheek to cheek with the village chiropractor. I head over to the kitchen to find Dev. When a waiter comes by with a tray full of dirty dishes, I ask if he'd get Dev to come out.

"Who?"

"Dev Sharma. The bar owner. The gin guy?"

"I know who he is, but he's gone."

"Back to his bar?"

"Nah. Said he had to go down to London tonight."

Would he leave without saying goodbye? I was a weepy mess the last time we were together, when he brought me back to the cottage. Maybe it's all too much for him.

I find Dev outside, closing the trunk to his car.

"Hey, I was just about to come find you," he says. "There's a plumbing disaster at my flat, and my tenant's away. I'm afraid I've got to head down to London."

"And I've got to shuffle off to Buffalo." I hate that I'm joking with him, but I'm afraid to be serious.

"Buffalo. Right."

"Do you have any idea where Buffalo is?" I ask.

"Kind of?"

"It's on Lake Erie. Does that help?"

"Geography's not my forte."

"It's very far away," I say.

"So, this is goodbye, then?" Dev takes a step toward me.

I don't have to try to remember his face. It's etched into my memory. I put out my hand, like I'm ready to shake and close a deal. Dev laughs and gives my hand a decisive, businesslike squeeze. And then he pulls me toward him. For a goodbye kiss, it's a great one. I put my hand on his chest, and feel the rhythm of his heart in my palm. I push him lightly away.

"Go," I say, and turn around quickly.

If this were one of Amity's romances, Dev would start to drive away but then I'd dash out and leap in front of his car. He'd get out yelling that I was crazy, that he could've run me over. I'd shout back something charming and nonsensical, and then we'd be kissing and crying, in each other's arms again, vowing to never part. But these days Amity can't do happy endings, and apparently neither can I.

CHAPTER FIFTY-SEVEN

Amity and I find Wyatt in the lobby, on his phone.

"Look at that smile. He can't contain it," Amity says.

Wyatt holds his hand over the phone and says, "I'm calling Bernard." He's jiggling his foot, pursing his lips as if to hold back a smile.

"Come on, come on," he whispers, and then he's smiling fully. "Oh my god, Bernard, it was amazing. I was amazing. I was Poirot and Miss Marple and DCI Foyle with dramatic pauses and everything." His smile is huge. "Yes, in front of everyone. Nope, no vomit. A miracle." He listens, cheeks flushed, eyes sparkling. "I do too."

Wyatt turns away, takes a few steps to distance himself, lowers his voice. He speaks too quietly for me to decipher his words, but I hear something for sure. There is love in his voice. He's bubbling over, not only because he wants to relive the moment but also because he's sharing it with the man he loves and who loves him back.

"I never bought all that nonsense about Bernard being tired of Wyatt," Amity says. "Who would be tired of Wyatt?"

"So why did Bernard send him away?"

"I think he had a better sense of what Wyatt needed to be happy than Wyatt did himself. Wyatt was never going to be fulfilled trying to take on what Bernard loved. He had to pursue his own passions."

"And you say you can't write happy endings."

Amity smiles. "This one wrote itself."

This is Wyatt's moment, and we revel in it like proud parents or, more accurately, like good friends. Because in the most unlikely of circumstances, that is what we have become.

On the way back to the cottage, there's little traffic in the village, so we all three walk in the road. It's started to rain, misty and light, and none of us are prepared, so we let the drops fall on our heads and our cheeks. Amity's face is glistening under the streetlights. Wyatt's freckles look darker and somehow more adorable. We talk about what's next, at the end of our respective flights: Amity all the way back to San Francisco, Wyatt to Newark, and me to Buffalo. Amity has some wildly brilliant ideas for her thriller and has already messaged her agent that she's going to try something new. Wyatt wants to find something back home that makes him feel as alive as he did solving this crime and presenting the solution to a live audience. My plan, if I have one, is less concrete. I want to sit with what I've learned about my mother and try to find out more. I want to understand the most important story she never told me.

The chance comes sooner than expected. As I walk back into the cottage, my phone rings. It's Germaine. Thanks to Edwina, who knows someone who knows a social worker who knows everything, she's found my grandfather, still alive, at the Derby Oaks Care Home. She suggests I delay my flight for a day so she can take me to visit him. I tell her I'll think about it, that I'll call her back. I'm not sure I'm brave enough.

Amity and Wyatt, not surprisingly, urge me to go.

"It might be your only chance," Amity says. "Who knows when you'll be back."

"Isn't it better to know him than to imagine him?" Wyatt says.

"The man whose carelessness set my mother's childhood on fire? Maybe not."

CHAPTER FIFTY-EIGHT

SATURDAY

Germaine picks me up early, right after Amity and Wyatt leave for the train station. She drives fast, which makes me even queasier than I already am. But I don't know if I want her to slow down, which would delay this meeting, or speed up so I can get it over with. I don't even know if I want to go.

"Pull over," I say.

"Are you going to be sick?" Germaine checks her rearview mirror as she starts to slow down.

"I don't know if I can do this. My grandfather sounds awful. Do I want to meet him? Is this what my mother would want?"

Germaine stops the car on the shoulder.

"I don't know, Cath. You seemed sure last night."

I try to clear my head, to remember why I thought this made sense.

"I wanted to see him for myself, because I'm tired of being kept in the dark, of not knowing anything, of being left to figure out everything and everyone on my own."

"Then it's for you, not for your mother."

"Right." I press down on my thighs to stop them from shaking. "So we proceed?"

"Yes."

There's still so much I don't know. Was my mother in touch with her father? Did he reach out to her? Did he care? Does he know that she's dead? I do not like the thought of having to deliver that information. He's old. What if it kills him?

Germaine pulls into the parking lot of the Derby Oaks Care Home, a sprawling brick complex that reminds me of my bland, 1970s-era middle school. I get out of the car, but Germaine stays put.

"You're not coming?"

"I assumed you'd want to do this alone."

She's right. I'm grateful for all the support, but I've had enough of my family's history being Willowthrop's favorite real mystery. I don't want a witness.

The lobby smells like roast chicken and cleaning fluid. The walls are decorated with thick hooked rugs in swirling patterns of brown and green. I sign the register and follow a nurse down a long corridor.

"Ready?" Her smile is tight, forced.

I'm expecting a giant, an ogre, some kind of devil. But when the door opens, there's only a frail man sitting up in bed. Everything about him seems insubstantial. He has filmy eyes, wisps of gray hair on his head, and patches of white stubble on his gaunt face, like he's used an electric shaver with a shaky hand. He's nearly eighty but looks older, maybe on account of living a hard life punctuated by too much drinking, smoking, and gambling. His long, thin arms rest on a blue wool blanket.

"Good morning, George," the nurse says, her voice cheery and loud. "This is your visitor. Your granddaughter."

It's so quiet I can hear the crackling of his breath. On the table beside his bed is a racing form and a calendar on the wrong month.

On the wall is a framed painting on velvet of an oak tree in autumn. The colors are garish, almost fluorescent.

"I'm Catherine." It comes out that way, the name my mother chose for me.

Has he heard what I've said? He stares at me, moving his mouth around like he's got something stuck in his teeth.

"Granddaughter, eh?"

"Yes, Susan Marie is my mother."

That sounds foreign; I feel like I'm talking about a stranger.

"You're Sukie's girl."

"That's right."

"You're a strapping thing."

Gosh. I didn't have that on my Bingo card.

"Not little like Sukie."

"My dad was tall."

"Huh." His fingers flutter on the blanket. "Come closer."

I'm reluctant to sit near him. I perch myself on the edge of the mattress.

"My mother wanted to bring me here. It's my first time in England."

"Is that right? Haven't heard anything from her. Not for years and years. She didn't write, not a word, so neither did I. So where is she, then? If she wanted to bring you here, why isn't she here?"

His manner makes me less afraid to tell him.

"She had a stroke, last year. She wasn't sick; it was sudden." For the first time, I wonder if my mother's stroke, which was so unexpected, was a long time coming, if burying her past took its toll.

"She's in hospital, then?"

"No, she isn't. Um, she died."

He juts out his lower lip, moves it right and left. Looks away from me and starts coughing lightly, and then harder. He wheezes

275

and gasps. I turn to the nurse. She pitches him forward, thumps on his back. Pushes the button to move his bed so he's more vertical.

"Is he okay?" I ask.

The nurse sighs. "Some days are harder than others." To my grandfather, she says, "There we go now, pet. You're fine."

He doesn't look fine. He looks pained.

"She didn't suffer," I say. "It happened very fast."

"My girl," he whispers. He's not looking at me. "Sukie."

Is he crying? This isn't what I wanted. I was going to be angry and strong. Why isn't my mother here? Why is this left to me, to tell him what's happened to his own daughter? I don't want to cry here but can't stop the tears. I wipe my nose with the back of my hand. This is all wrong, all of it. I have so many questions: How could he send away his own daughter? Why didn't he write to her? Why did she stay away for so long? But I can't bring myself to ask.

"In the drawer," he says, waving a hand toward his night table. "My wallet."

What the hell? Is he going to give me money?

"I don't need—"

"Get my wallet," he croaks.

I find the wallet, cracked leather, and give it to him. His hands are shaking. It takes him a while to slide something out. It's a photograph, frayed on the edges and crinkled, like it's been in there for a long time, maybe since shortly after it was taken. A family in front of a small stone house. George, with a full head of hair and a muscular body, his arm around Ann, who's leaning against his shoulder and smiling at the camera. Her hair is swept back off her face, but I can tell it is thick, like mine. She's holding the hand of a little girl in a sleeveless shirt and shorts.

It's a beautiful picture and it is horrifying. A portrait of all that was lost.

"Take it," he says. His eyes are watery, his lips quivering.

"I can take a photograph of it with my phone, and you can keep it," I say.

"I want you to have it." He watches me put the photograph in my bag. "She was better off there. Cheeky thing. She was better off."

"I don't know," I say. "I know nothing about it."

As I'm trying to figure out what to say, he rests his head on the pillow and closes his eyes. His breathing slows into a steady rhythm.

"He tires easily," the nurse says. "Do you want to come back later?"

"I don't think so."

I tear off a blank edge of the racing form and take a pen from my bag. I write down my name and address and phone number. I can't imagine that we'll talk again, but it seems the right thing to do. In large letters, I add, "It was nice to visit with you." Maybe not what my mother would do, but like Germaine said, she's not here. It's only me.

I hand the slip of paper to the nurse.

"Can you make sure he sees this?"

"Of course," she says.

In the car, Germaine says, "So?"

I tell her it was worse and better than I thought. He's a sad, angry man, but not without feeling. On the drive home, I open the window and lean my face out to feel the country air on my cheeks. The hills are lush and inviting. I try to remember that line from Sherlock Holmes that Amity quoted on our first day in the village. Something about hellish cruelty and hidden wickedness, a pretty village and a sordid crime. I think I get it now. The secrets of strangers are pure pleasure. Murder, revenge, lies, abandonment—they're a respite from the mess and confusion of our own lives. Fictional chaos is a holiday, a beautiful distraction. We can go along for the ride and shiver from the danger without worrying that we'll get hurt. And in the end, all questions will be answered, all actions explained. Everything will be clear and put back in its place. The sun will come up, the bus will run its route, the nosy neighbor will resume her watch, and the beauty at the bakery will smile and ask which kind of savory pie we'd like today. Fake mysteries are like roller coasters at an amusement park, thrills and relief without pain.

PART III

A Letter

CHAPTER FIFTY-NINE

FIVE MONTHS LATER—NOVEMBER

Today is a year since my mother died. I declined Aurora's invitation to fly to Florida to swim with manatees in her honor. I also nixed Mr. Groberg's suggestion that I take a long walk somewhere my mom loved, because I'm in Buffalo, which she hated, and it's pouring, a freezing rain that should be snow. On days like this, my mom and I would read, so that's what I decide to do. I heat up some spiced cider and bring it to the living room. I stretch out on the couch, my toes tucked under a blanket my grandmother made, and I begin to read.

There was no possibility of taking a walk that day. . . .

As usual, I'm swept into the story immediately, sharing Jane Eyre's outrage at being treated so badly by the relatives who have taken her in. The wind howls around my house, and soon it's raving "in furious gusts" outside the awful Lowood Institution, where Jane is sent to school. She's such a resilient little thing.

Since learning the truth about my mother, I've thought a lot about coping and the myriad ways that people react to what befalls them.

I don't know why hardship makes one person mean and another kind, someone a realist and someone else a dreamer, why someone has an inner compass and someone else is forever lost. Maybe it's DNA, or some chance encounters, a wise word or a helping hand at the right time. Maybe it's the difference between having been hungry too long and or having been fed. Who am I to judge?

I've been thinking about my grandfather too. I wasn't surprised that I never heard from him or to learn, three months after I got home, that he passed away in his sleep. The note from the nursing home said it was a gentle death, that he wasn't in any pain, but I find that hard to believe. Leaving the world in a room like that, alone, with no one to hold your hand or wipe your brow? Not how I'd like to take my final bow.

I go back into the kitchen and warm up some lentil soup, my book open in one hand while I stir with the other. Now Jane is a governess at Thornfield Hall, and, of course, I'm picturing North Lees Hall in Hathersage and remembering standing there with Dev. At this moment, what's in *Jane Eyre* seems more real to me than everything that happened during my week in Derbyshire. If I hadn't been in regular touch with Wyatt and Amity and Germaine, and wasn't maintaining a warm, if infrequent correspondence with Dev, I'd be tempted to believe the whole thing had been a dream.

Now Mr. Rochester is disguised as a gypsy woman, his face hidden by a black bonnet as he tries to discern Jane's true feelings for him. He challenges her to turn toward love.

"You are cold, because you are alone; no contact strikes the fire from you that is in you."

A rumble outside. It's the FedEx truck. Through the window, I watch the driver run up the path, head down against the slanting rain. A rap on the kitchen door. He thrusts out a package. Inside, I pull the tab and open it.

It's from a law firm in Sheffield, England, the office of a solicitor called Angus Darpiddle, a name absurd enough to make me think this a ruse, perhaps an invitation to Willowthrop's next murder week. I scan the words with a feeling of déjà vu, which I realize is an actual memory of finding an unexpected document related to my mother and England. Mr. Darpiddle writes to inform me that two months before his demise, George Martin Crowley, my grandfather, revised his last will and testament. He left all his possessions to me. I have to read it again. *He left all his possessions to you.* I read on, shocked to discover that my grandfather's worldly goods were more than some empty bottles of booze and old racing forms. His "estate," as Mr. Darpiddle calls it, consists of eight thousand pounds in a savings account at the Derbyshire Community Bank, 353 pounds in BetUK, which I suppose is his bookie, and a dwelling where he resided for nearly eight years before moving into Derby Oaks Care Home. This must be the cottage that he won from his gambling buddy in a bet.

I laugh out loud. I am an English heiress. Eight thousand pounds and a dilapidated cottage aren't exactly "fit for a lord," but still. I can't wait to tell Amity.

"Neglected and with only intermittent tenants, the dwelling, which was once a small storage barn, may be in a state of disrepair," Mr. Darpiddle writes. "We assume you will want to sell the property and are prepared to assist with all necessary investigations, transactions, and legal proceedings."

He has included a few photographs. The "dwelling," as he calls it, is a sturdy stone building with a thick wooden door. The cottage appears to be in a field or pasture. The property includes a garden and a shed. According to an enclosed map, the cottage is on the edge of Bakewell, three miles from the center of Willowthrop. My grandfather returned nearly to the scene of his crime.

I'm tempted to email Germaine, to ask how much she thinks the cottage is worth. It can't be much. Probably whoever purchases it will knock down the dwelling, clear the property, and build a new home, a bland brick one like the house where Stanley and Pippa Grange pretended to live in wedded misery. The photographs of the cottage interior are too dark to make out clearly, but the place looks to be in decent shape.

The kitchen is small and mostly taken up by a solid country table. The walls are white, the ceiling made of thick wooden logs like in a mountain cabin. In the sitting room, there are stone walls, wood frames around the windows, a woodburning stove in a tiled corner. Old but comfortable-looking furniture.

As I look at the pictures, something strange happens. My mother called it "vision," the ability to look at something unformed, or dilapidated, or tacky—a room or a house or even an old dress—and see how it could be made into something wonderful.

"I don't have it," I used to tell her, thinking that vision was some magical skill that I'd failed to inherit.

"Don't be ridiculous," she'd say, always impatient when I found it difficult to be like her.

But now I can imagine the change. I hold up a photograph of the garden. I squint, and I can see it: the land cleared of weeds and replanted with flowers and vegetables. The roof fixed, the walkway lined with sedum, hollyhock crawling up a trellis. Sunflowers as big as a giant's hands. The front door sanded and stained. Dare I open it?

I move back into the living room and sit down on the couch, knocking my copy of *Jane Eyre* onto the floor. How funny to learn of an inheritance as Jane did. To have something in a book happen to me. Can a life be changed by a letter in the mail? Is that all it takes?

My mother would love this. *It's a sign*, she'd say. *You must go! This is the next phase of your life. Run toward it.*

And maybe I can. Maybe chasing after something new is not always delusional, a run from discomfort. Maybe for me, it's a chance to shape my destiny.

I may have been right in learning not to trust my mother, in girding myself for disappointment. But that doesn't mean I have to discount everything she believed in. I put the papers and photographs back in the envelope and close the clasp, thinking of what I might tell Mr. Angus Darpiddle.

I am coming, I will write, to accept my grandfather's unexpected gift, and claim what is mine.

PART IV

The Peak

CHAPTER SIXTY

ONE YEAR SINCE MURDER WEEK—JUNE

The countryside is lusher than I remembered. Through the taxi window, the bright green pastures, the bushes and trees, the whole landscape looks swollen with water, like it's moments from spilling over. It's succor after the dry spell at home, where I took Mr. Groberg's advice and put in a sprinkler system so I wouldn't have to worry that the family renting my house will forget to water.

We stop at a traffic light beside a bicycle rental shop, where a young couple is strapping a baby into the carrier on the back of a bike. They kiss the baby's cheeks and lean over to kiss each other. It seems like a good omen, for which I'm grateful. I'm here in England without a ticket home. I've got my inheritance and rent from my new tenants in Buffalo, and I'll have a small salary from a part-time job at The Book and Hook. Kim doubts I'll be able to tolerate being an employee after owning my own business, but she was too excited about taking over the optician shop to notice that the only thing that made me sad was how easy it was to walk away. For the first time, I'm going to try to figure out what I want to do, instead of merely continuing what I've always done.

"Are you sure this is the place, duck?" the driver says.

We're on the edge of a large field. I recognize the cottage from the photographs, but now it seems narrower and taller, and more like a storage barn. It has a wooden door that looks impenetrable and only one small window facing the front. It is not inviting.

The skeleton key is under the mat, as promised. The door, which is even thicker than I imagined, opens directly into the kitchen, which, despite a low ceiling and a lot of dust, is a pleasant surprise. There's a long, sturdy wooden table, shelves stacked with old ceramic plates, two white cabinets, and a small electric stove. I can see myself making breakfast here, scrambled eggs from my own chickens, which I've never wanted to raise until this moment. Taped to the refrigerator, which is barely chin height, is a note from Germaine. She's left me milk, eggs, bread and butter, bacon, apples, and coffee. In the door is a bottle of white wine.

In the sitting room, the only other room on the first floor, there's a leather couch that's covered with a musty wool blanket. There's also a rocking chair, a small rickety bookshelf, and a few oversize old pillows in a wicker basket on the floor near the woodstove. Up the steep, narrow stairs is a bedroom, with a solid dresser and a mattress that doesn't seem half bad. The windows are small, but the view over the hills couldn't be prettier.

I'm glad I waited until June to return; it's nice weather for getting the house and garden in shape. Amity and Wyatt have promised to come and help. She'll be here in July for the swan census and the official opening of Hadley Hall. Wyatt, who is getting lots of work now as an audiobook narrator, has carved out a week in September to return to Derbyshire to claim his prize by playing the dead body in a Masterpiece Mystery show. He tells me he's been practicing by doing corpse pose.

I spend the first day cleaning, throwing out moth-eaten old linens and blankets, scrubbing the tiny bathroom. Germaine comes by with more cleaning supplies and hand-me-downs—a quilt, a set of sheets, a braided rug, some towels. The second night, she brings Indian food, and we eat curry and drink beer. The next day a pickup truck pulls up to the cottage. Sally, the vicar, unloads an old bicycle with a basket for me to use until I get a car. I haven't ventured into town yet, too nervous about what I might find.

On my fourth morning, I'm in the garden struggling to yank out a wisteria vine when the gate creaks.

"I don't think that's a fair fight."

The sun gives a lustrous shine to Dev's hair. He looks taller than I remembered.

"Fair to me or to the wisteria?"

"I was going to say to you," Dev says, "but I can see you're stronger than I thought. Bold of you to take on gardening."

"Isn't it though?"

What a fool I was.

"Wisteria is tenacious," Dev says, rolling up his sleeves. "You have to go deep." He reaches for my shovel. "May I?"

I step aside and watch as he digs the shovel down around the largest root. He puts his foot on the metal blade and hinges it back. He moves around the root, spearing the shovel and hinging, spearing and hinging.

"You don't have to do this," I say.

He pauses. "I know."

"I'm working on getting a green thumb. See?"

He stakes the shovel in the ground and takes my hand. He flips it palm up, looks down at my fingers, touches my thumb.

"No sign of progress," he says.

"Really? You don't see the tinge of green?"

I don't know if he can feel my hand tremble, but his is steady.

We work together, both gripping the wooden handle, pushing the shovel into the ground and prying the blade to coax the roots to release their hold. It's nearly too much for me, working by his side like this. Finally, the root comes out in a knot that is bigger and heavier than I could have imagined. We drag it to the side of the garden.

"I almost forgot," Dev says. "I have some photographs for you." He takes an envelope from his shirt pocket. "I found them in a box in the basement—these are from the seventies, when your mum was a girl. I thought you might find them interesting, to get a sense of her life here. The one on top I'm told is your grandmother."

"Seriously?" Does he know what a gift this is? In the photo, she looks only a little older than I am now. She's holding a bicycle, with a basket, of course, her head thrown back in laughter. She looks tall, like me, and has thick, unruly hair, like mine. I run a finger lightly over her face. I wish I could tip her chin forward and gaze right into her eyes.

"This is amazing," I say.

"I thought you'd like that one."

"I love how she looks," I say.

"I do too," Dev says. "She looks like you."

There's so much I want to say to him, but the combination of his presence and these old photographs is overwhelming. I leaf through them, knowing I'll look at them more carefully later. They seem like they're from another era, and I guess they are. Children on a swing, a crowd of kids at a school fair, boys playing by the river. I stop at one of a little girl with blond hair, holding the hand of an older girl.

"That one's special," Dev says.

The younger girl is tiny, knock-kneed, a little dirty and with her hair a mess, like she's been running around outside on a hot day. I could look at her forever. For so long, my only physical connection to my mother's childhood was the Melling School book, which I've brought with me. Now I can see her when she was young and honest.

"When was this from?" I say.

"It says on the back."

I flip it over. Someone has scrawled "1978, Sukie and Polly."

"That's Polly?"

Dev smiles and nods.

"I still can't get over that our mothers knew each other," I say.

"It's wild, I know."

The two girls in the photograph seem so happy and carefree, like they're out on an adventure, enjoying the countryside, the fine weather, each other's company. Like days like this will be theirs forever. My mom and Dev's, together. It's magical.

"Do you think that, somehow, we knew?" I say.

"That our mothers brought us together?"

"Yes, exactly."

"Not in the slightest," Dev says.

"Oh." I can't help being disappointed.

But then Dev takes my hand.

"What I feel for you, Cath, has absolutely nothing to do with our mothers."

I can't speak, but it doesn't matter. Dev leans in and kisses me, and whatever hesitancy I had about seeing him again has vanished. He is not only still here in Willowthrop, he is here in my garden, with me. And this time, I am all in.

When we come up for air, Dev says he wants to ask me something. I kiss him before he can say more. I know what his question is anyway. Finally, I answer.

"I am not going to bolt," I say. "I promise."

"Brilliant of you to let me know, but I was going to ask if you'd come down to the bar tonight. I'm trying out a new menu of cocktails."

"No more Hanky Panky?"

"I'll make you something better."

He glances at my bicycle leaning on the fence.

"You can ride down; I'll drive you home."

I point to the cottage. "Here? This is my home?"

"How about that?" Dev says. "This is your home."

Hand in hand, we walk out of the garden. I watch his little car disappear over the hill. I walk into the pasture, where the grass is still low. In the distance, a narrow footpath cuts across the slope. I pick up my pace as I climb the hill, the breeze pushing my hair off my shoulders. I am ready to explore, to roam the countryside that was once my mother's playground, to walk along the river where she thought she'd be safe. I can follow in her footsteps and forge new paths.

I don't know exactly what I'm doing here or if I can make this place my own. But I'm getting used to the idea of taking a leap and trusting that I'll find my way. I may never know what makes someone broken or whole or why someone stays or goes. But I can accept that some things, even important, life-changing things, remain a mystery.

ACKNOWLEDGMENTS

Writers often have a hard time saying where their ideas come from, but the origin of this book is no mystery. It began when Noelle Salazar, an author friend I know only online, posted photographs of her trip to England's Peak District. Enchanted, I asked Noelle if she would share her itinerary. Several months later, my sister Laura and I were in Derbyshire exploring the Peak District, which felt like stepping into the pages of our favorite novels. By the time I got home, I knew where I'd set my next novel. Thank you, Noelle, for introducing me to this magical landscape.

My sisters, Laura Dukess and Linda Dukess, are the most voracious readers I know and the only other members of my first and favorite book club. Laura, thank you for being the best traveling companion and for delighting in everything we encountered in the Peak District (even, like Amity, mushy peas). Our trip to Bakewell, the model for fictional Willowthrop, would be one of my favorite memories even if it hadn't inspired this book. Linda, thank you for reading countless drafts and for being as helpful a therapist for my fictional characters as you are for real people.

To Karen Pittelman, thank you for your uncanny ability to understand the heart of a story before it's formed and for pushing me to get it right. I hope to never write a novel without you.

ACKNOWLEDGMENTS

Thanks to all the writer friends who read drafts, offered advice, and shared wisdom as fellow travelers, especially Margaret Anastas, Genine Babakian, Suzy Becker, Christina Clancy, Jeanine Cummins, Sam Grieve, Lauren Kennedy, Steve Lewis, Annabel Monaghan, Kristin van Ogtrop, Sally Schwartz, Lindy Sinclair, and Erica Youngren. You all enrich my life and my writing.

Thanks to Jill Sigelbaum for helpful insights.

Thanks to Josie Fanelli of Kurt Sauer Opticians in Larchmont, New York, for sharing her story and inspiring Cath Little's career.

Thank you to the Virginia Center for the Creative Arts, where I figured out my fake murder and made the delightful discovery that many of my fellow writers in residence, even serious poets, harbored a soft spot for a good English village murder mystery.

Thank you to my editor, Hannah Braaten at Scout Press, for falling in love with this novel and shepherding it to publication with intelligence, good cheer, and efficiency. Thank you to everyone at Scout Press and Gallery Books, especially Jennifer Bergstrom, Alison Callahan, Hope Herr-Cardillo, Sally Marvin, Christine Masters, Erica Ferguson, Lucy Nalen, Sophie Normil, Sarah Schlick, and Kell Wilson. Thank you, Vi-An Nguyen, for the brilliant cover illustration and design.

Doug Stewart, of Sterling Lord Literistic, Inc., remains the best literary agent I could imagine. Thank you, Doug, for believing in me through the ups and downs and for being so good at what you do. Also at Sterling Lord, thank you to Tyler Monson, Szilvia Molnar, and Amanda Price.

Thank you to my mother, Mona Dukess, for showing me the artist's way.

And finally, thanks to Steve, Joe, and Johnny Liesman, for having faith that my chaotic writing process would turn into something. Even though you make fun of the shows I watch on television, you three are my favorite characters of all.